SINA GRACE · SIOBHAN KEENAN · CATHY LE

Ghosted in L.A.

VOL. 3

Published by

BOOM! BOX™

Ross Richie..CEO & Founder
Joy Huffman..CFO
Matt Gagnon...Editor-in-Chief
Filip Sablik.................................President, Publishing & Marketing
Stephen Christy.......................................President, Development
Lance Kreiter......................Vice President, Licensing & Merchandising
Arune Singh..Vice President, Marketing
Bryce Carlson.............Vice President, Editorial & Creative Strategy
Kate Henning...Director, Operations
Spencer Simpson...Director, Sales
Scott Newman.............................Manager, Production Design
Elyse Strandberg......................................Manager, Finance
Sierra Hahn...Executive Editor
Jeanine Schaefer.......................................Executive Editor
Dafna Pleban..Senior Editor
Shannon Watters...Senior Editor
Eric Harburn...Senior Editor
Matthew Levine...Editor
Sophie Philips-Roberts.............................Associate Editor
Amanda LaFranco.......................................Associate Editor
Jonathan Manning....................................Associate Editor
Gavin Gronenthal.......................................Assistant Editor
Gwen Waller...Assistant Editor
Allyson Gronowitz..Assistant Editor
Ramiro Portnoy...Assistant Editor
Kenzie Rzonca...Assistant Editor
Shelby Netschke..Editorial Assistant
Michelle Ankley...Design Coordinator
Marie Krupina...Production Designer
Grace Park..Production Designer
Chelsea Roberts......................................Production Designer
Samantha Knapp.......................Production Design Assistant
José Meza..Live Events Lead
Stephanie Hocutt.............................Digital Marketing Lead
Esther Kim......................................Marketing Coordinator
Breanna Sarpy.............................Live Events Coordinator
Amanda Lawson...............................Marketing Assistant
Holly Aitchison.............................Digital Sales Coordinator
Morgan Perry.................................Retail Sales Coordinator
Megan Christopher........................Operations Coordinator
Rodrigo Hernandez........................Operations Coordinator
Zipporah Smith....................................Operations Assistant
Jason Lee..Senior Accountant
Sabrina Lesin......................................Accounting Assistant

BOOm! BOX™

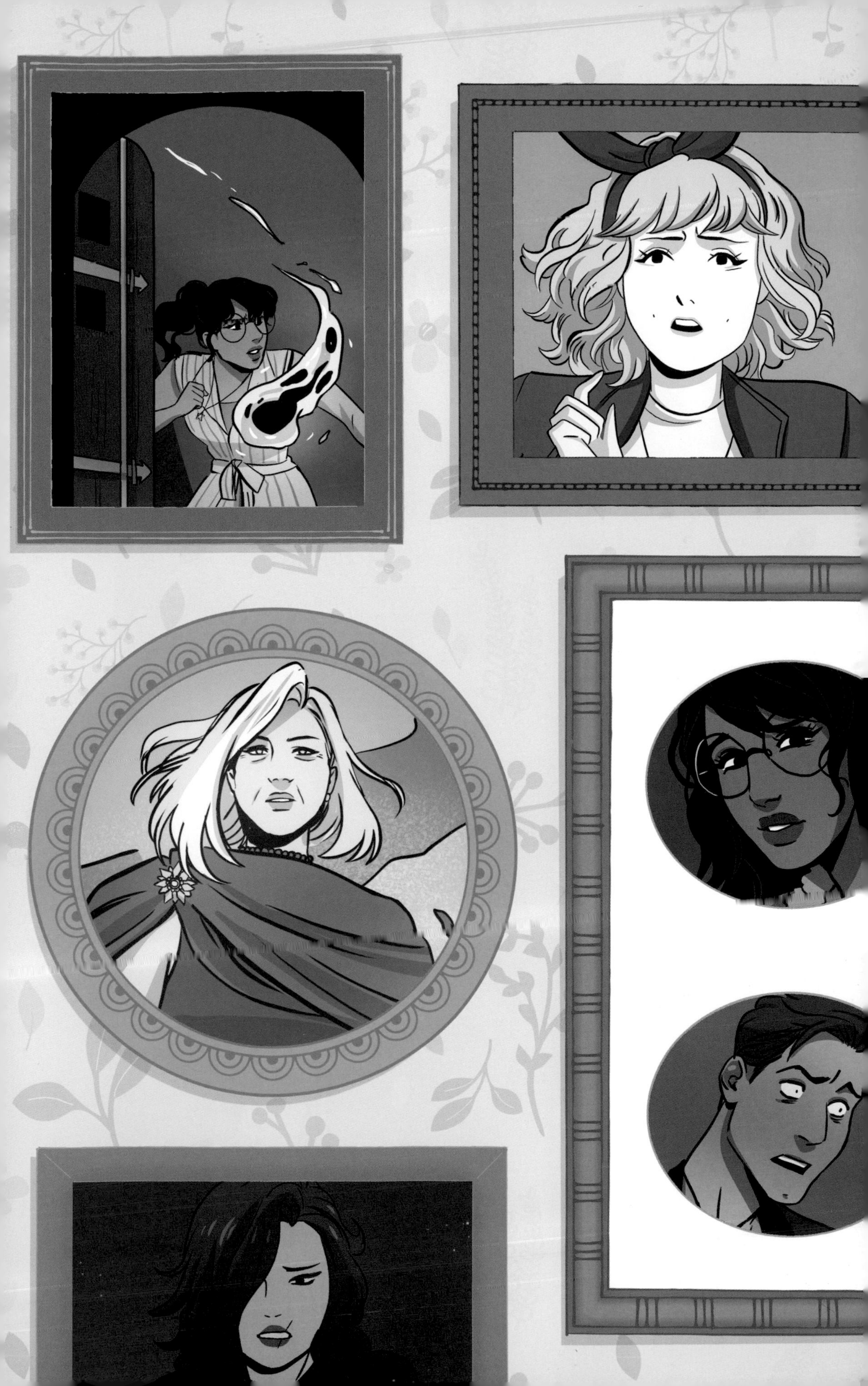

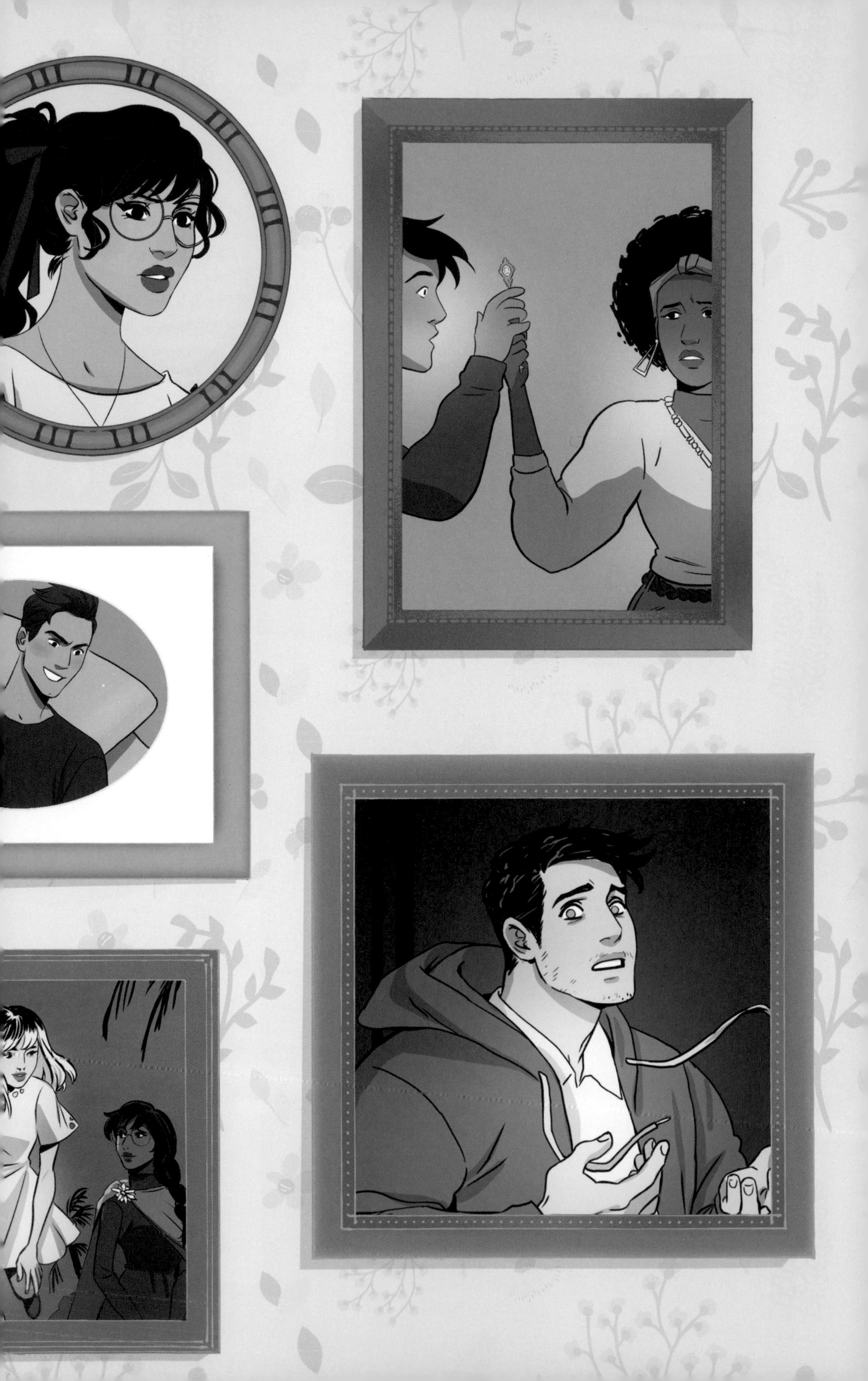

Created & Written by .... **Sina Grace**

Illustrated by .... **Siobhan Keenan**
With .... Sina Grace
Inking Assistance .... Lea Caballero

Colors by .... **Cathy Le**
With .... **Jeremy Lawson & Natalia Nesterenko**

Letters by .... **DC Hopkins**

Cover by .... **Siobhan Keenan**

Series Designers .... **Michelle Ankley & Grace Park**
Collection Designer .... **Marie Krupina**
Assistant Editor .... **Allyson Gronowitz**
Editor .... **Shannon Watters**

Special Thanks to Francesco Segala,
Vico Ortiz, and Elena Megalos.

Chapter Nine

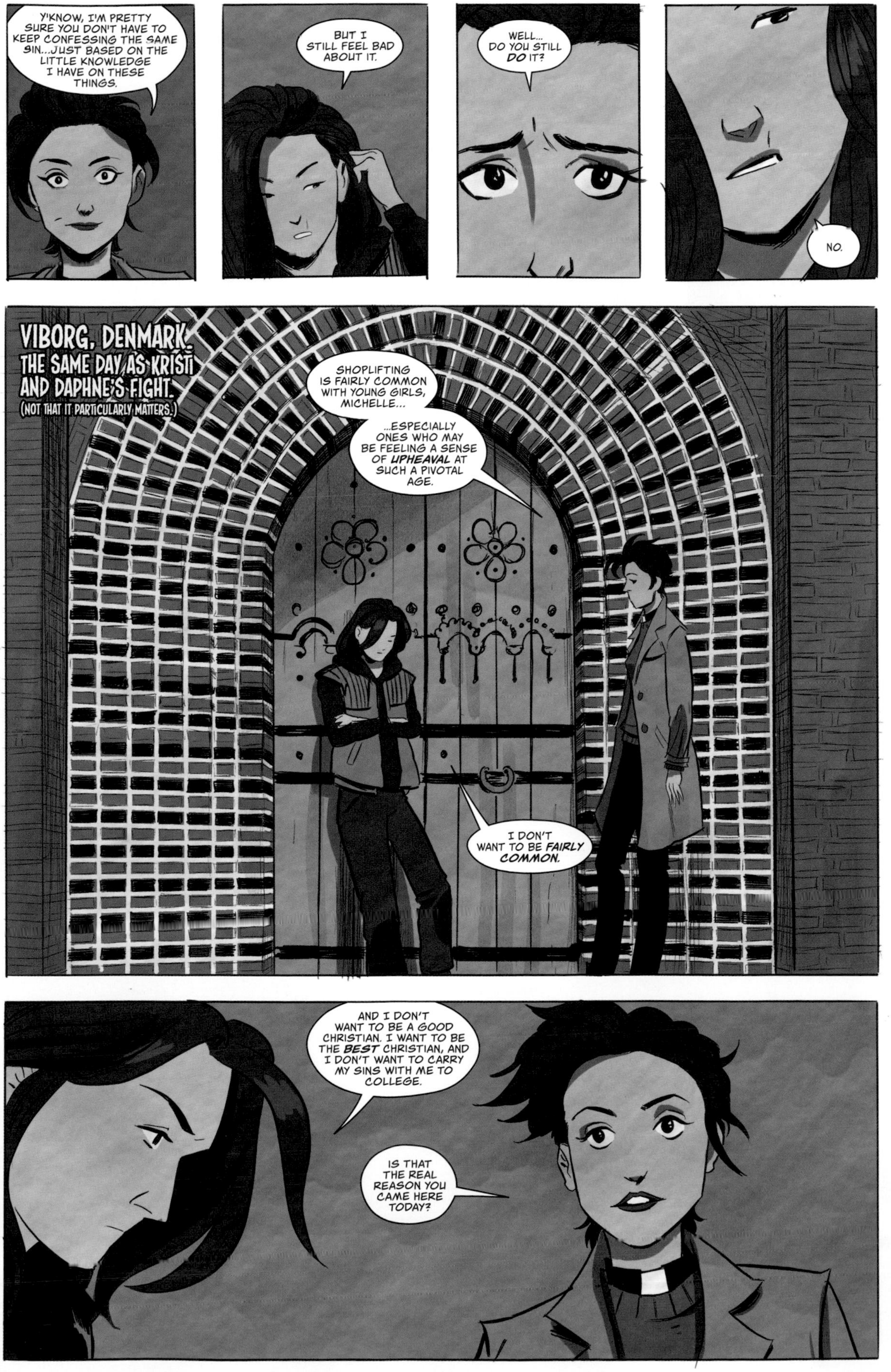
Y'KNOW, I'M PRETTY SURE YOU DON'T HAVE TO KEEP CONFESSING THE SAME SIN...JUST BASED ON THE LITTLE KNOWLEDGE I HAVE ON THESE THINGS.
BUT I STILL FEEL BAD ABOUT IT.
WELL... DO YOU STILL DO IT?
NO.
VIBORG, DENMARK. THE SAME DAY AS KRISTI AND DAPHNE'S FIGHT.
(NOT THAT IT PARTICULARLY MATTERS.)
SHOPLIFTING IS FAIRLY COMMON WITH YOUNG GIRLS, MICHELLE...
...ESPECIALLY ONES WHO MAY BE FEELING A SENSE OF UPHEAVAL AT SUCH A PIVOTAL AGE.
I DON'T WANT TO BE FAIRLY COMMON.
AND I DON'T WANT TO BE A GOOD CHRISTIAN. I WANT TO BE THE BEST CHRISTIAN, AND I DON'T WANT TO CARRY MY SINS WITH ME TO COLLEGE.
IS THAT THE REAL REASON YOU CAME HERE TODAY?

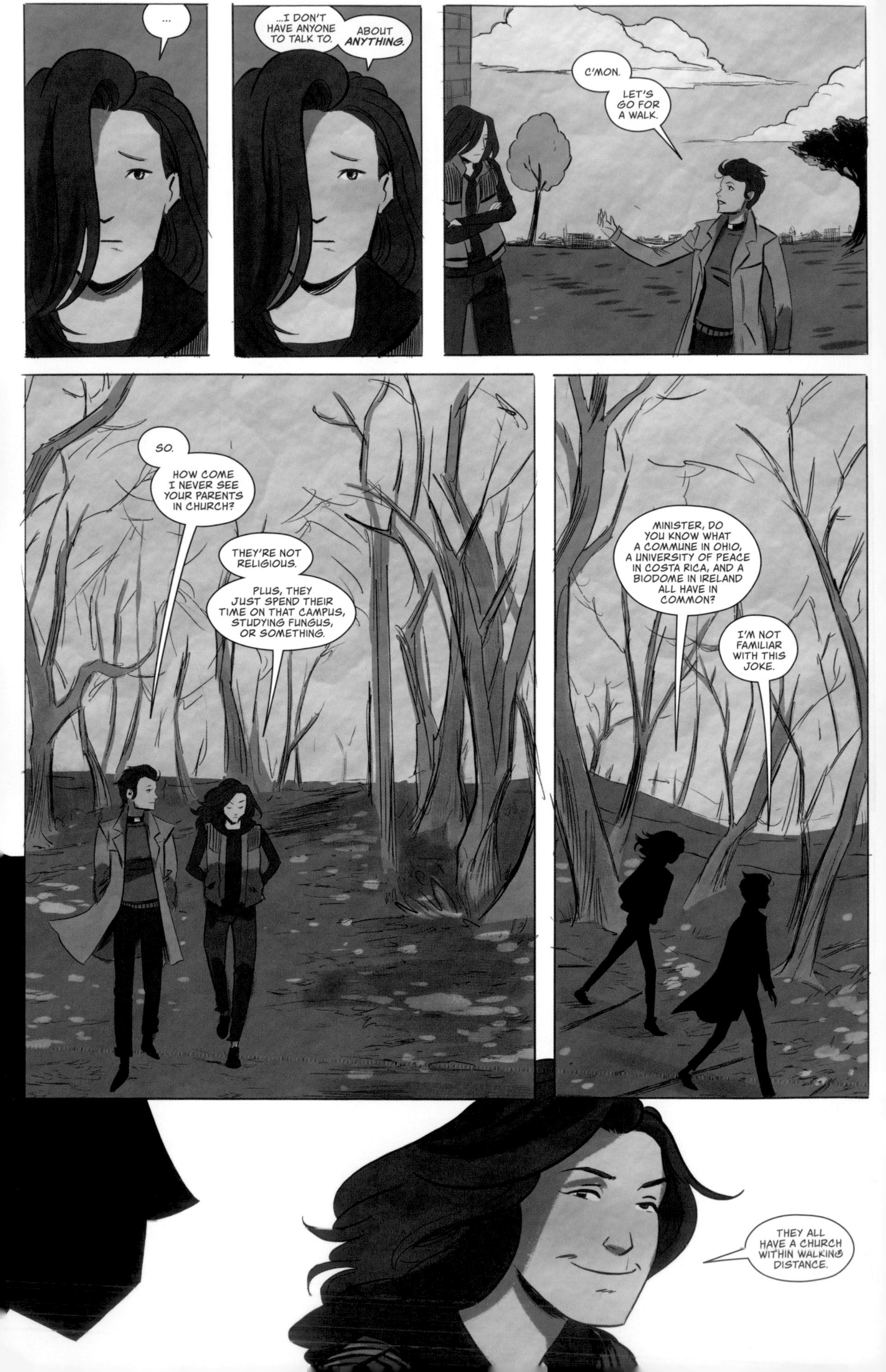
...
...I DON'T HAVE ANYONE TO TALK TO.
ABOUT ANYTHING.
C'MON.
LET'S GO FOR A WALK.
SO.
HOW COME I NEVER SEE YOUR PARENTS IN CHURCH?
THEY'RE NOT RELIGIOUS.
PLUS, THEY JUST SPEND THEIR TIME ON THAT CAMPUS, STUDYING FUNGUS, OR SOMETHING.
MINISTER, DO YOU KNOW WHAT A COMMUNE IN OHIO, A UNIVERSITY OF PEACE IN COSTA RICA, AND A BIODOME IN IRELAND ALL HAVE IN COMMON?
I'M NOT FAMILIAR WITH THIS JOKE.
THEY ALL HAVE A CHURCH WITHIN WALKING DISTANCE.

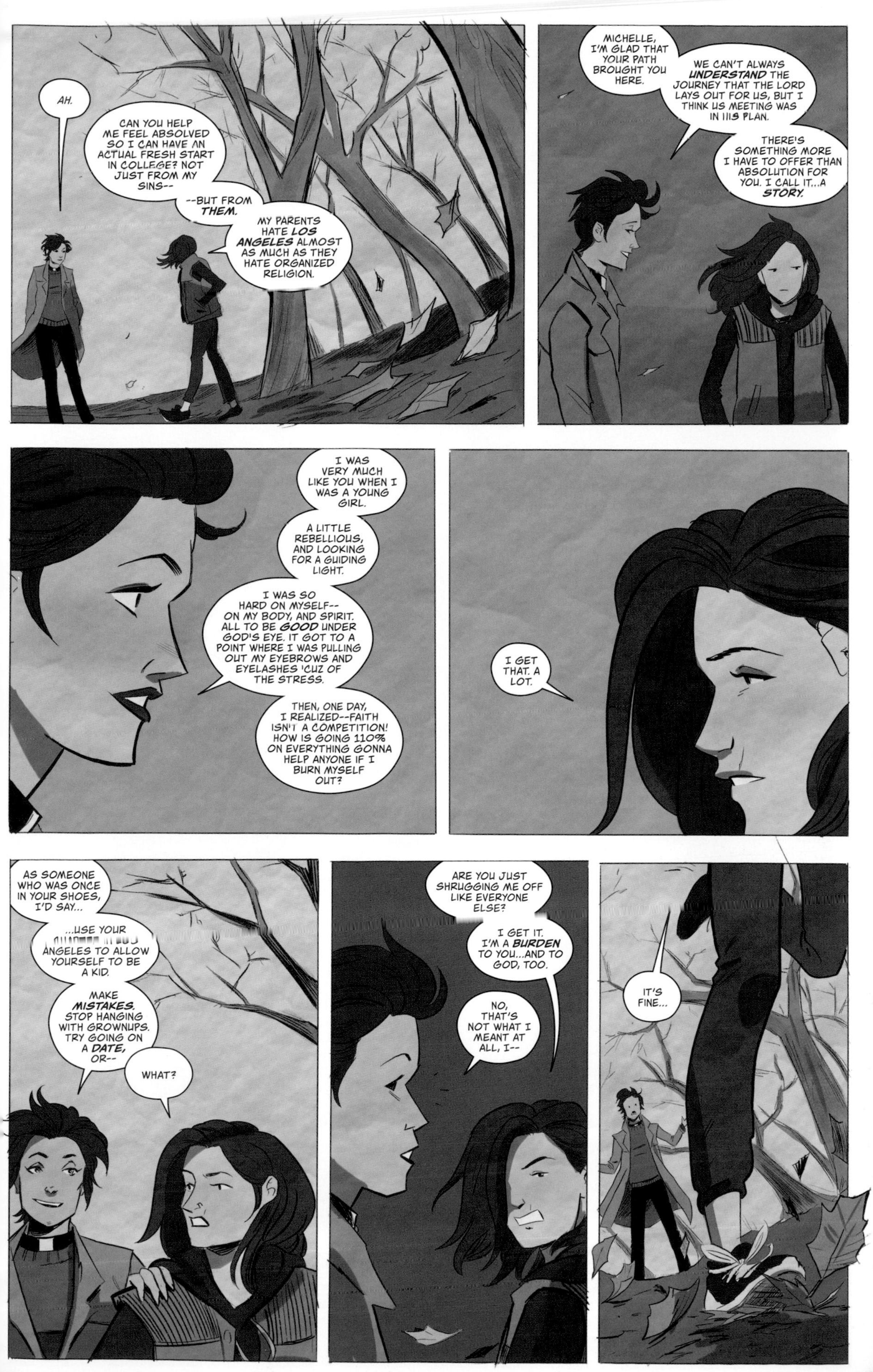
AH.
CAN YOU HELP ME FEEL ABSOLVED SO I CAN HAVE AN ACTUAL FRESH START IN COLLEGE? NOT JUST FROM MY SINS--
--BUT FROM THEM.
MY PARENTS HATE LOS ANGELES ALMOST AS MUCH AS THEY HATE ORGANIZED RELIGION.
MICHELLE, I'M GLAD THAT YOUR PATH BROUGHT YOU HERE.
WE CAN'T ALWAYS UNDERSTAND THE JOURNEY THAT THE LORD LAYS OUT FOR US, BUT I THINK US MEETING WAS IN HIS PLAN.
THERE'S SOMETHING MORE I HAVE TO OFFER THAN ABSOLUTION FOR YOU. I CALL IT...A STORY.
I WAS VERY MUCH LIKE YOU WHEN I WAS A YOUNG GIRL.
A LITTLE REBELLIOUS, AND LOOKING FOR A GUIDING LIGHT.
I WAS SO HARD ON MYSELF--ON MY BODY, AND SPIRIT. ALL TO BE GOOD UNDER GOD'S EYE. IT GOT TO A POINT WHERE I WAS PULLING OUT MY EYEBROWS AND EYELASHES 'CUZ OF THE STRESS.
THEN, ONE DAY, I REALIZED--FAITH ISN'T A COMPETITION! HOW IS GOING 110% ON EVERYTHING GONNA HELP ANYONE IF I BURN MYSELF OUT?
I GET THAT. A LOT.
AS SOMEONE WHO WAS ONCE IN YOUR SHOES, I'D SAY...
...USE YOUR ANGELES TO ALLOW YOURSELF TO BE A KID.
MAKE MISTAKES. STOP HANGING WITH GROWNUPS. TRY GOING ON A DATE, OR--
WHAT?
ARE YOU JUST SHRUGGING ME OFF LIKE EVERYONE ELSE?
I GET IT. I'M A BURDEN TO YOU...AND TO GOD, TOO.
NO, THAT'S NOT WHAT I MEANT AT ALL, I--
IT'S FINE...

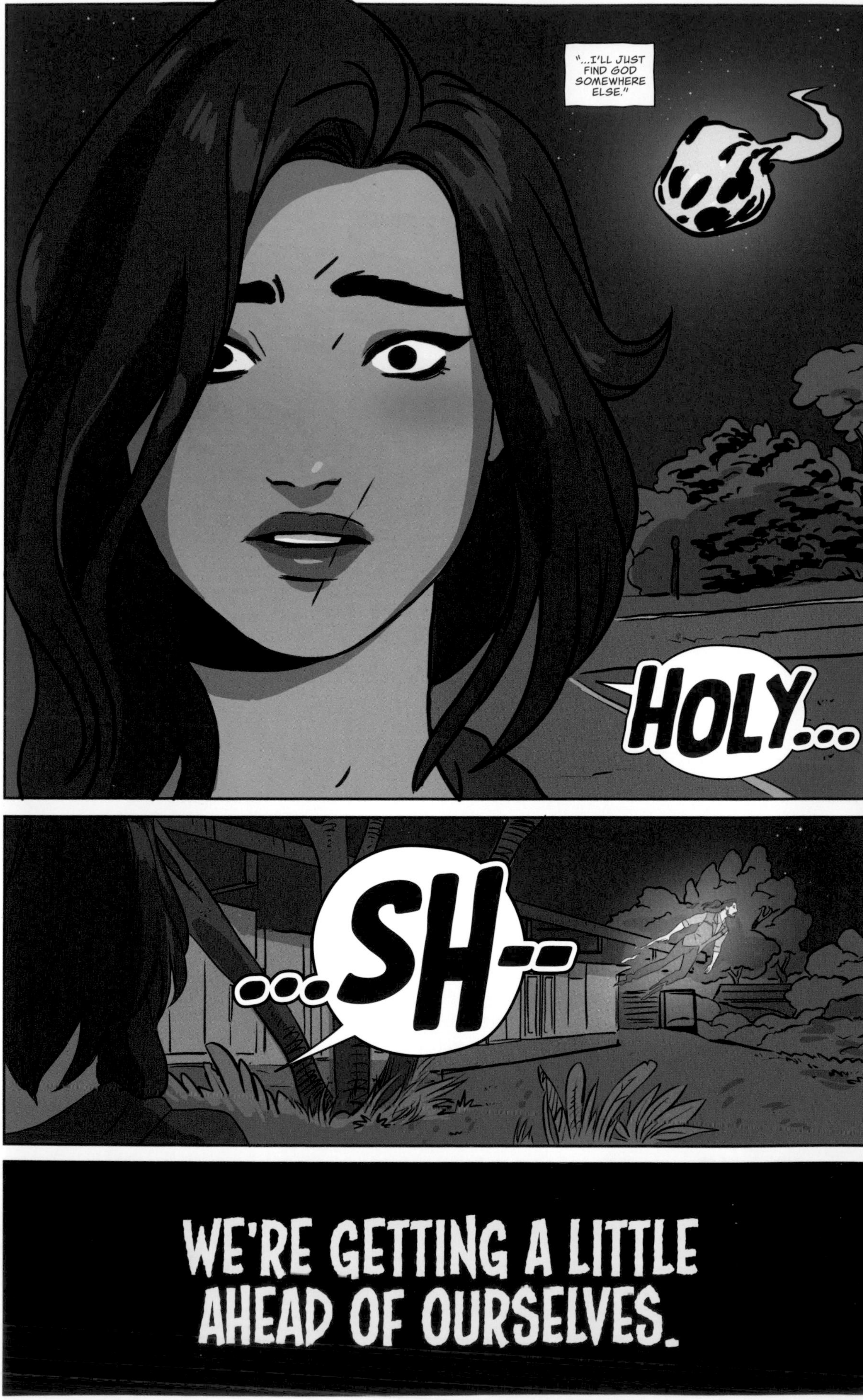
"...I'LL JUST FIND GOD SOMEWHERE ELSE."
HOLY...
...SH-..
WE'RE GETTING A LITTLE AHEAD OF OURSELVES.

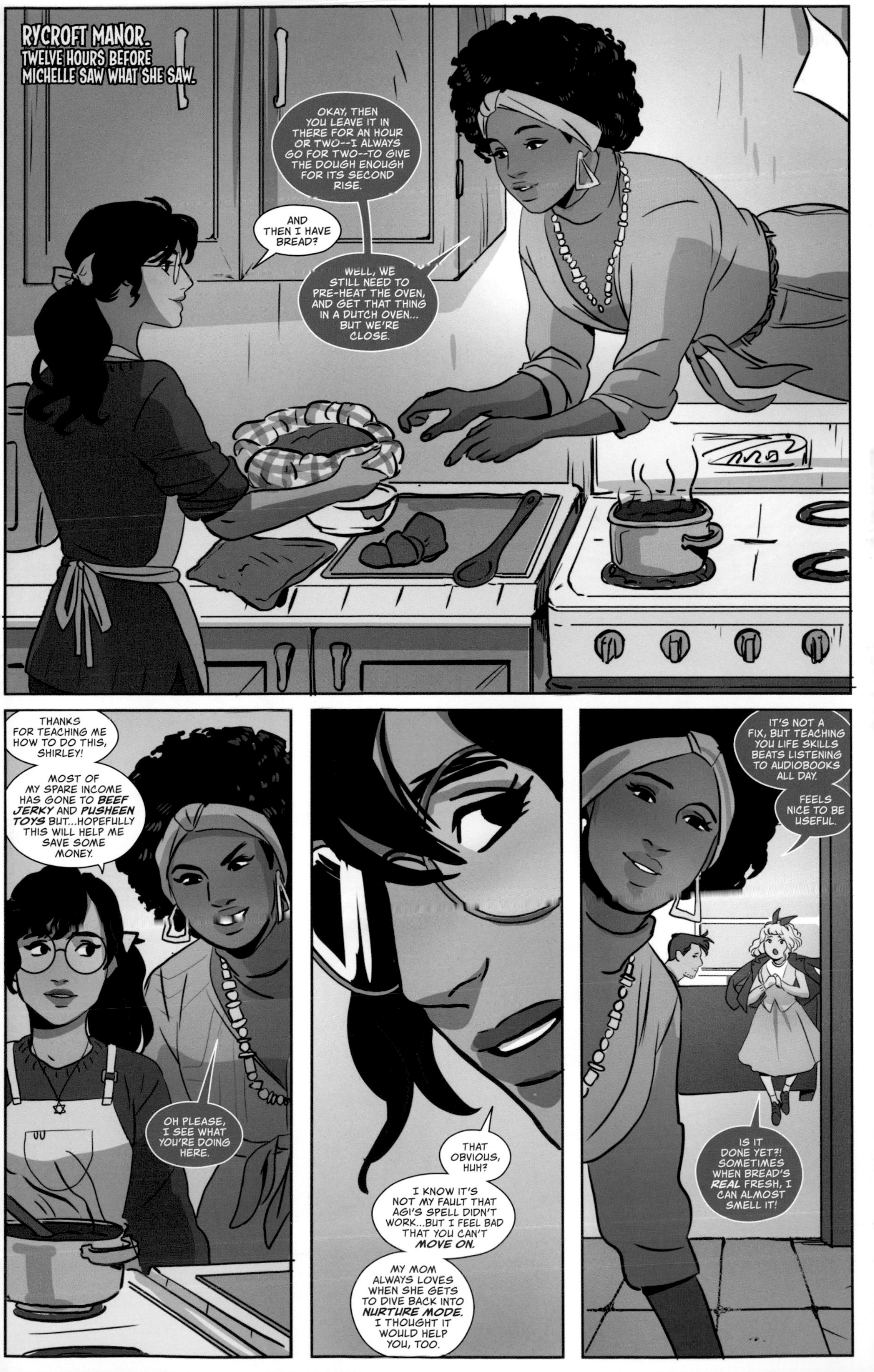
RYCROFT MANOR. TWELVE HOURS BEFORE MICHELLE SAW WHAT SHE SAW.
OKAY, THEN YOU LEAVE IT IN THERE FOR AN HOUR OR TWO--I ALWAYS GO FOR TWO--TO GIVE THE DOUGH ENOUGH FOR ITS SECOND RISE.
AND THEN I HAVE BREAD?
WELL, WE STILL NEED TO PRE-HEAT THE OVEN, AND GET THAT THING IN A DUTCH OVEN... BUT WE'RE CLOSE.
THANKS FOR TEACHING ME HOW TO DO THIS, SHIRLEY!
MOST OF MY SPARE INCOME HAS GONE TO BEEF JERKY AND PUSHEEN TOYS BUT...HOPEFULLY THIS WILL HELP ME SAVE SOME MONEY.
OH PLEASE, I SEE WHAT YOU'RE DOING HERE.
THAT OBVIOUS, HUH?
I KNOW IT'S NOT MY FAULT THAT AGI'S SPELL DIDN'T WORK...BUT I FEEL BAD THAT YOU CAN'T MOVE ON.
MY MOM ALWAYS LOVES WHEN SHE GETS TO DIVE BACK INTO NURTURE MODE. I THOUGHT IT WOULD HELP YOU, TOO.
IT'S NOT A FIX, BUT TEACHING YOU LIFE SKILLS BEATS LISTENING TO AUDIOBOOKS ALL DAY.
FEELS NICE TO BE USEFUL.
IS IT DONE YET?! SOMETIMES WHEN BREAD'S REAL FRESH, I CAN ALMOST SMELL IT!

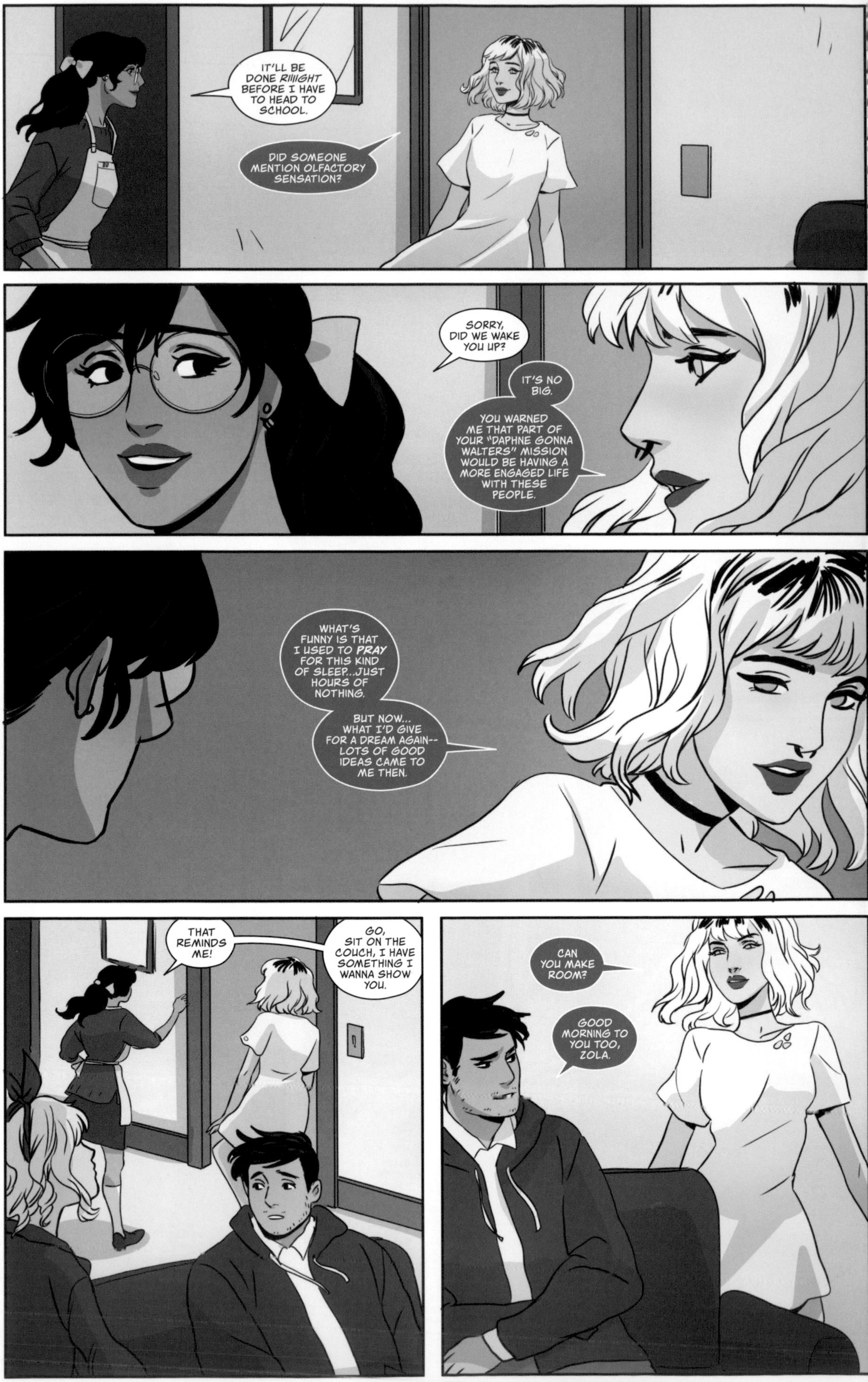
IT'LL BE DONE RIIIIGHT BEFORE I HAVE TO HEAD TO SCHOOL.
DID SOMEONE MENTION OLFACTORY SENSATION?
SORRY, DID WE WAKE YOU UP?
IT'S NO BIG.
YOU WARNED ME THAT PART OF YOUR "DAPHNE GONNA WALTERS" MISSION WOULD BE HAVING A MORE ENGAGED LIFE WITH THESE PEOPLE.
WHAT'S FUNNY IS THAT I USED TO PRAY FOR THIS KIND OF SLEEP...JUST HOURS OF NOTHING.
BUT NOW... WHAT I'D GIVE FOR A DREAM AGAIN-- LOTS OF GOOD IDEAS CAME TO ME THEN.
THAT REMINDS ME!
GO, SIT ON THE COUCH, I HAVE SOMETHING I WANNA SHOW YOU.
CAN YOU MAKE ROOM?
GOOD MORNING TO YOU TOO, ZOLA.

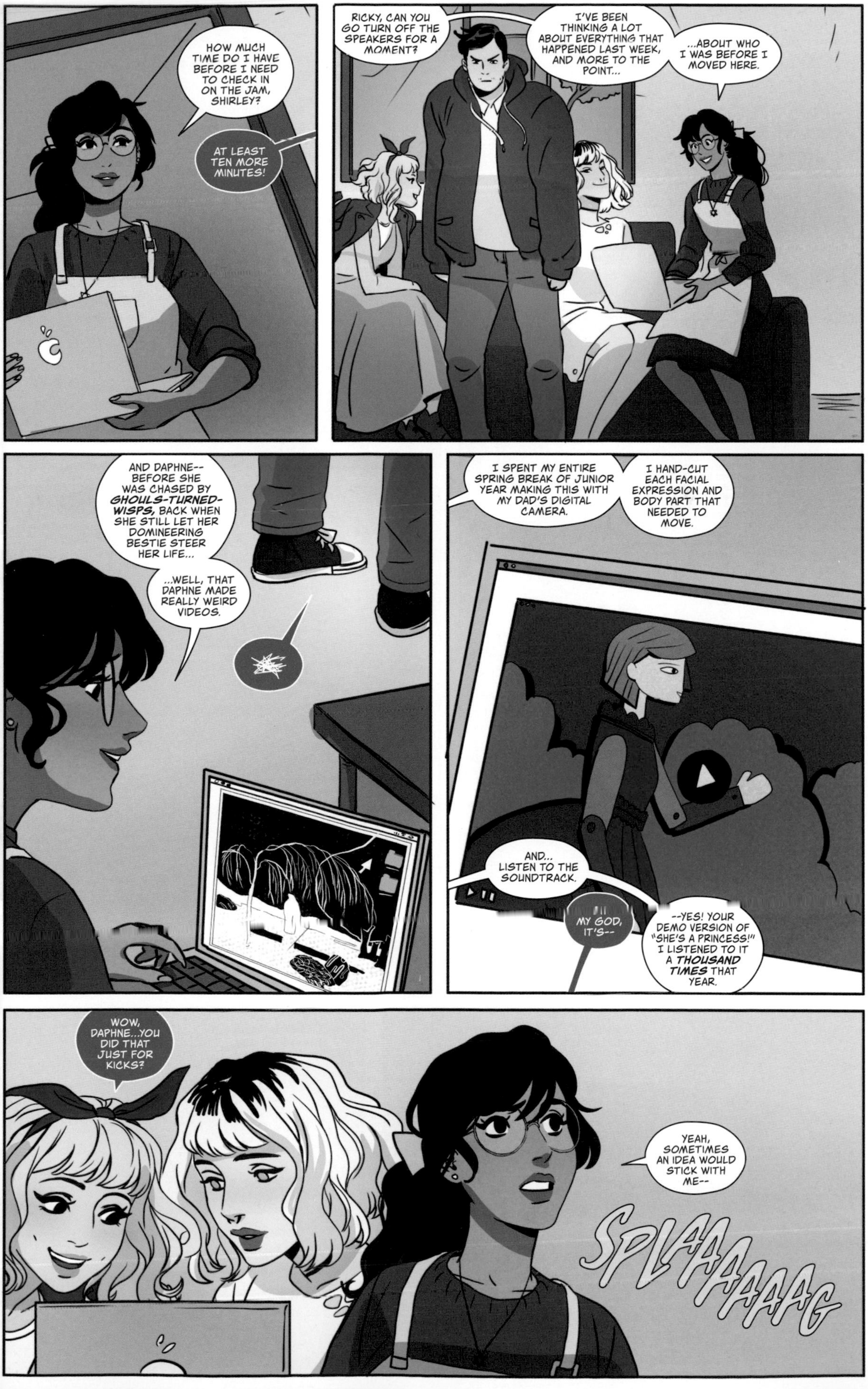
HOW MUCH TIME DO I HAVE BEFORE I NEED TO CHECK IN ON THE JAM, SHIRLEY?
AT LEAST TEN MORE MINUTES!
RICKY, CAN YOU GO TURN OFF THE SPEAKERS FOR A MOMENT?
I'VE BEEN THINKING A LOT ABOUT EVERYTHING THAT HAPPENED LAST WEEK, AND MORE TO THE POINT...
...ABOUT WHO I WAS BEFORE I MOVED HERE.
AND DAPHNE-- BEFORE SHE WAS CHASED BY *GHOULS-TURNED-WISPS,* BACK WHEN SHE STILL LET HER DOMINEERING BESTIE STEER HER LIFE...
...WELL, THAT DAPHNE MADE REALLY WEIRD VIDEOS.
I SPENT MY ENTIRE SPRING BREAK OF JUNIOR YEAR MAKING THIS WITH MY DAD'S DIGITAL CAMERA.
I HAND-CUT EACH FACIAL EXPRESSION AND BODY PART THAT NEEDED TO MOVE.
AND... LISTEN TO THE SOUNDTRACK.
MY GOD, IT'S--
--YES! YOUR DEMO VERSION OF "SHE'S A PRINCESS!" I LISTENED TO IT A *THOUSAND TIMES* THAT YEAR.
WOW, DAPHNE...YOU DID THAT JUST FOR KICKS?
YEAH, SOMETIMES AN IDEA WOULD STICK WITH ME--
SPLAAAAAAG

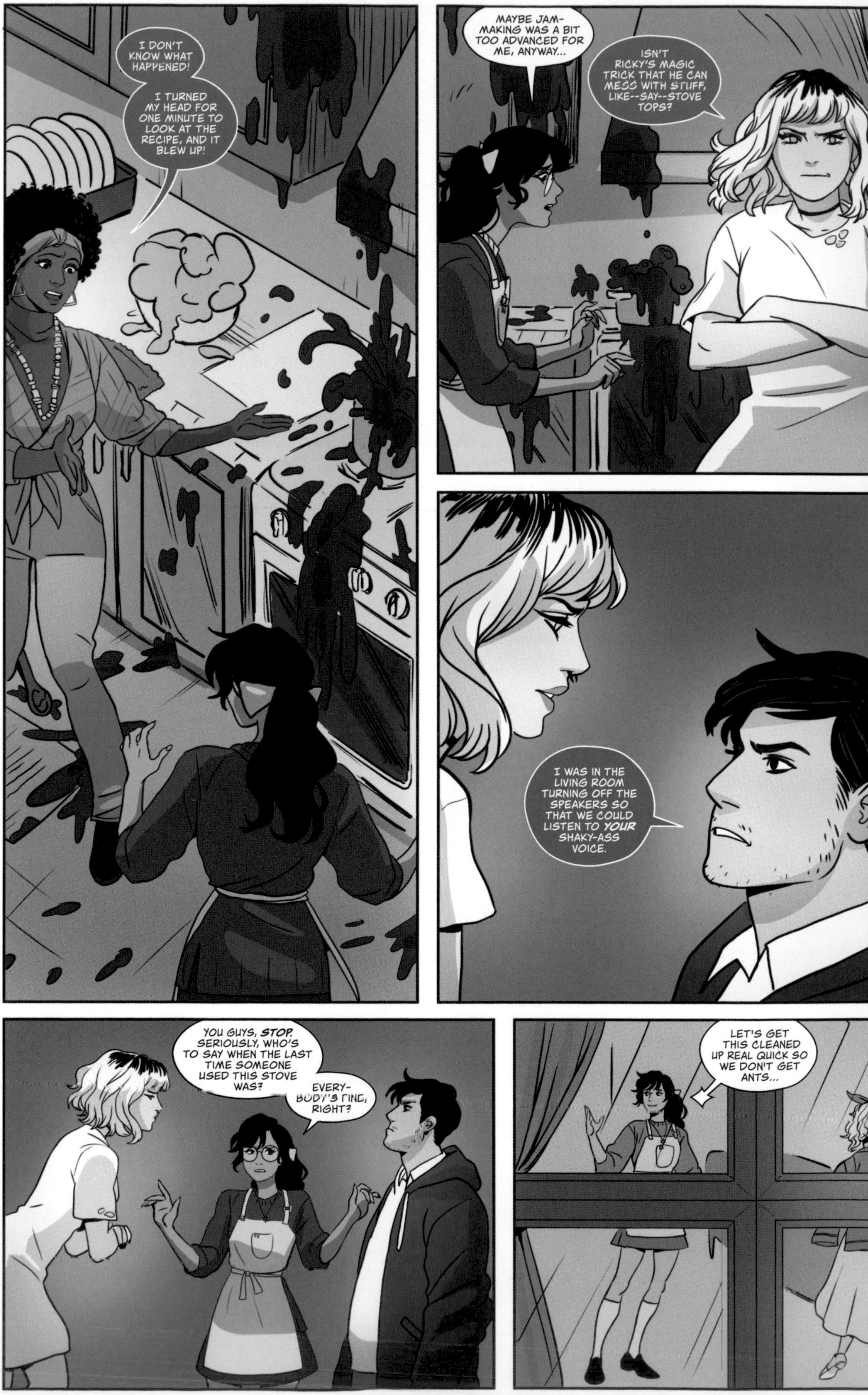
I DON'T KNOW WHAT HAPPENED!
I TURNED MY HEAD FOR ONE MINUTE TO LOOK AT THE RECIPE, AND IT BLEW UP!
MAYBE JAM-MAKING WAS A BIT TOO ADVANCED FOR ME, ANYWAY...
ISN'T RICKY'S MAGIC TRICK THAT HE CAN MESS WITH STUFF, LIKE--SAY--STOVE TOPS?
I WAS IN THE LIVING ROOM TURNING OFF THE SPEAKERS SO THAT WE COULD LISTEN TO YOUR SHAKY-ASS VOICE.
YOU GUYS, STOP. SERIOUSLY, WHO'S TO SAY WHEN THE LAST TIME SOMEONE USED THIS STOVE WAS?
EVERY-BODY'S FINE, RIGHT?
LET'S GET THIS CLEANED UP REAL QUICK SO WE DON'T GET ANTS...

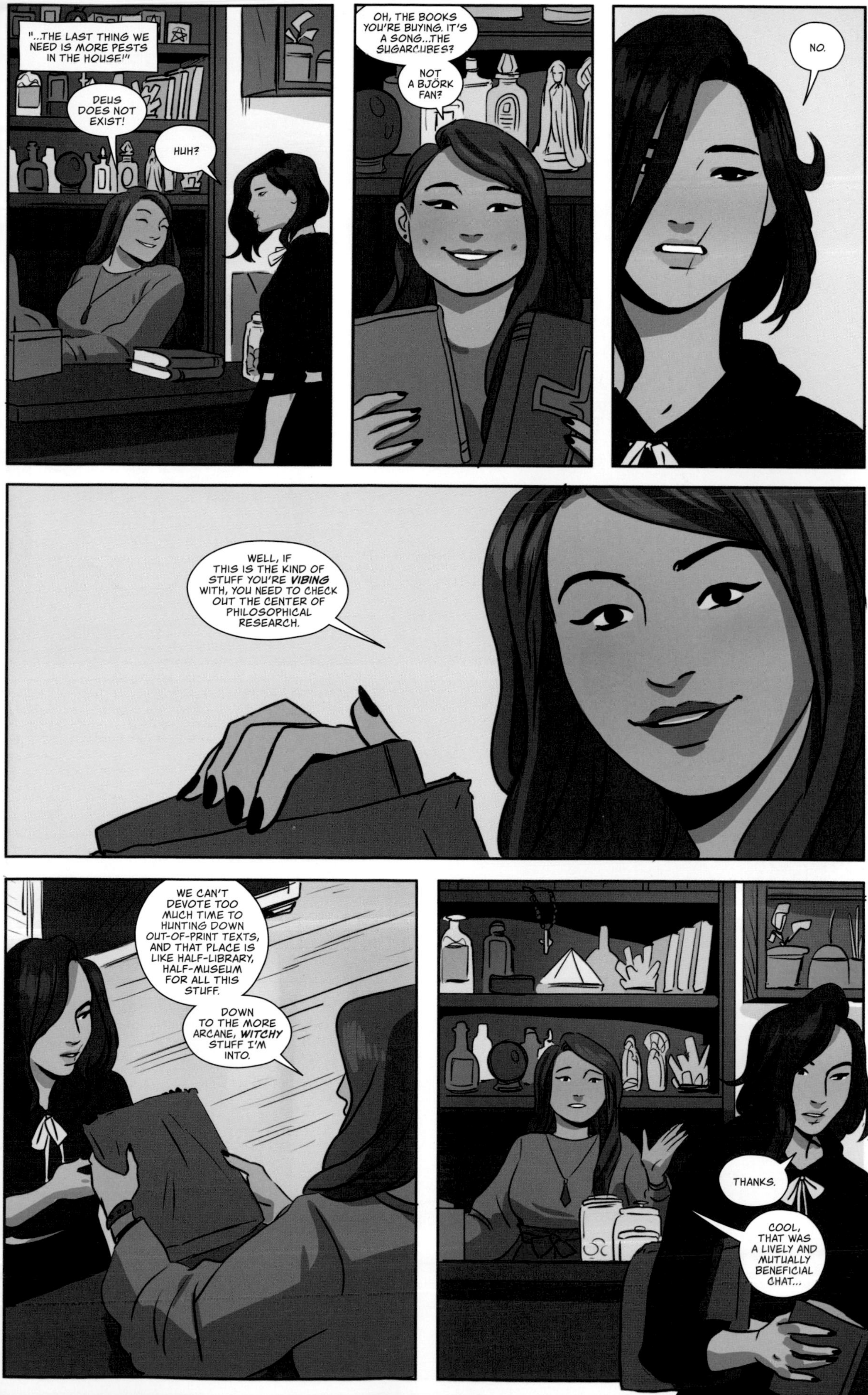
"...THE LAST THING WE NEED IS MORE PESTS IN THE HOUSE!"
DEUS DOES NOT EXIST!
HUH?
OH, THE BOOKS YOU'RE BUYING. IT'S A SONG...THE SUGARCUBES?
NOT A BJÖRK FAN?
NO.
WELL, IF THIS IS THE KIND OF STUFF YOU'RE *VIBING* WITH, YOU NEED TO CHECK OUT THE CENTER OF PHILOSOPHICAL RESEARCH.
WE CAN'T DEVOTE TOO MUCH TIME TO HUNTING DOWN OUT-OF-PRINT TEXTS, AND THAT PLACE IS LIKE HALF-LIBRARY, HALF-MUSEUM FOR ALL THIS STUFF.
DOWN TO THE MORE ARCANE, *WITCHY* STUFF I'M INTO.
THANKS.
COOL, THAT WAS A LIVELY AND MUTUALLY BENEFICIAL CHAT...

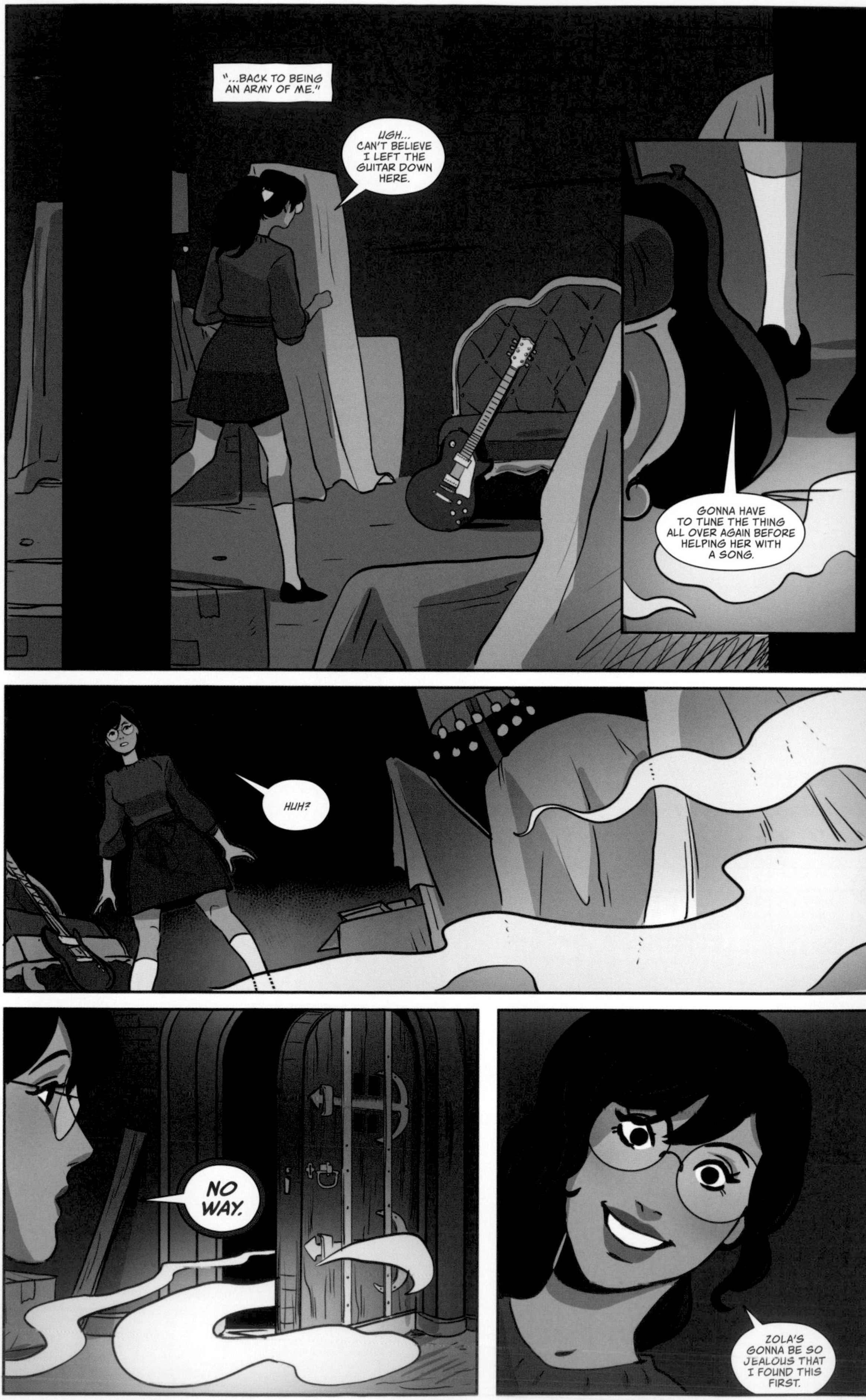
"...BACK TO BEING AN ARMY OF ME."
UGH... CAN'T BELIEVE I LEFT THE GUITAR DOWN HERE.
GONNA HAVE TO TUNE THE THING ALL OVER AGAIN BEFORE HELPING HER WITH A SONG.
HUH?
NO WAY.
ZOLA'S GONNA BE SO JEALOUS THAT I FOUND THIS FIRST.

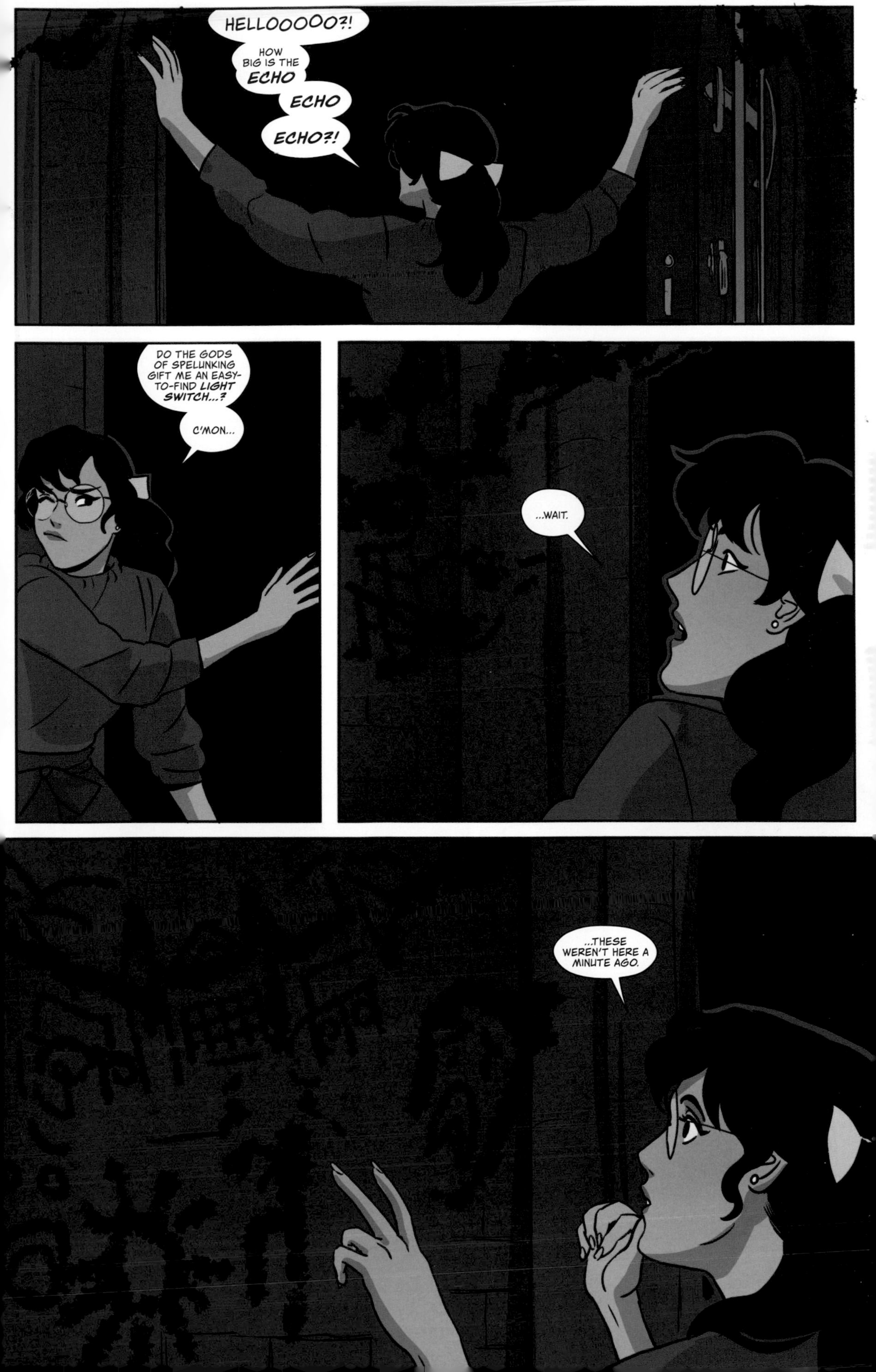
HELLOOOOO?!
HOW BIG IS THE ECHO
ECHO
ECHO?!
DO THE GODS OF SPELUNKING GIFT ME AN EASY-TO-FIND LIGHT SWITCH...?
C'MON...
...WAIT.
...THESE WEREN'T HERE A MINUTE AGO.

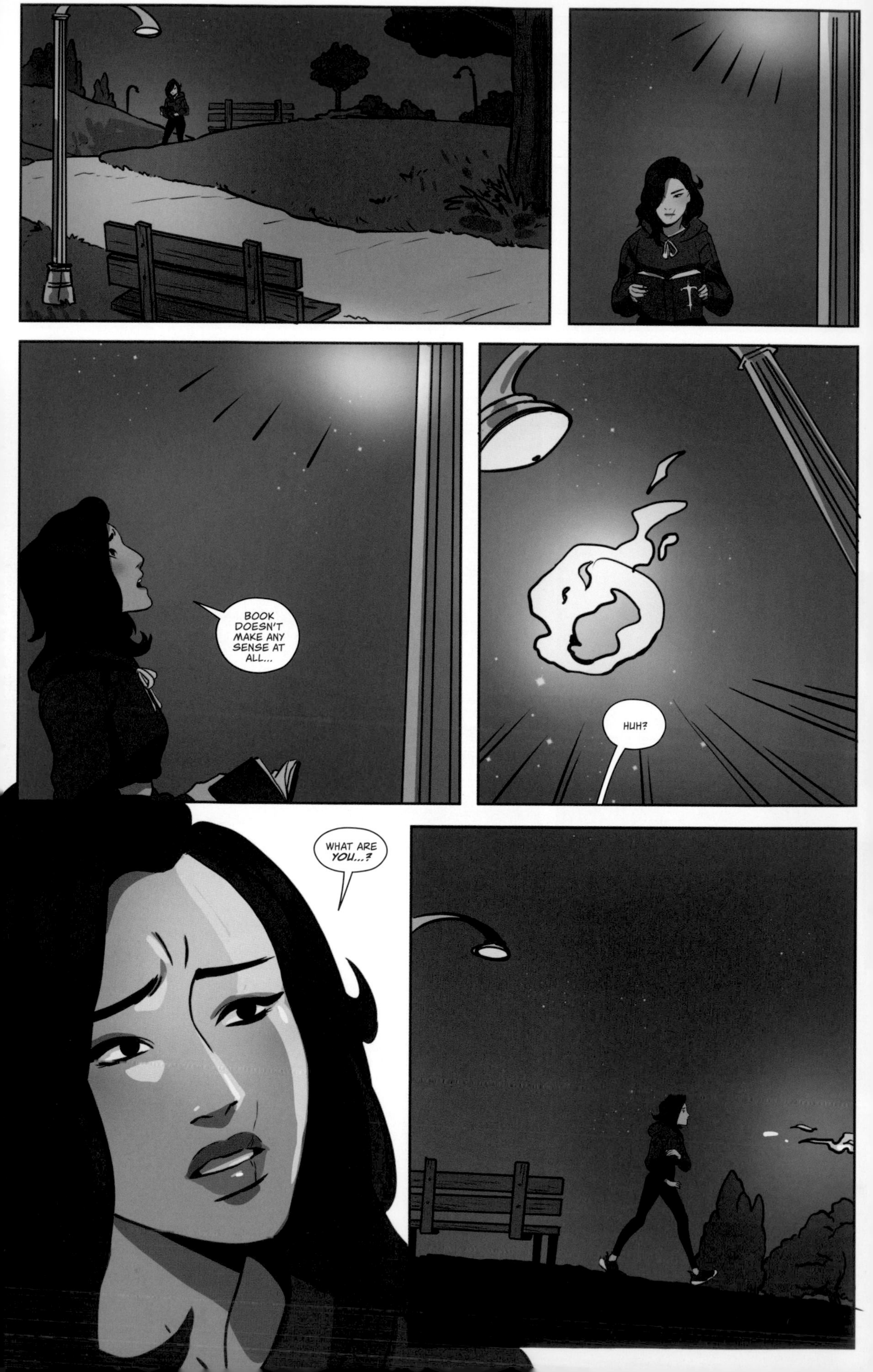
BOOK DOESN'T MAKE ANY SENSE AT ALL...
HUH?
WHAT ARE YOU...?

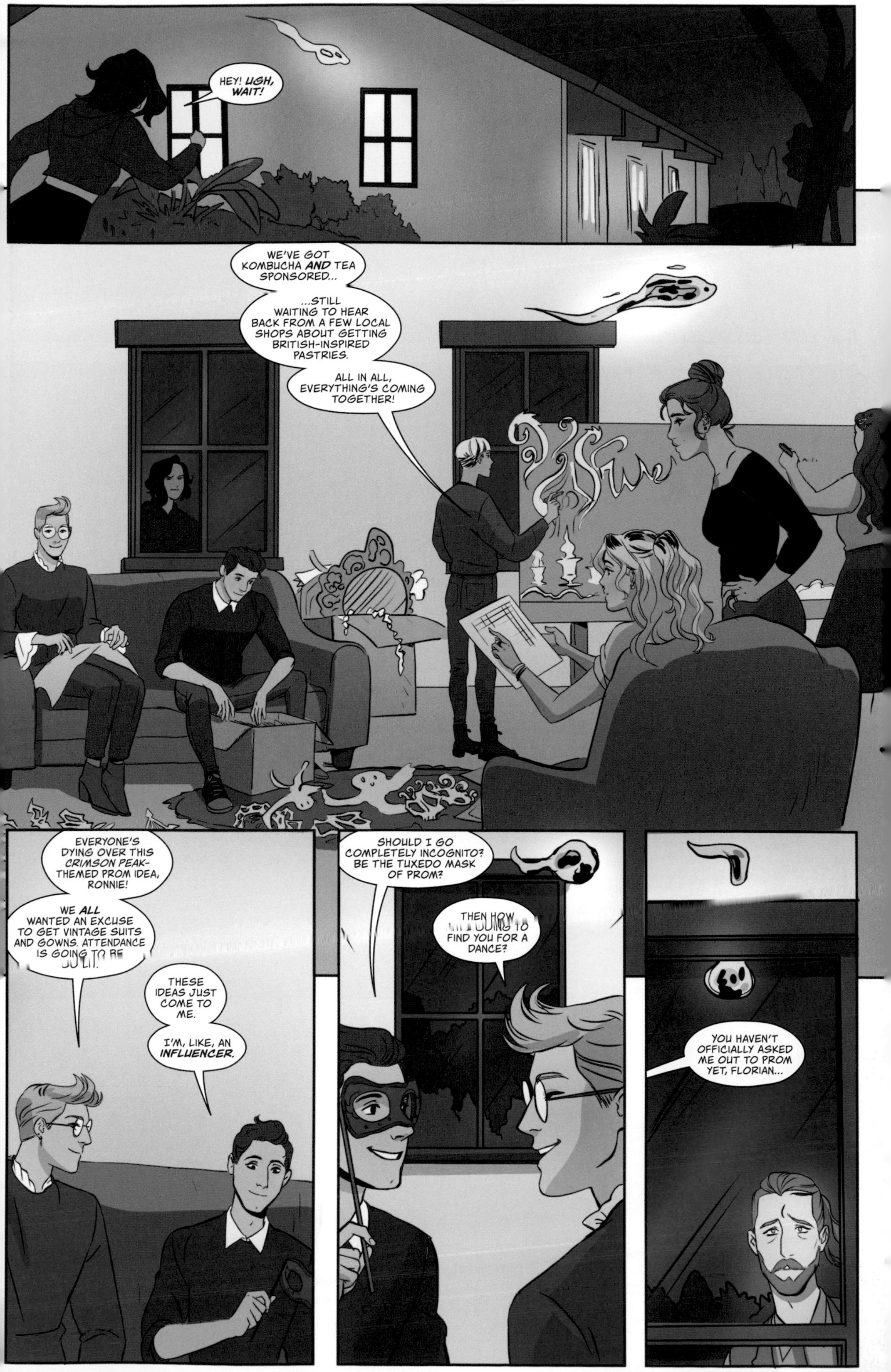
HEY! UGH, WAIT!
WE'VE GOT KOMBUCHA AND TEA SPONSORED...
...STILL WAITING TO HEAR BACK FROM A FEW LOCAL SHOPS ABOUT GETTING BRITISH-INSPIRED PASTRIES.
ALL IN ALL, EVERYTHING'S COMING TOGETHER!
EVERYONE'S DYING OVER THIS CRIMSON PEAK-THEMED PROM IDEA, RONNIE!
WE ALL WANTED AN EXCUSE TO GET VINTAGE SUITS AND GOWNS. ATTENDANCE IS GOING TO BE LIT.
THESE IDEAS JUST COME TO ME.
I'M, LIKE, AN INFLUENCER.
SHOULD I GO COMPLETELY INCOGNITO? BE THE TUXEDO MASK OF PROM?
THEN HOW TO FIND YOU FOR A DANCE?
YOU HAVEN'T OFFICIALLY ASKED ME OUT TO PROM YET, FLORIAN...

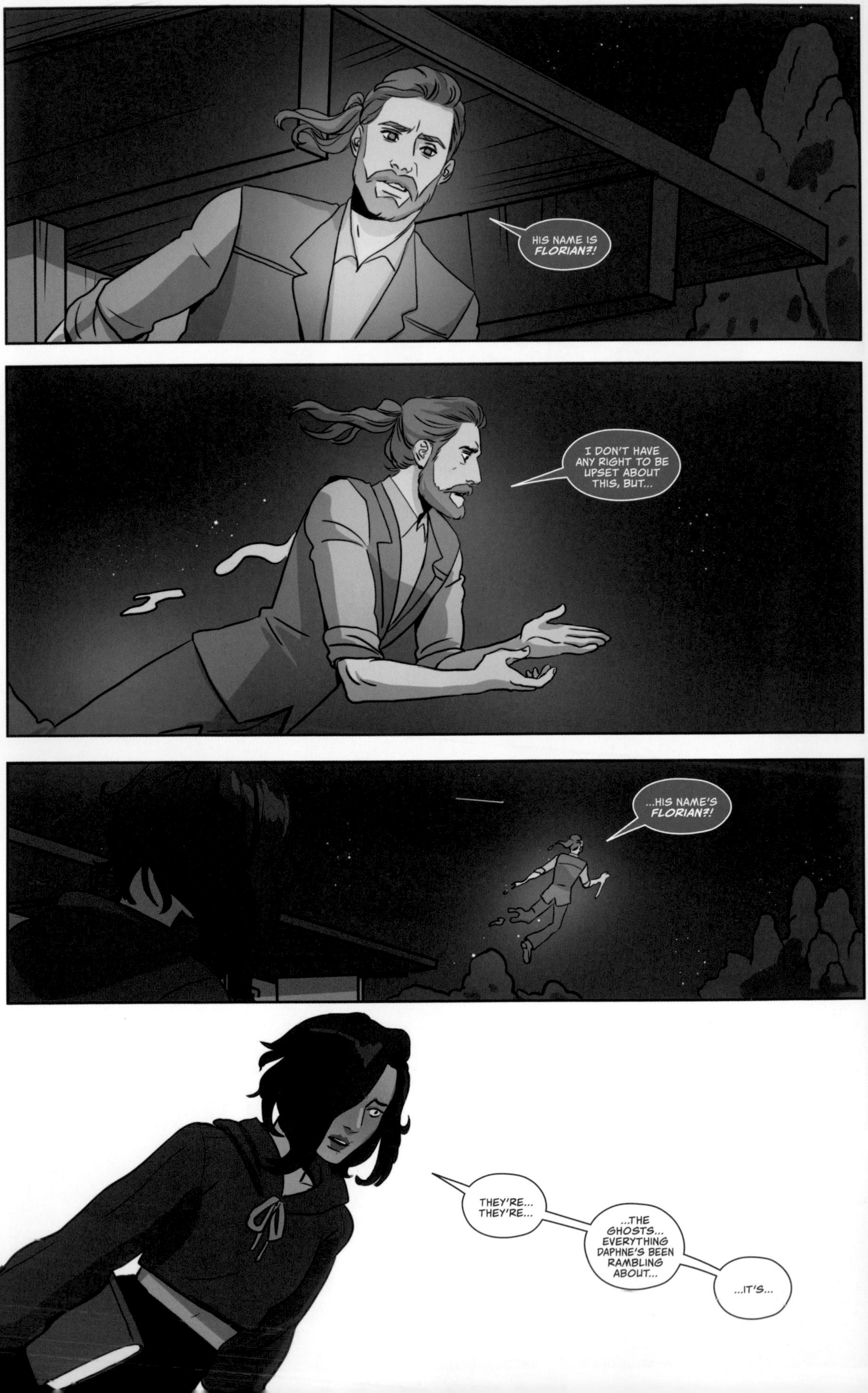
HIS NAME IS *FLORIAN?!*
I DON'T HAVE ANY RIGHT TO BE UPSET ABOUT THIS, BUT...
...HIS NAME'S *FLORIAN?!*
THEY'RE... THEY'RE...
...THE GHOSTS... EVERYTHING DAPHNE'S BEEN RAMBLING ABOUT...
...IT'S...

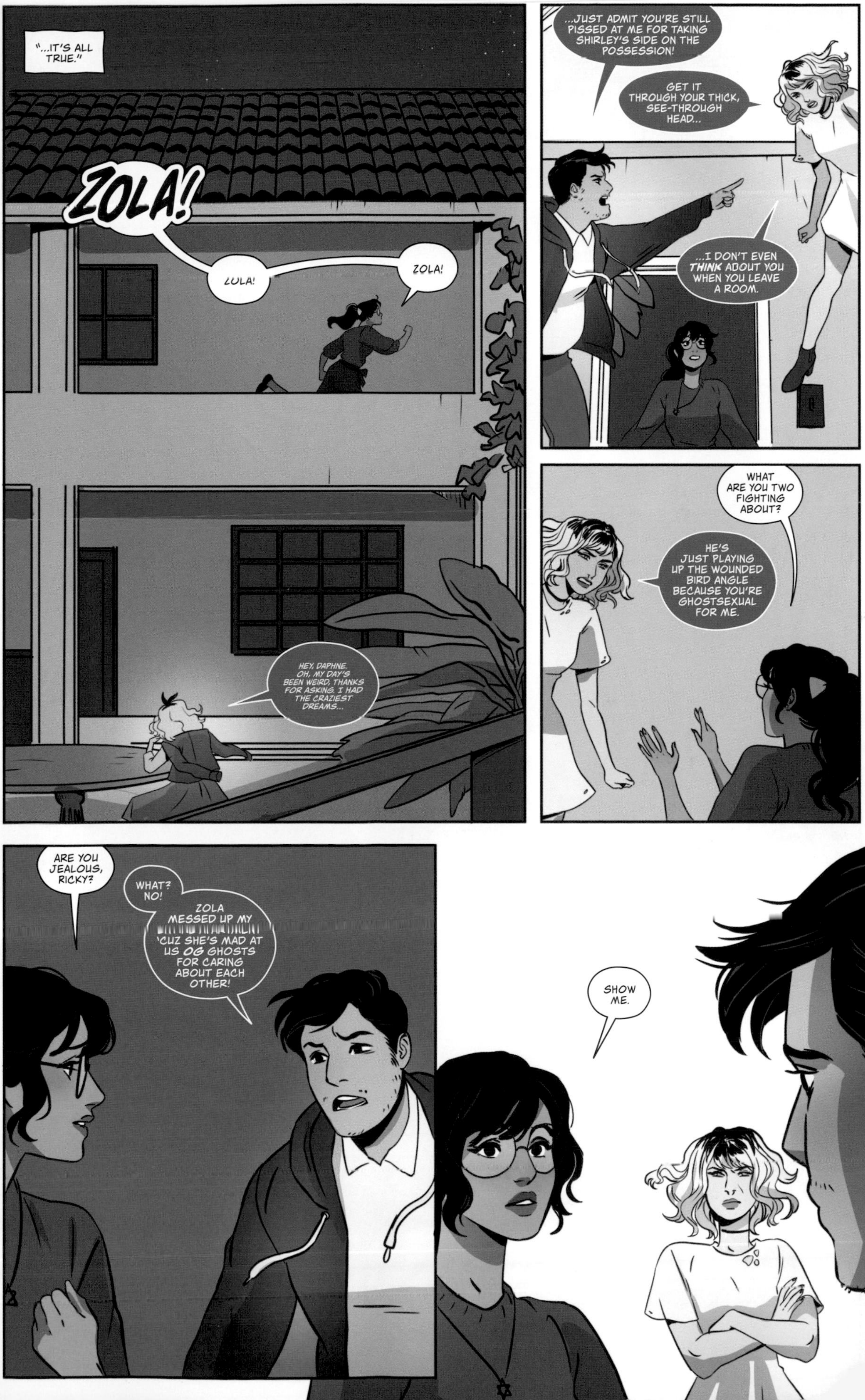

"...IT'S ALL TRUE."
ZOLA!
ZOLA!
ZOLA!
HEY, DAPHNE. OH, MY DAY'S BEEN WEIRD, THANKS FOR ASKING. I HAD THE CRAZIEST DREAMS...
...JUST ADMIT YOU'RE STILL PISSED AT ME FOR TAKING SHIRLEY'S SIDE ON THE POSSESSION!
GET IT THROUGH YOUR THICK, SEE-THROUGH HEAD...
...I DON'T EVEN THINK ABOUT YOU WHEN YOU LEAVE A ROOM.
WHAT ARE YOU TWO FIGHTING ABOUT?
HE'S JUST PLAYING UP THE WOUNDED BIRD ANGLE BECAUSE YOU'RE GHOSTSEXUAL FOR ME.
ARE YOU JEALOUS, RICKY?
WHAT? NO!
ZOLA MESSED UP MY
'CUZ SHE'S MAD AT US OG GHOSTS FOR CARING ABOUT EACH OTHER!
SHOW ME.

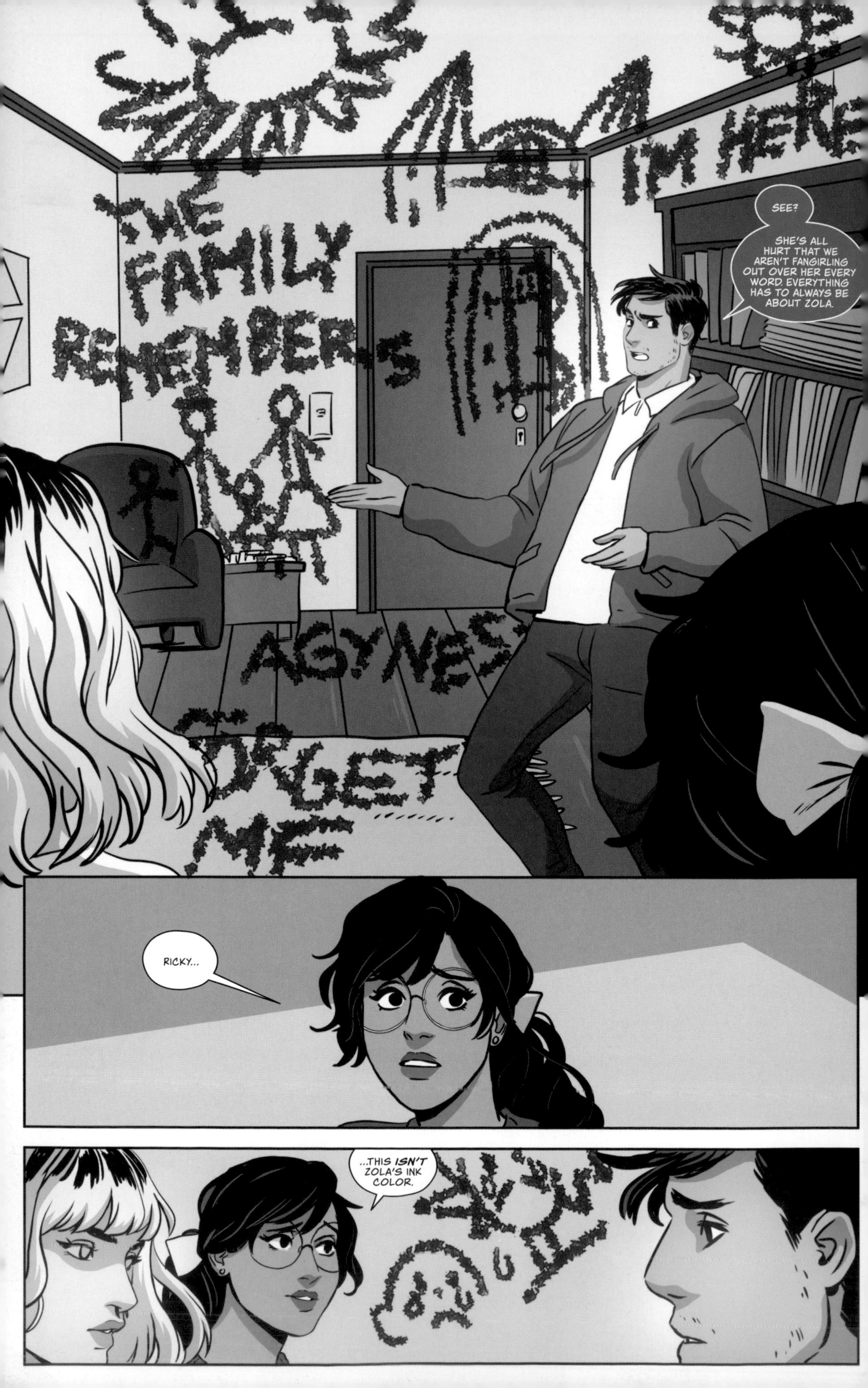
IM HERE
THE FAMILY REMEMBERS
AGYNES
SEE?
SHE'S ALL HURT THAT WE AREN'T FANGIRLING OUT OVER HER EVERY WORD. EVERYTHING HAS TO ALWAYS BE ABOUT ZOLA.
RICKY...
...THIS *ISN'T* ZOLA'S INK COLOR.

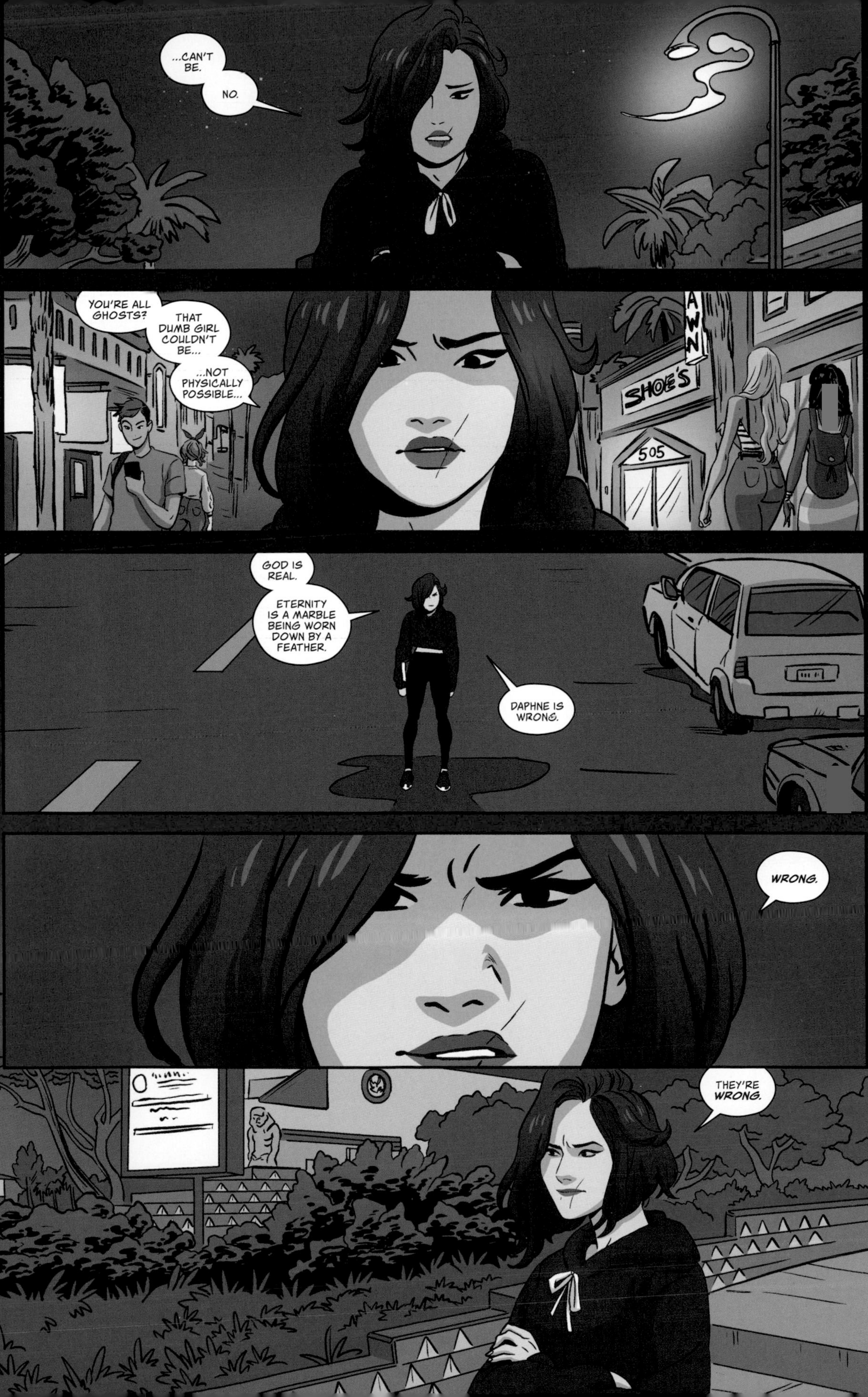
...CAN'T BE.
NO.
YOU'RE ALL GHOSTS?
THAT DUMB GIRL COULDN'T BE...
...NOT PHYSICALLY POSSIBLE...
SHOE'S
505
GOD IS REAL.
ETERNITY IS A MARBLE BEING WORN DOWN BY A FEATHER.
DAPHNE IS WRONG.
WRONG.
THEY'RE WRONG.

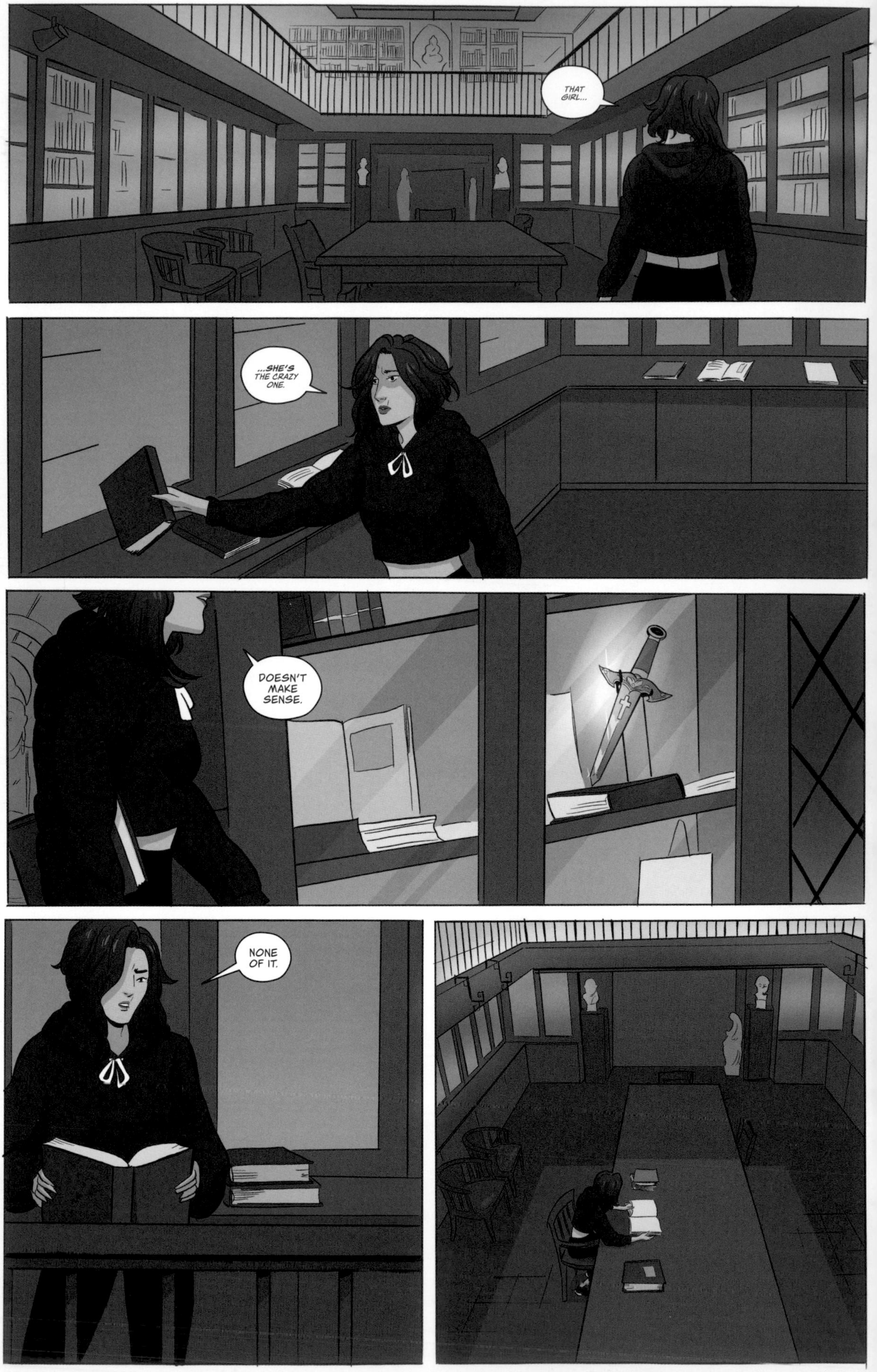
THAT GIRL...
...SHE'S THE CRAZY ONE.
DOESN'T MAKE SENSE.
NONE OF IT.

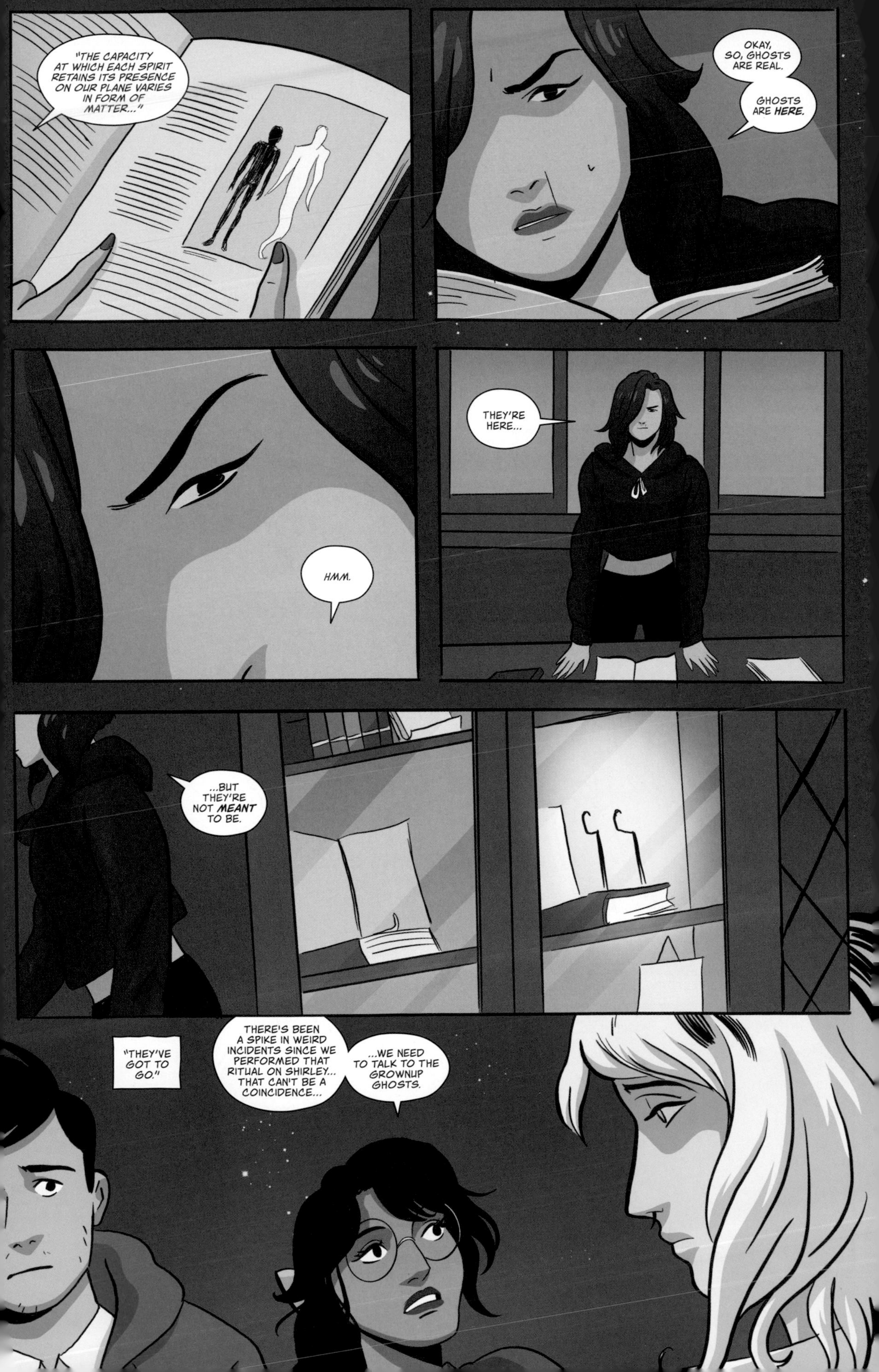
"THE CAPACITY AT WHICH EACH SPIRIT RETAINS ITS PRESENCE ON OUR PLANE VARIES IN FORM OF MATTER..."
OKAY, SO, GHOSTS ARE REAL.
GHOSTS ARE HERE.
HMM.
THEY'RE HERE...
...BUT THEY'RE NOT MEANT TO BE.
"THEY'VE GOT TO GO."
THERE'S BEEN A SPIKE IN WEIRD INCIDENTS SINCE WE PERFORMED THAT RITUAL ON SHIRLEY... THAT CAN'T BE A COINCIDENCE...
...WE NEED TO TALK TO THE GROWNUP GHOSTS.

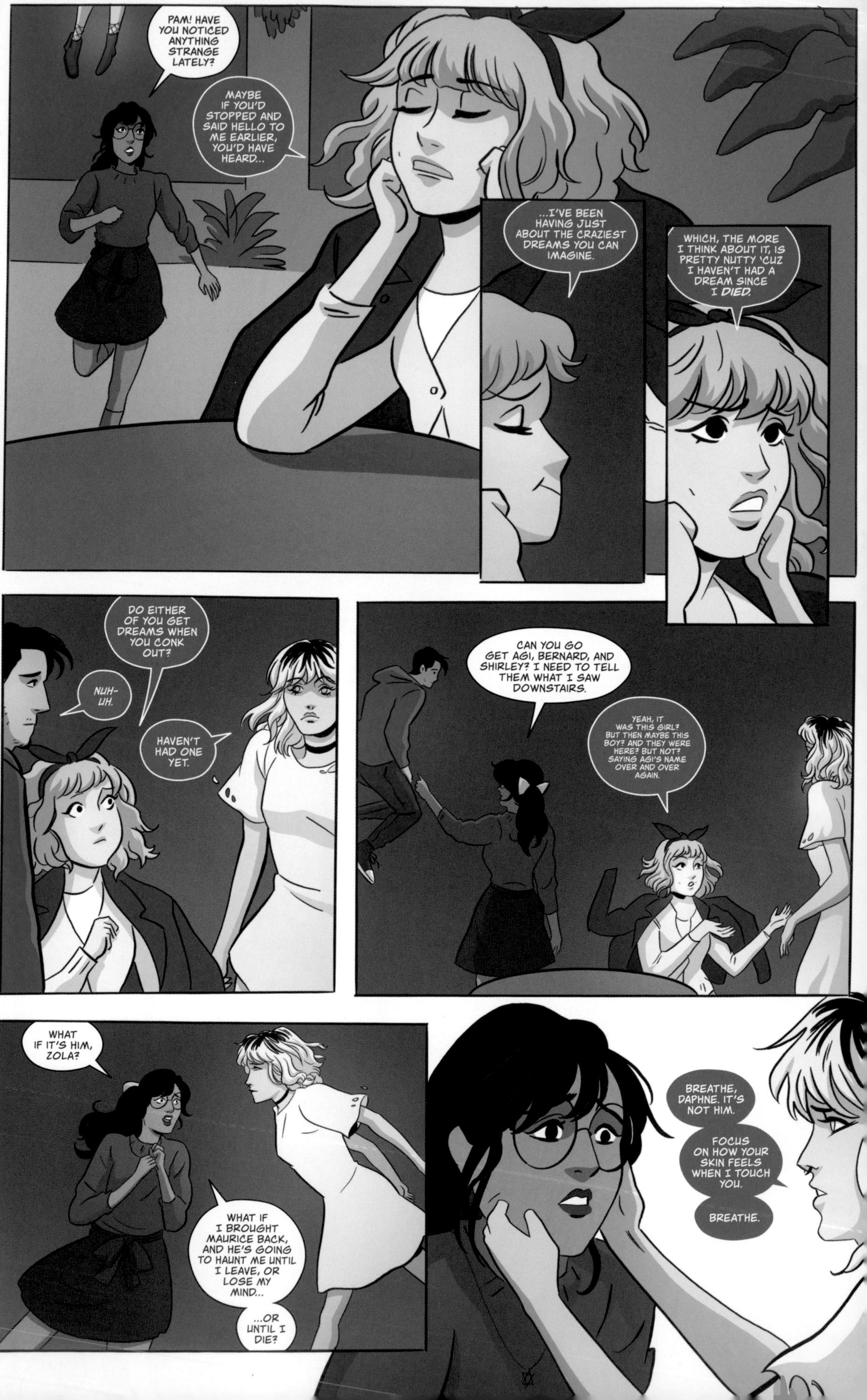
PAM! HAVE YOU NOTICED ANYTHING STRANGE LATELY?
MAYBE IF YOU'D STOPPED AND SAID HELLO TO ME EARLIER, YOU'D HAVE HEARD...
...I'VE BEEN HAVING JUST ABOUT THE CRAZIEST DREAMS YOU CAN IMAGINE.
WHICH, THE MORE I THINK ABOUT IT, IS PRETTY NUTTY 'CUZ I HAVEN'T HAD A DREAM SINCE I *DIED*.
DO EITHER OF YOU GET DREAMS WHEN YOU CONK OUT?
NUH-UH.
HAVEN'T HAD ONE YET.
CAN YOU GO GET AGI, BERNARD, AND SHIRLEY? I NEED TO TELL THEM WHAT I SAW DOWNSTAIRS.
YEAH, IT WAS THIS GIRL? BUT THEN MAYBE THIS BOY? AND THEY WERE HERE? BUT NOT? SAYING AGI'S NAME OVER AND OVER AGAIN.
WHAT IF IT'S HIM, ZOLA?
WHAT IF I BROUGHT MAURICE BACK, AND HE'S GOING TO HAUNT ME UNTIL I LEAVE, OR LOSE MY MIND...
...OR UNTIL I DIE?
BREATHE, DAPHNE. IT'S NOT HIM.
FOCUS ON HOW YOUR SKIN FEELS WHEN I TOUCH YOU.
BREATHE.

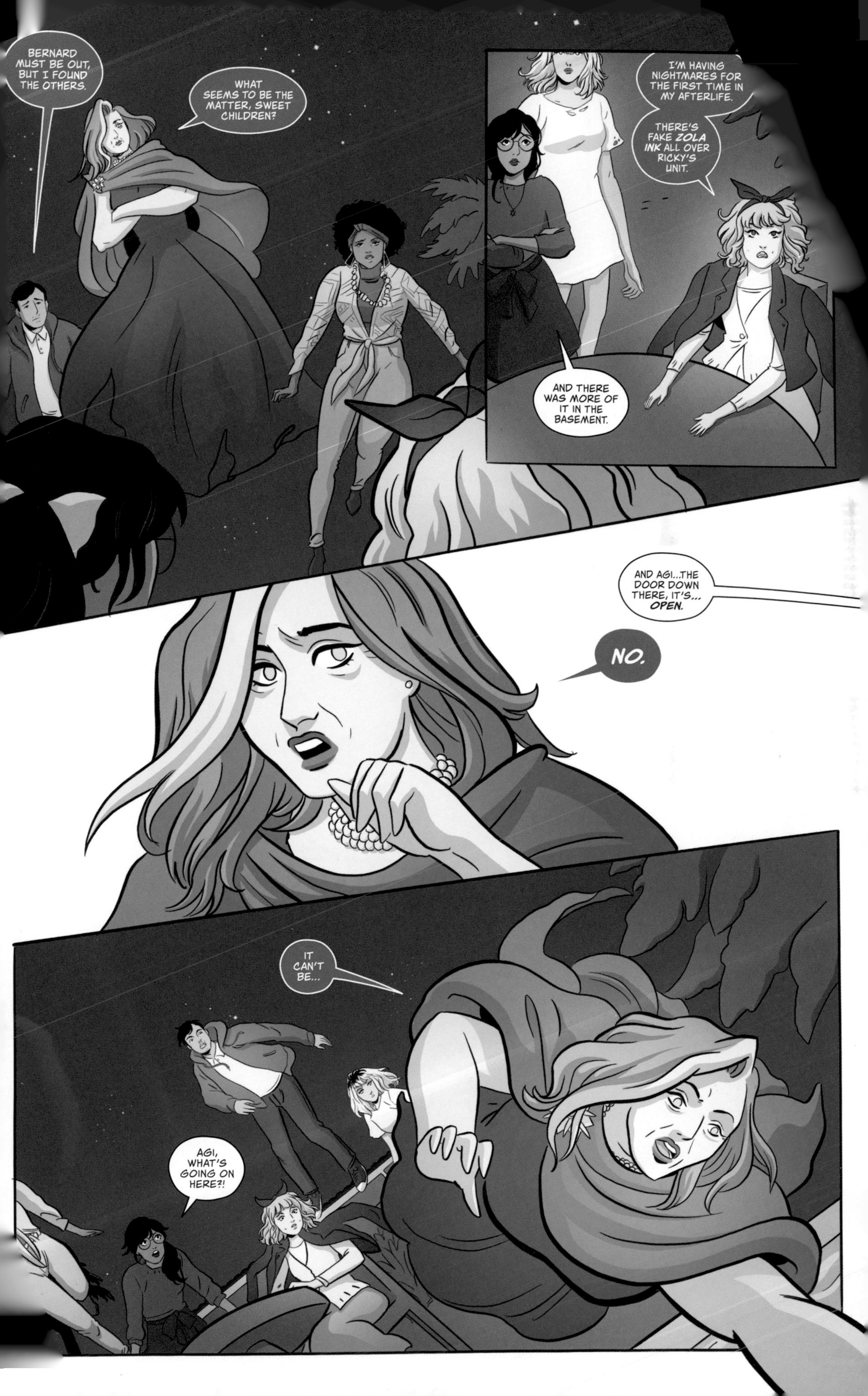
BERNARD MUST BE OUT, BUT I FOUND THE OTHERS.
WHAT SEEMS TO BE THE MATTER, SWEET CHILDREN?
I'M HAVING NIGHTMARES FOR THE FIRST TIME IN MY AFTERLIFE.
THERE'S FAKE ZOLA INK ALL OVER RICKY'S UNIT.
AND THERE WAS MORE OF IT IN THE BASEMENT.
AND AGI...THE DOOR DOWN THERE, IT'S... OPEN.
NO.
IT CAN'T BE...
AGI, WHAT'S GOING ON HERE?!

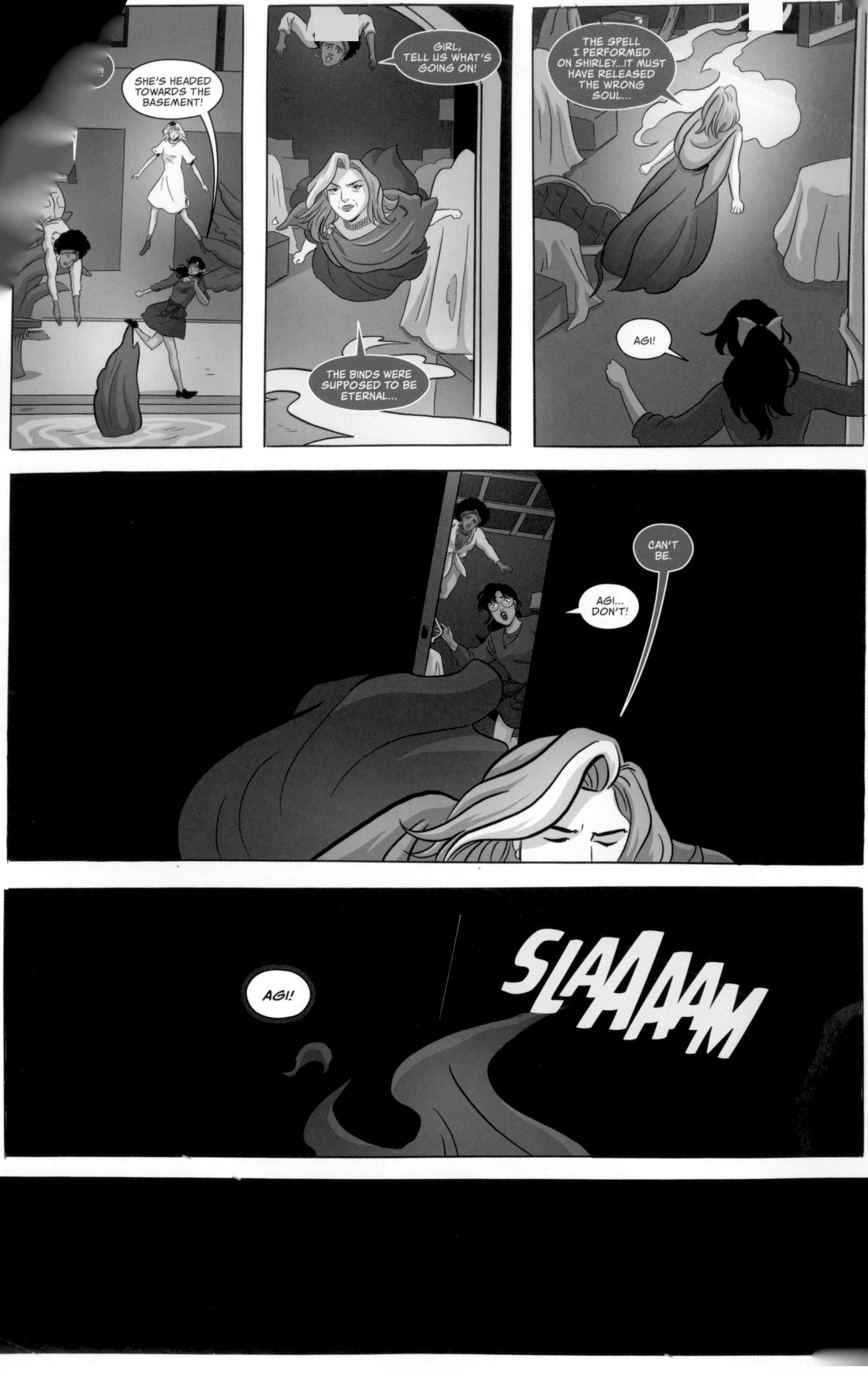
SHE'S HEADED TOWARDS THE BASEMENT!
GIRL, TELL US WHAT'S GOING ON!
THE BINDS WERE SUPPOSED TO BE ETERNAL...
THE SPELL I PERFORMED ON SHIRLEY...IT MUST HAVE RELEASED THE WRONG SOUL...
AGI!
CAN'T BE.
AGI... DON'T!
AGI!
SLAAAAM

Chapter Ten

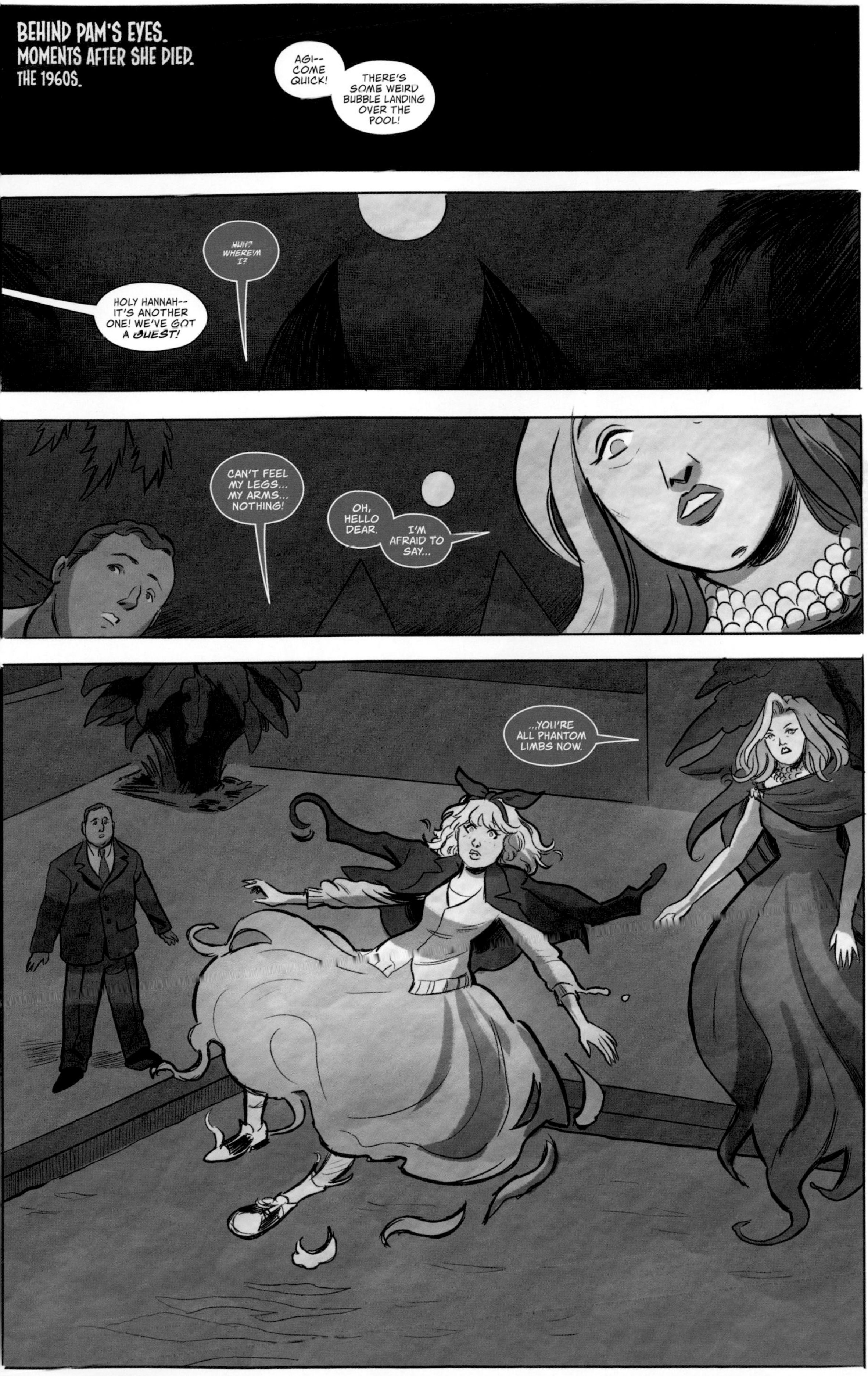
BEHIND PAM'S EYES. MOMENTS AFTER SHE DIED. THE 1960S.
AGI-- COME QUICK!
THERE'S SOME WEIRD BUBBLE LANDING OVER THE POOL!
HUH? WHERE'M I?
HOLY HANNAH-- IT'S ANOTHER ONE! WE'VE GOT A GUEST!
CAN'T FEEL MY LEGS... MY ARMS... NOTHING!
OH, HELLO DEAR.
I'M AFRAID TO SAY...
...YOU'RE ALL PHANTOM LIMBS NOW.

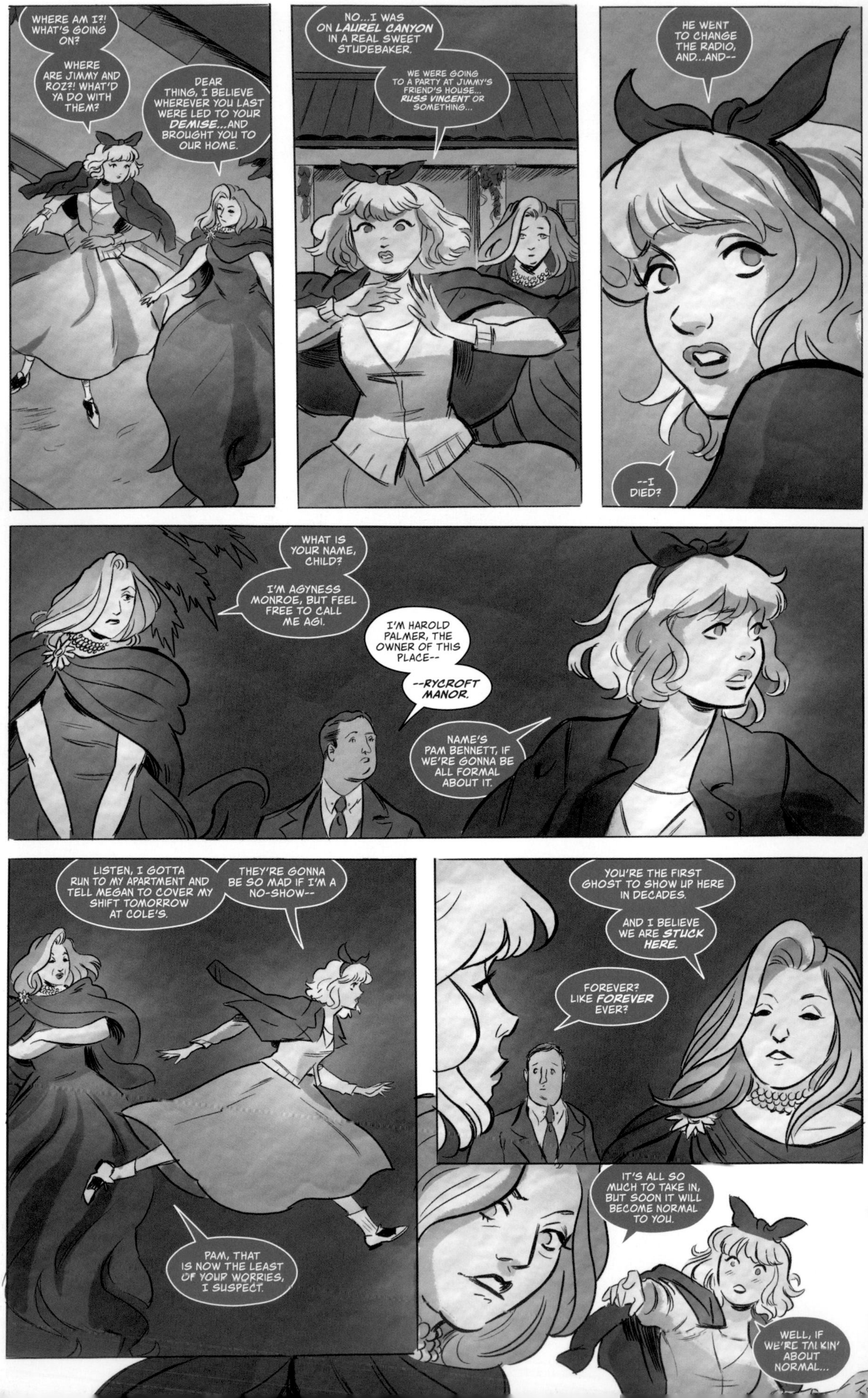
WHERE AM I?! WHAT'S GOING ON?
WHERE ARE JIMMY AND ROZ?! WHAT'D YA DO WITH THEM?
DEAR THING, I BELIEVE WHEREVER YOU LAST WERE LED TO YOUR DEMISE...AND BROUGHT YOU TO OUR HOME.
NO...I WAS ON LAUREL CANYON IN A REAL SWEET STUDEBAKER.
WE WERE GOING TO A PARTY AT JIMMY'S FRIEND'S HOUSE... RUSS VINCENT OR SOMETHING...
HE WENT TO CHANGE THE RADIO, AND...AND--
--I DIED?
WHAT IS YOUR NAME, CHILD?
I'M AGYNESS MONROE, BUT FEEL FREE TO CALL ME AGI.
I'M HAROLD PALMER, THE OWNER OF THIS PLACE--
--RYCROFT MANOR.
NAME'S PAM BENNETT, IF WE'RE GONNA BE ALL FORMAL ABOUT IT.
LISTEN, I GOTTA RUN TO MY APARTMENT AND TELL MEGAN TO COVER MY SHIFT TOMORROW AT COLE'S.
THEY'RE GONNA BE SO MAD IF I'M A NO-SHOW--
PAM, THAT IS NOW THE LEAST OF YOUR WORRIES, I SUSPECT.
YOU'RE THE FIRST GHOST TO SHOW UP HERE IN DECADES.
AND I BELIEVE WE ARE STUCK HERE.
FOREVER? LIKE FOREVER EVER?
IT'S ALL SO MUCH TO TAKE IN, BUT SOON IT WILL BECOME NORMAL TO YOU.
WELL, IF WE'RE TALKIN' ABOUT NORMAL...

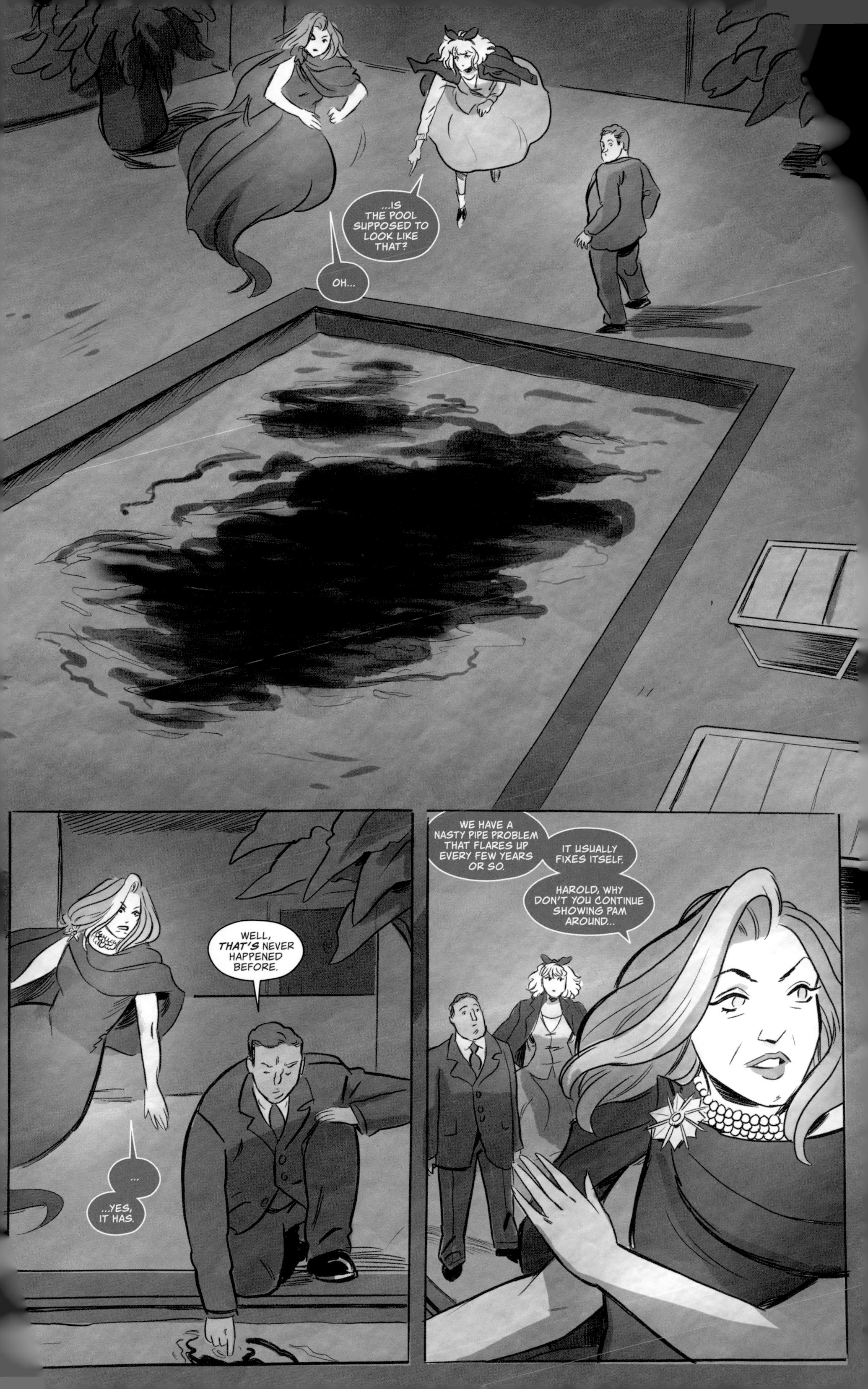
...IS THE POOL SUPPOSED TO LOOK LIKE THAT?
OH...
WELL, THAT'S NEVER HAPPENED BEFORE.
...
...YES, IT HAS.
WE HAVE A NASTY PIPE PROBLEM THAT FLARES UP EVERY FEW YEARS OR SO.
IT USUALLY FIXES ITSELF.
HAROLD, WHY DON'T YOU CONTINUE SHOWING PAM AROUND...

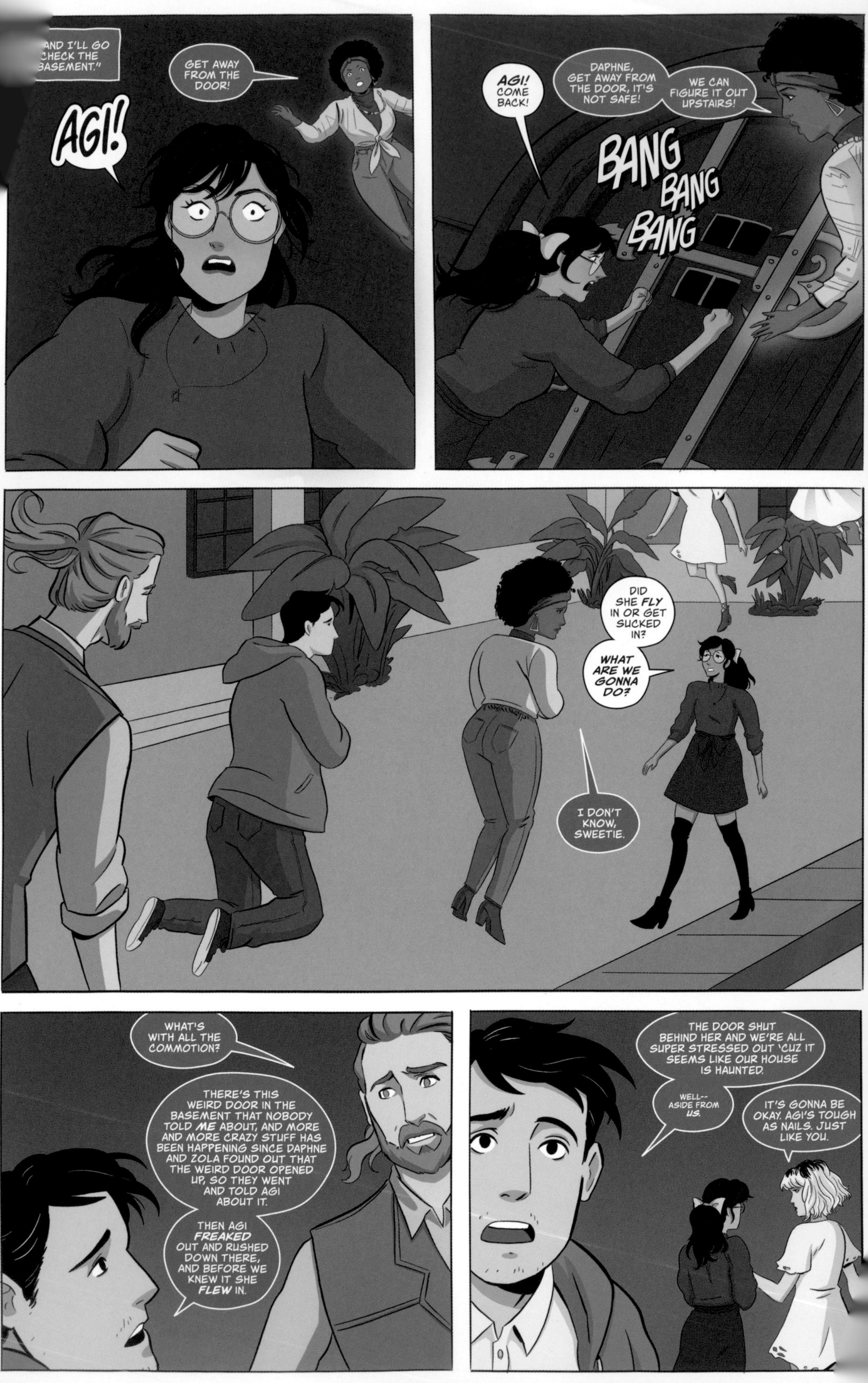
"AND I'LL GO CHECK THE BASEMENT."
GET AWAY FROM THE DOOR!
AGI!
AGI! COME BACK!
DAPHNE, GET AWAY FROM THE DOOR, IT'S NOT SAFE!
WE CAN FIGURE IT OUT UPSTAIRS!
BANG
BANG
BANG
DID SHE FLY IN OR GET SUCKED IN?
WHAT ARE WE GONNA DO?
I DON'T KNOW, SWEETIE.
WHAT'S WITH ALL THE COMMOTION?
THERE'S THIS WEIRD DOOR IN THE BASEMENT THAT NOBODY TOLD ME ABOUT, AND MORE AND MORE CRAZY STUFF HAS BEEN HAPPENING SINCE DAPHNE AND ZOLA FOUND OUT THAT THE WEIRD DOOR OPENED UP, SO THEY WENT AND TOLD AGI ABOUT IT.
THEN AGI FREAKED OUT AND RUSHED DOWN THERE, AND BEFORE WE KNEW IT SHE FLEW IN.
THE DOOR SHUT BEHIND HER AND WE'RE ALL SUPER STRESSED OUT 'CUZ IT SEEMS LIKE OUR HOUSE IS HAUNTED.
WELL-- ASIDE FROM US.
IT'S GONNA BE OKAY. AGI'S TOUGH AS NAILS. JUST LIKE YOU.

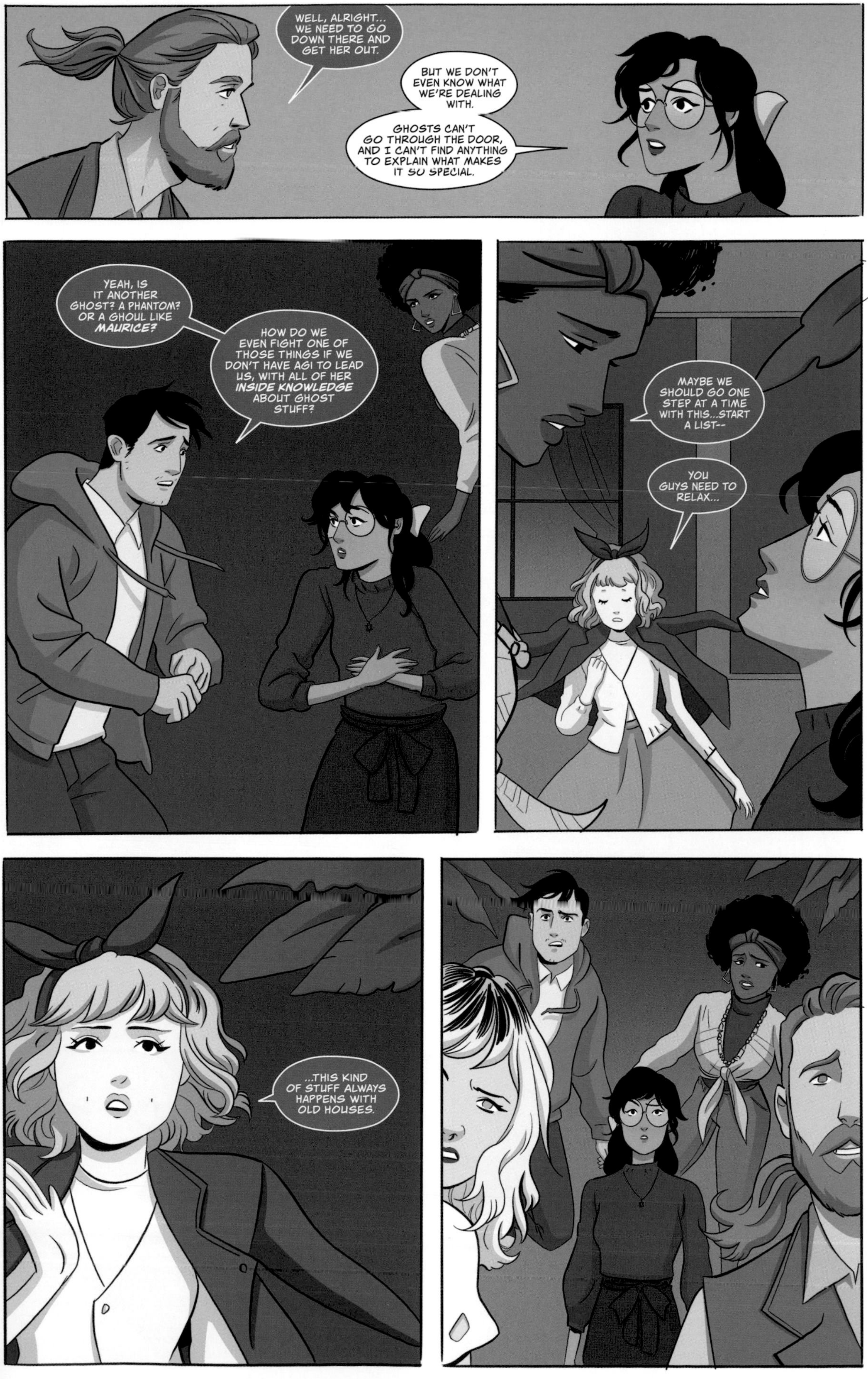
WELL, ALRIGHT... WE NEED TO GO DOWN THERE AND GET HER OUT.
BUT WE DON'T EVEN KNOW WHAT WE'RE DEALING WITH.
GHOSTS CAN'T GO THROUGH THE DOOR, AND I CAN'T FIND ANYTHING TO EXPLAIN WHAT MAKES IT SO SPECIAL.
YEAH, IS IT ANOTHER GHOST? A PHANTOM? OR A GHOUL LIKE MAURICE?
HOW DO WE EVEN FIGHT ONE OF THOSE THINGS IF WE DON'T HAVE AGI TO LEAD US, WITH ALL OF HER INSIDE KNOWLEDGE ABOUT GHOST STUFF?
MAYBE WE SHOULD GO ONE STEP AT A TIME WITH THIS...START A LIST--
YOU GUYS NEED TO RELAX...
...THIS KIND OF STUFF ALWAYS HAPPENS WITH OLD HOUSES.

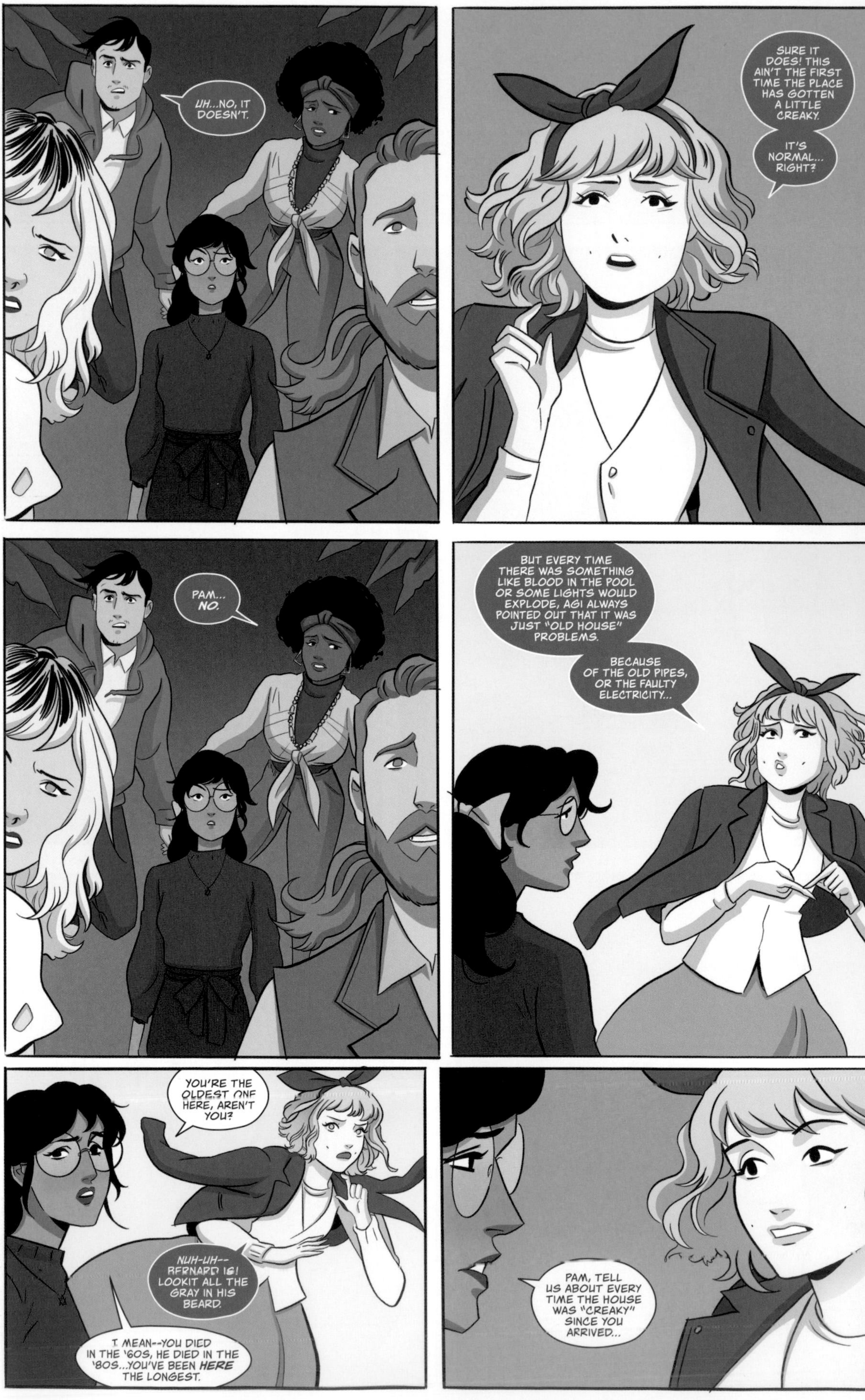
UH...NO, IT DOESN'T.
SURE IT DOES! THIS AIN'T THE FIRST TIME THE PLACE HAS GOTTEN A LITTLE CREAKY.
IT'S NORMAL... RIGHT?
PAM... NO.
BUT EVERY TIME THERE WAS SOMETHING LIKE BLOOD IN THE POOL OR SOME LIGHTS WOULD EXPLODE, AGI ALWAYS POINTED OUT THAT IT WAS JUST "OLD HOUSE" PROBLEMS.
BECAUSE OF THE OLD PIPES, OR THE FAULTY ELECTRICITY...
YOU'RE THE OLDEST ONE HERE, AREN'T YOU?
NUH-UH-- BERNARD IS! LOOKIT ALL THE GRAY IN HIS BEARD.
I MEAN--YOU DIED IN THE '60S, HE DIED IN THE '80S...YOU'VE BEEN HERE THE LONGEST.
PAM, TELL US ABOUT EVERY TIME THE HOUSE WAS "CREAKY" SINCE YOU ARRIVED...

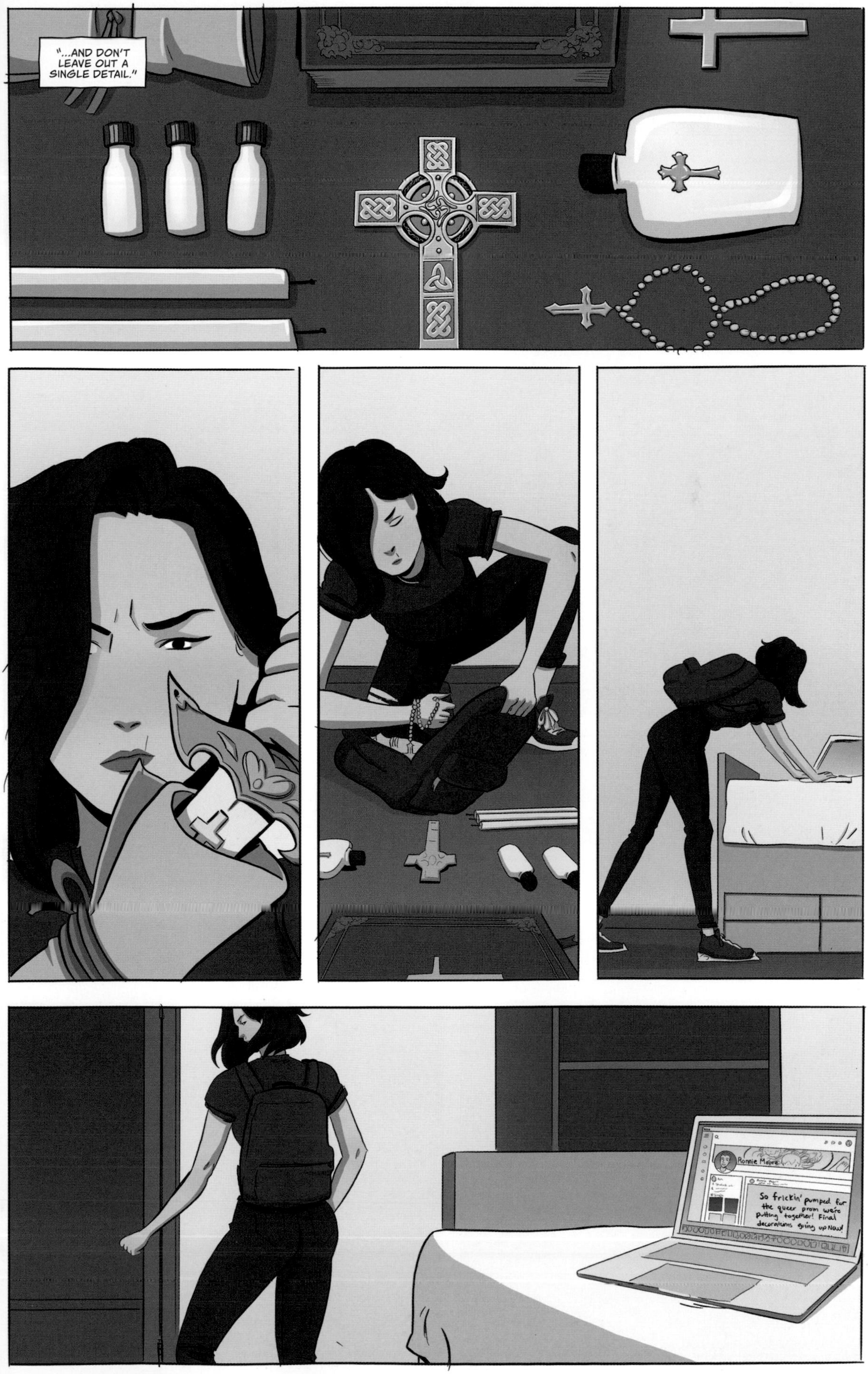
"...AND DON'T LEAVE OUT A SINGLE DETAIL."
Ronnie Moore
So frickin' pumped for the queer prom we're putting together! Final decorations going up Now!

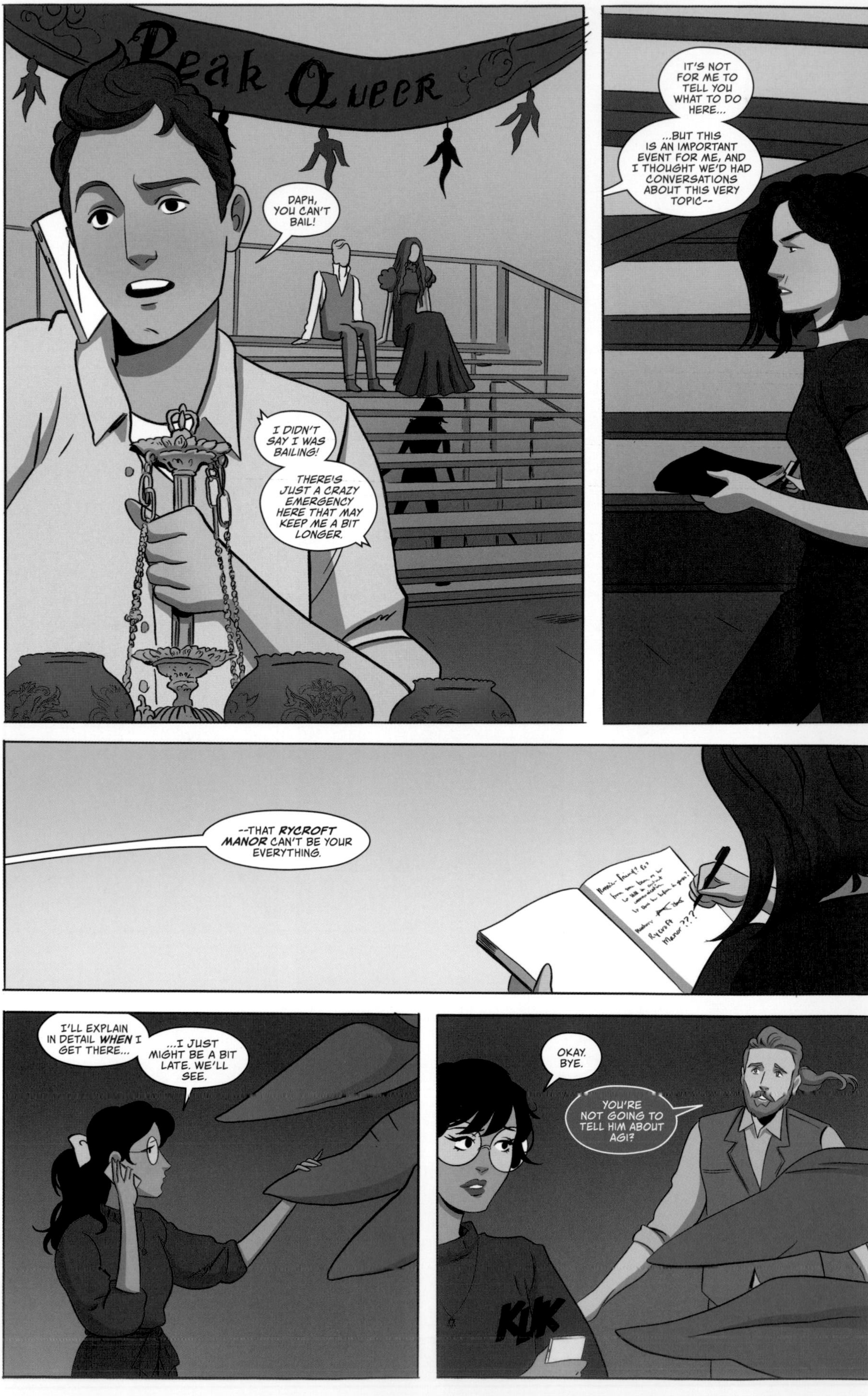
Peak Queer
DAPH, YOU CAN'T BAIL!
I DIDN'T SAY I WAS BAILING!
THERE'S JUST A CRAZY EMERGENCY HERE THAT MAY KEEP ME A BIT LONGER.
IT'S NOT FOR ME TO TELL YOU WHAT TO DO HERE...
...BUT THIS IS AN IMPORTANT EVENT FOR ME, AND I THOUGHT WE'D HAD CONVERSATIONS ABOUT THIS VERY TOPIC--
--THAT RYCROFT MANOR CAN'T BE YOUR EVERYTHING.
I'LL EXPLAIN IN DETAIL WHEN I GET THERE...
...I JUST MIGHT BE A BIT LATE. WE'LL SEE.
OKAY. BYE.
YOU'RE NOT GOING TO TELL HIM ABOUT AGI?
KLIK

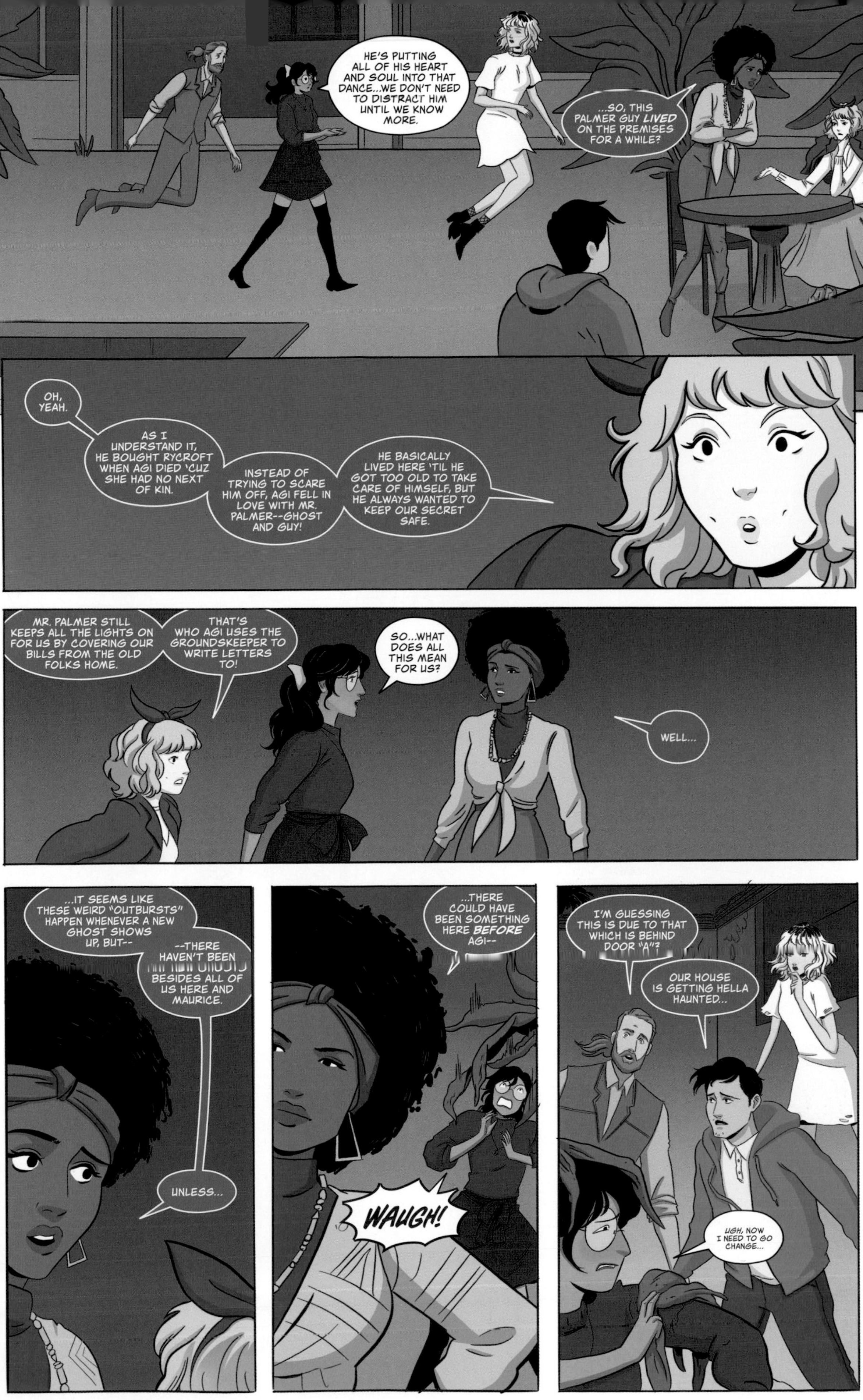
HE'S PUTTING ALL OF HIS HEART AND SOUL INTO THAT DANCE...WE DON'T NEED TO DISTRACT HIM UNTIL WE KNOW MORE.
...SO, THIS PALMER GUY LIVED ON THE PREMISES FOR A WHILE?
OH, YEAH.
AS I UNDERSTAND IT, HE BOUGHT RYCROFT WHEN AGI DIED 'CUZ SHE HAD NO NEXT OF KIN.
INSTEAD OF TRYING TO SCARE HIM OFF, AGI FELL IN LOVE WITH MR. PALMER--GHOST AND GUY!
HE BASICALLY LIVED HERE 'TIL HE GOT TOO OLD TO TAKE CARE OF HIMSELF, BUT HE ALWAYS WANTED TO KEEP OUR SECRET SAFE.
MR. PALMER STILL KEEPS ALL THE LIGHTS ON FOR US BY COVERING OUR BILLS FROM THE OLD FOLKS HOME.
THAT'S WHO AGI USES THE GROUNDSKEEPER TO WRITE LETTERS TO!
SO...WHAT DOES ALL THIS MEAN FOR US?
WELL...
...IT SEEMS LIKE THESE WEIRD "OUTBURSTS" HAPPEN WHENEVER A NEW GHOST SHOWS UP, BUT--
--THERE HAVEN'T BEEN
BESIDES ALL OF US HERE AND MAURICE.
UNLESS...
...THERE COULD HAVE BEEN SOMETHING HERE BEFORE AGI--
WAUGH!
I'M GUESSING THIS IS DUE TO THAT WHICH IS BEHIND DOOR "A"?
OUR HOUSE IS GETTING HELLA HAUNTED...
UGH, NOW I NEED TO GO CHANGE...

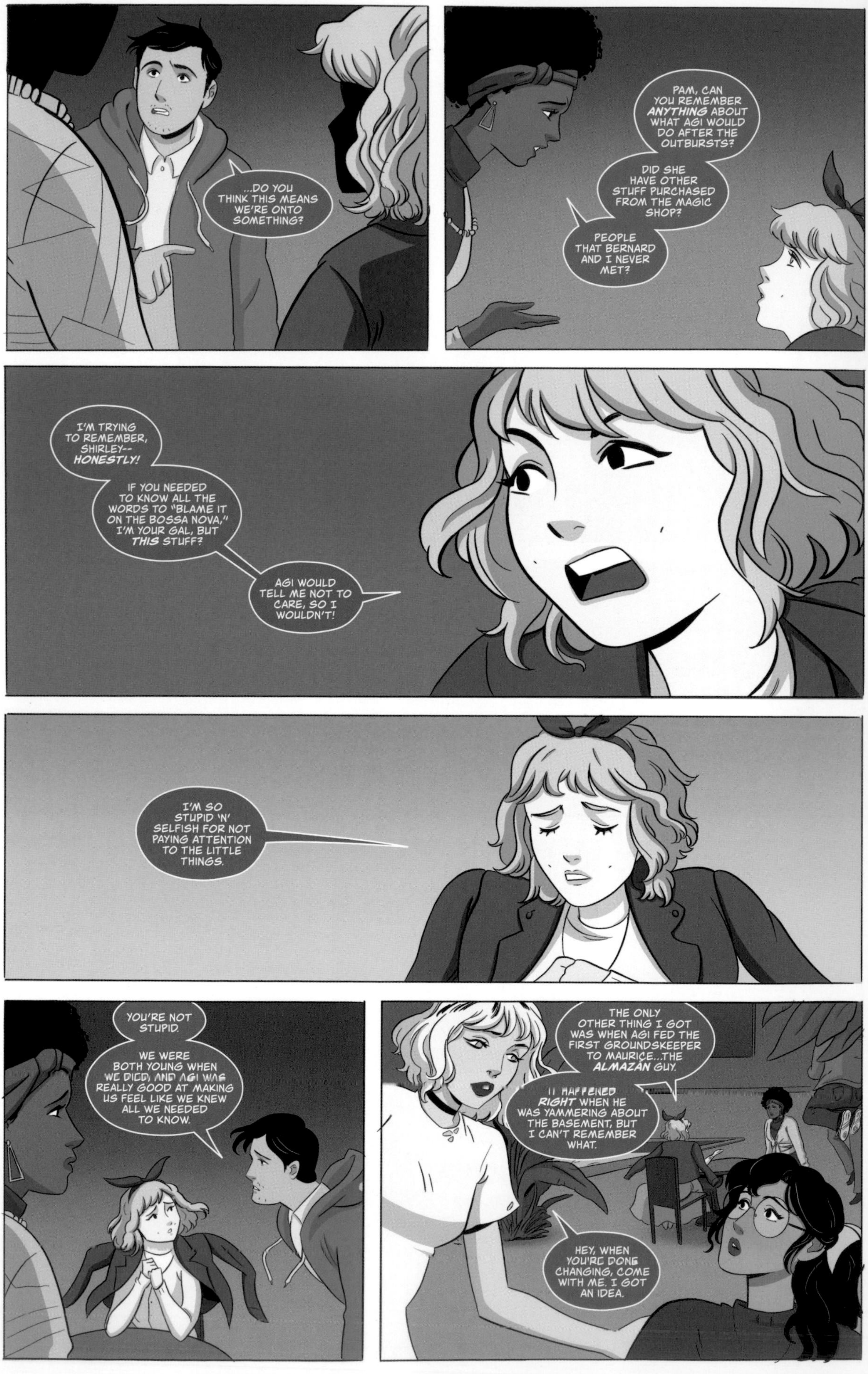
...DO YOU THINK THIS MEANS WE'RE ONTO SOMETHING?
PAM, CAN YOU REMEMBER ANYTHING ABOUT WHAT AGI WOULD DO AFTER THE OUTBURSTS?
DID SHE HAVE OTHER STUFF PURCHASED FROM THE MAGIC SHOP?
PEOPLE THAT BERNARD AND I NEVER MET?
I'M TRYING TO REMEMBER, SHIRLEY-- HONESTLY!
IF YOU NEEDED TO KNOW ALL THE WORDS TO "BLAME IT ON THE BOSSA NOVA," I'M YOUR GAL, BUT THIS STUFF?
AGI WOULD TELL ME NOT TO CARE, SO I WOULDN'T!
I'M SO STUPID 'N' SELFISH FOR NOT PAYING ATTENTION TO THE LITTLE THINGS.
YOU'RE NOT STUPID.
WE WERE BOTH YOUNG WHEN WE DIED, AND AGI WAS REALLY GOOD AT MAKING US FEEL LIKE WE KNEW ALL WE NEEDED TO KNOW.
THE ONLY OTHER THING I GOT WAS WHEN AGI FED THE FIRST GROUNDSKEEPER TO MAURICE...THE ALMAZÁN GUY.
IT HAPPENED RIGHT WHEN HE WAS YAMMERING ABOUT THE BASEMENT, BUT I CAN'T REMEMBER WHAT.
HEY, WHEN YOU'RE DONE CHANGING, COME WITH ME. I GOT AN IDEA.

AGI MAY BE REACHABLE.

IF WHATEVER IS TRAPPED IN THERE CAN MESS WITH US FROM BEHIND THE DOOR...MAYBE AGI CAN, TOO.

IT'S SAFE TO SAY THAT THIS *THING* IS OUR KIND OF SUPERNATURAL, RIGHT?

SO, BY LAW OF WEIRD, CREEPY MAGIC STUFF...MAYBE WE CAN USE MY INK AS A TWO-SIDED ETCH-A-SKETCH.

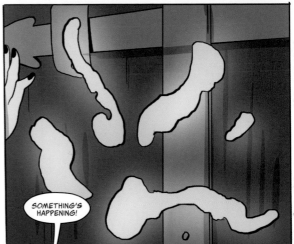

SOMETHING'S HAPPENING!

KEY... JEWELRY.

IS IT THAT EPIC BROOCH AGI'S ALWAYS WEARING?

NO, SHE WAS WEARING THAT WHEN SHE WENT IN...

HUH.

I'M STUMPED.

I'M NOT.

I KNOW WHAT IT MEANS.

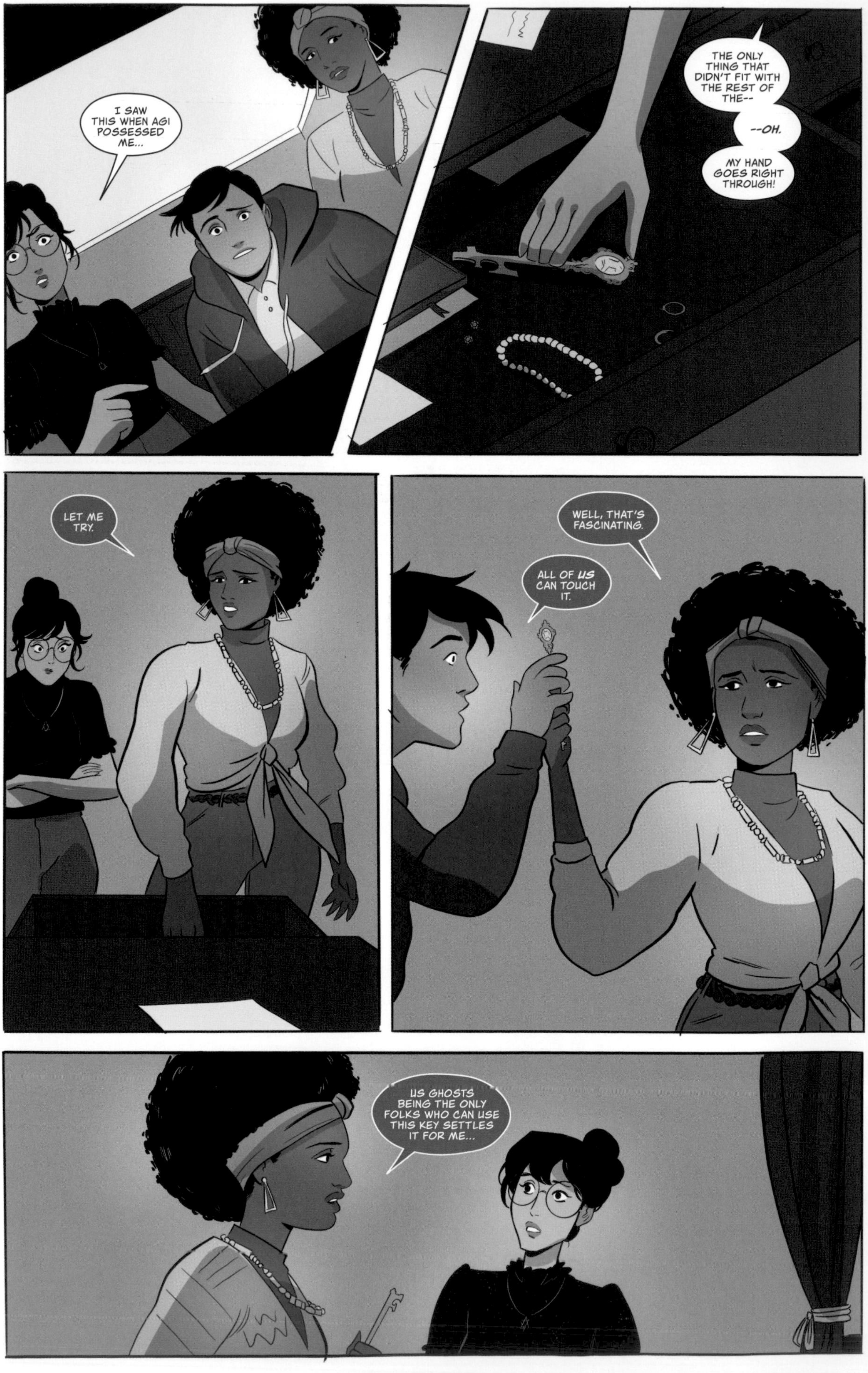
I SAW THIS WHEN AGI POSSESSED ME...
THE ONLY THING THAT DIDN'T FIT WITH THE REST OF THE--
--OH.
MY HAND GOES RIGHT THROUGH!
LET ME TRY.
WELL, THAT'S FASCINATING.
ALL OF US CAN TOUCH IT.
US GHOSTS BEING THE ONLY FOLKS WHO CAN USE THIS KEY SETTLES IT FOR ME...

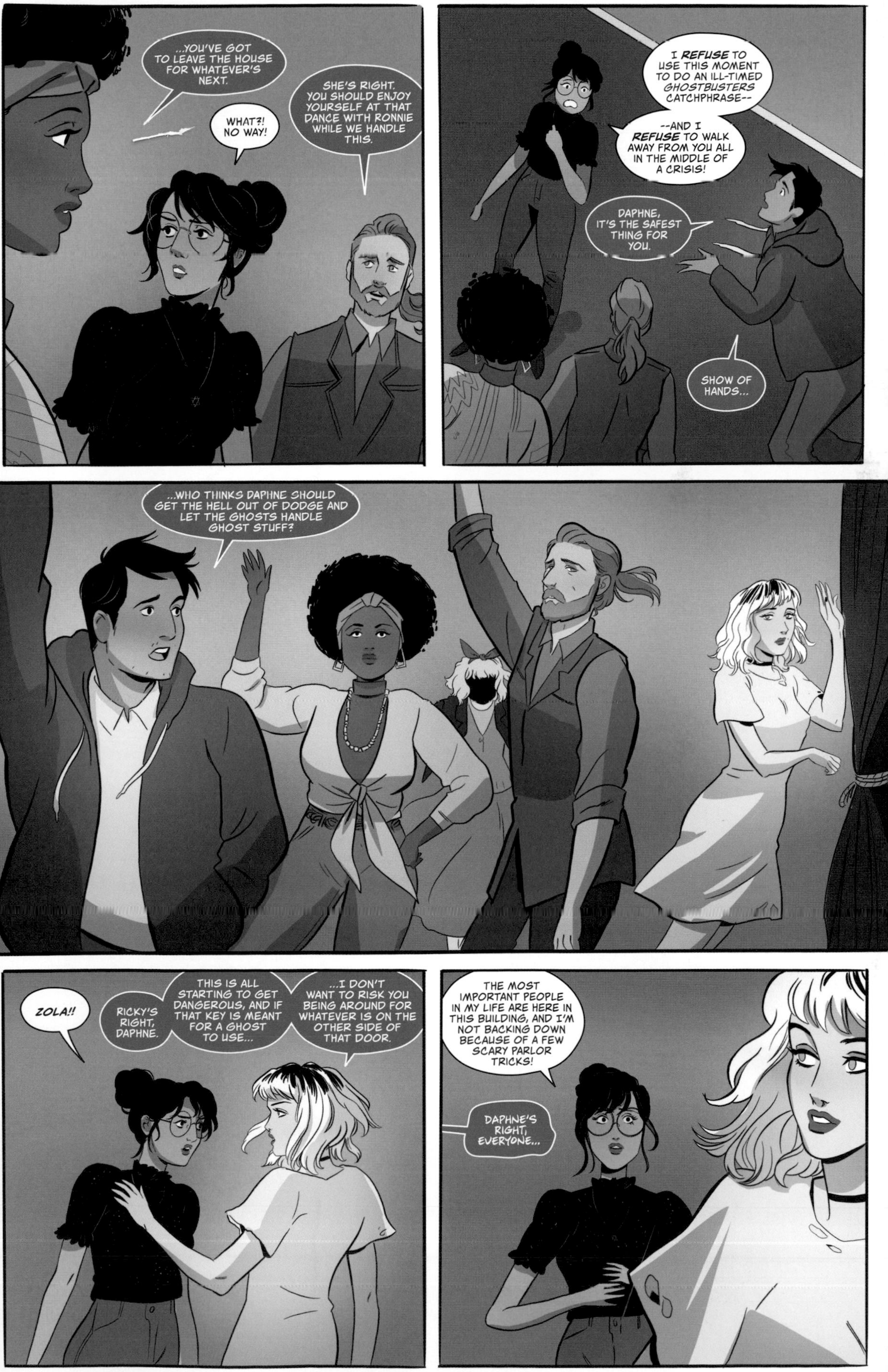
...YOU'VE GOT TO LEAVE THE HOUSE FOR WHATEVER'S NEXT.
WHAT?! NO WAY!
SHE'S RIGHT. YOU SHOULD ENJOY YOURSELF AT THAT DANCE WITH RONNIE WHILE WE HANDLE THIS.
I REFUSE TO USE THIS MOMENT TO DO AN ILL-TIMED GHOSTBUSTERS CATCHPHRASE--
--AND I REFUSE TO WALK AWAY FROM YOU ALL IN THE MIDDLE OF A CRISIS!
DAPHNE, IT'S THE SAFEST THING FOR YOU.
SHOW OF HANDS...
...WHO THINKS DAPHNE SHOULD GET THE HELL OUT OF DODGE AND LET THE GHOSTS HANDLE GHOST STUFF?
ZOLA!!
RICKY'S RIGHT, DAPHNE.
THIS IS ALL STARTING TO GET DANGEROUS, AND IF THAT KEY IS MEANT FOR A GHOST TO USE...
...I DON'T WANT TO RISK YOU BEING AROUND FOR WHATEVER IS ON THE OTHER SIDE OF THAT DOOR.
THE MOST IMPORTANT PEOPLE IN MY LIFE ARE HERE IN THIS BUILDING, AND I'M NOT BACKING DOWN BECAUSE OF A FEW SCARY PARLOR TRICKS!
DAPHNE'S RIGHT, EVERYONE...

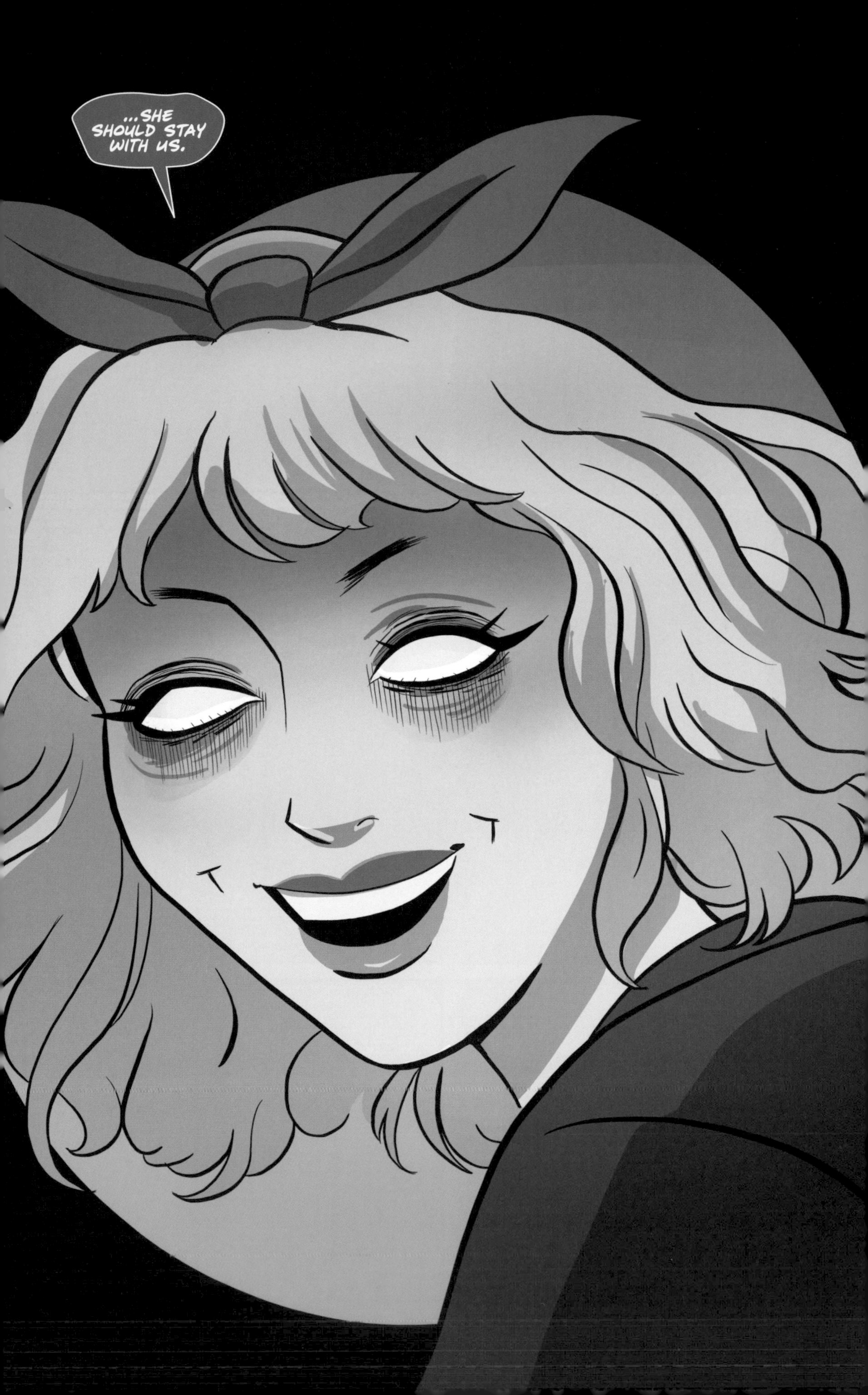
...SHE SHOULD STAY WITH US.

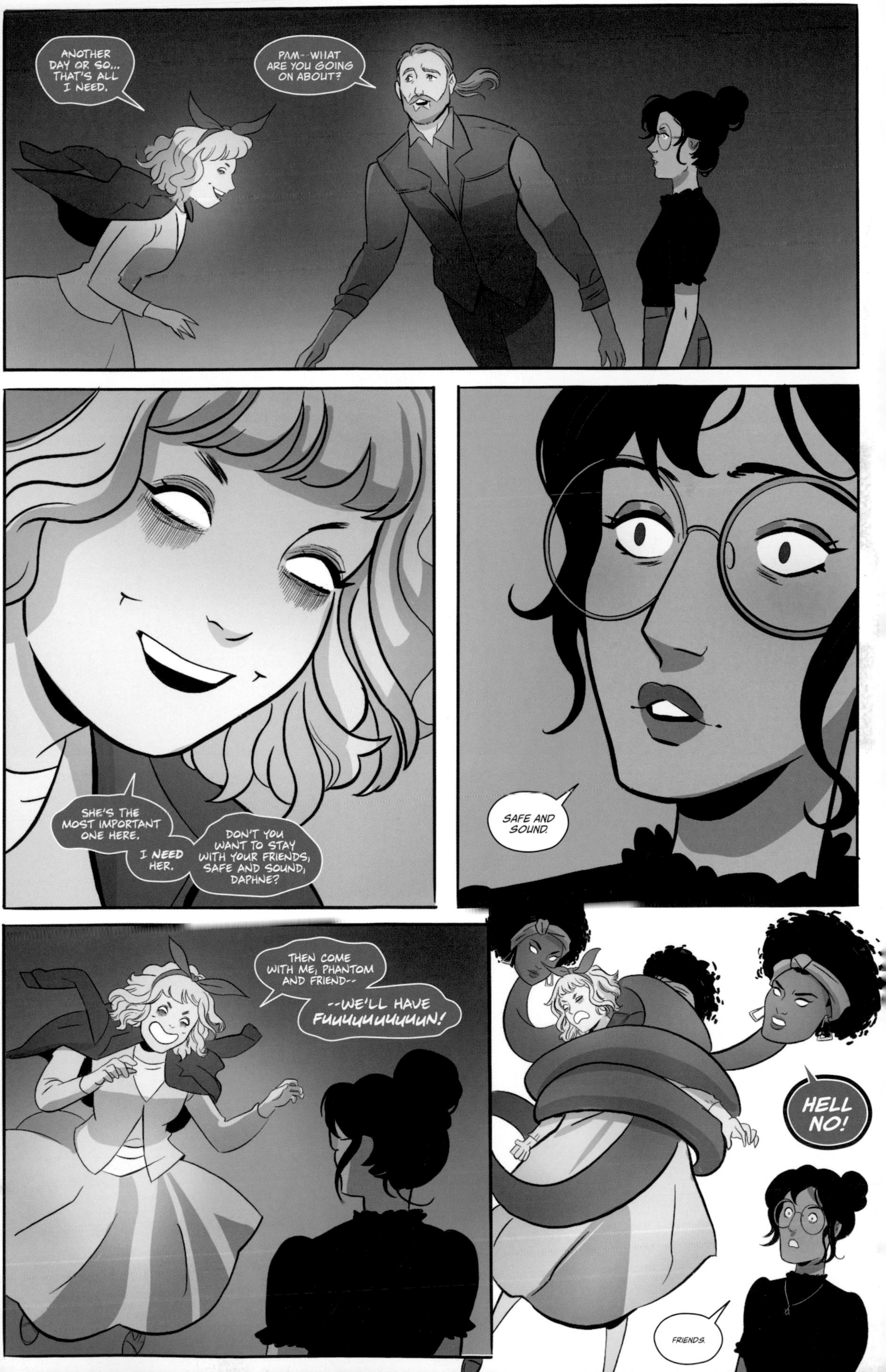
ANOTHER DAY OR SO... THAT'S ALL I NEED.
PAM-- WHAT ARE YOU GOING ON ABOUT?
SHE'S THE MOST IMPORTANT ONE HERE.
I NEED HER.
DON'T YOU WANT TO STAY WITH YOUR FRIENDS, SAFE AND SOUND, DAPHNE?
SAFE AND SOUND.
THEN COME WITH ME, PHANTOM AND FRIEND--
--WE'LL HAVE FUUUUUUUUUN!
HELL NO!
FRIENDS.

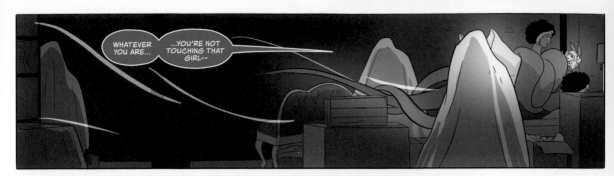

WHATEVER YOU ARE... ...YOU'RE NOT TOUCHING THAT GIRL--

--AND YOU WON'T HURT AGI!

WHUDDD

TOO LATE!!

SHIRLEY? WHAT ARE WE DOING DOWN HERE?

THIS THING, THIS GHOST OR WHATEVER THE HELL, IS STARTING TO GET SOME NERVE...

"...WE GOTTA SORT OUT A PLAN, AND QUICK."

OMYGOD IT'S GETTING STRONGER AND IT WANTS ME.

BREATHE, DAPHNE.

YOU'RE RIGHT. IT IS GETTING STRONGER, BUT WE'RE GOING TO HANDLE THE PROBLEM.

NOW DO YOU SEE THAT YOU'VE GOT TO GET OUT OF HERE?

ZOLA...I CAN'T STOP SHAKING.

LET'S GET YOU IN A DRESS AND OFF TO THAT DANCE. THIS ISN'T YOUR FIGHT.

EVERYONE ELSE, WAIT FOR ME BEFORE YOU DO ANYTHING...

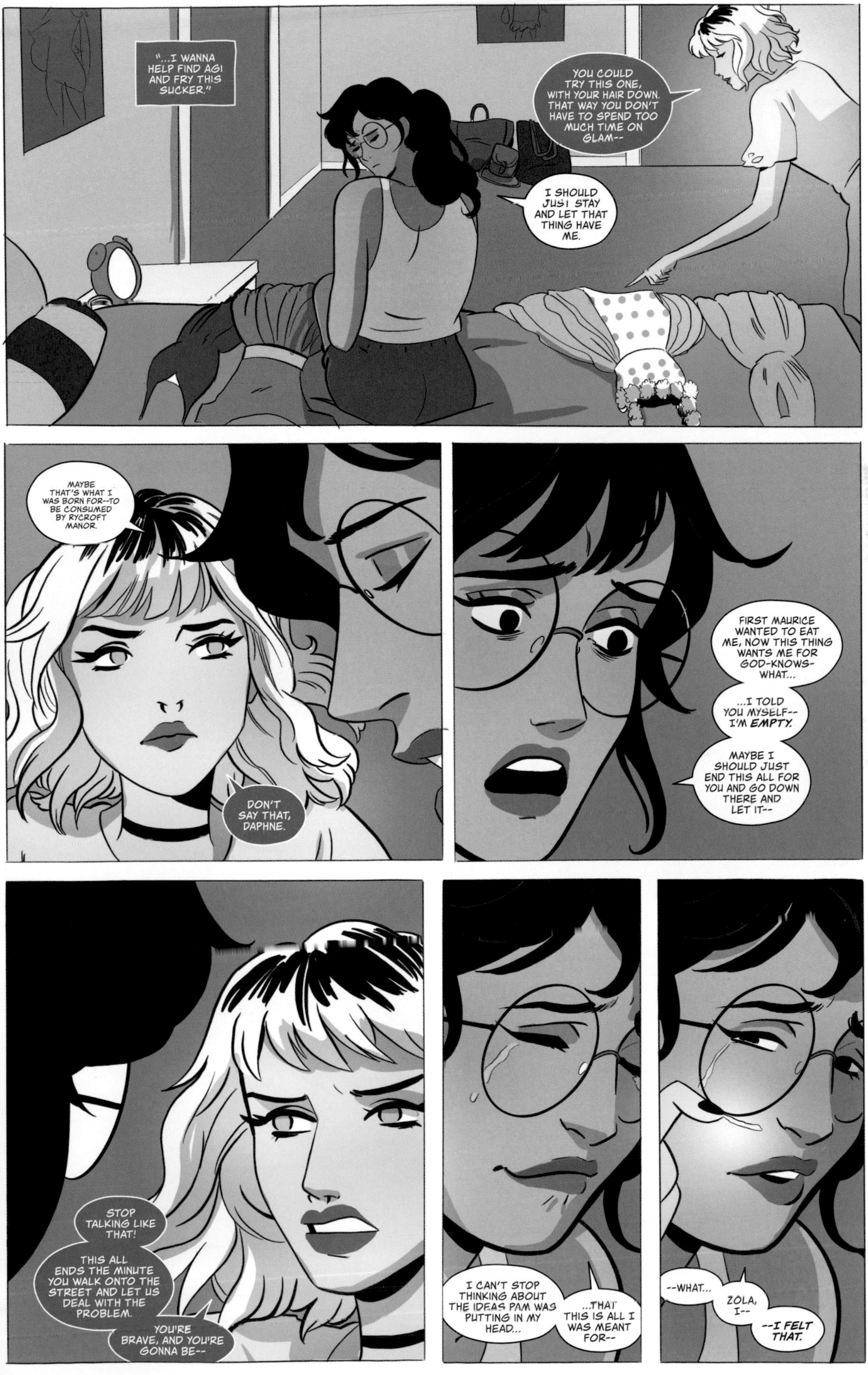
"...I WANNA HELP FIND AGI AND FRY THIS SUCKER."
YOU COULD TRY THIS ONE, WITH YOUR HAIR DOWN. THAT WAY YOU DON'T HAVE TO SPEND TOO MUCH TIME ON GLAM--
I SHOULD JUST STAY AND LET THAT THING HAVE ME.
MAYBE THAT'S WHAT I WAS BORN FOR--TO BE CONSUMED BY RYCROFT MANOR.
DON'T SAY THAT, DAPHNE.
FIRST MAURICE WANTED TO EAT ME, NOW THIS THING WANTS ME FOR GOD-KNOWS-WHAT...
...I TOLD YOU MYSELF--I'M *EMPTY.*
MAYBE I SHOULD JUST END THIS ALL FOR YOU AND GO DOWN THERE AND LET IT--
STOP TALKING LIKE THAT!
THIS ALL ENDS THE MINUTE YOU WALK ONTO THE STREET AND LET US DEAL WITH THE PROBLEM.
YOU'RE BRAVE, AND YOU'RE GONNA BE--
I CAN'T STOP THINKING ABOUT THE IDEAS PAM WAS PUTTING IN MY HEAD...
...THAT THIS IS ALL I WAS MEANT FOR--
--WHAT...
ZOLA, I--
--I FELT THAT.

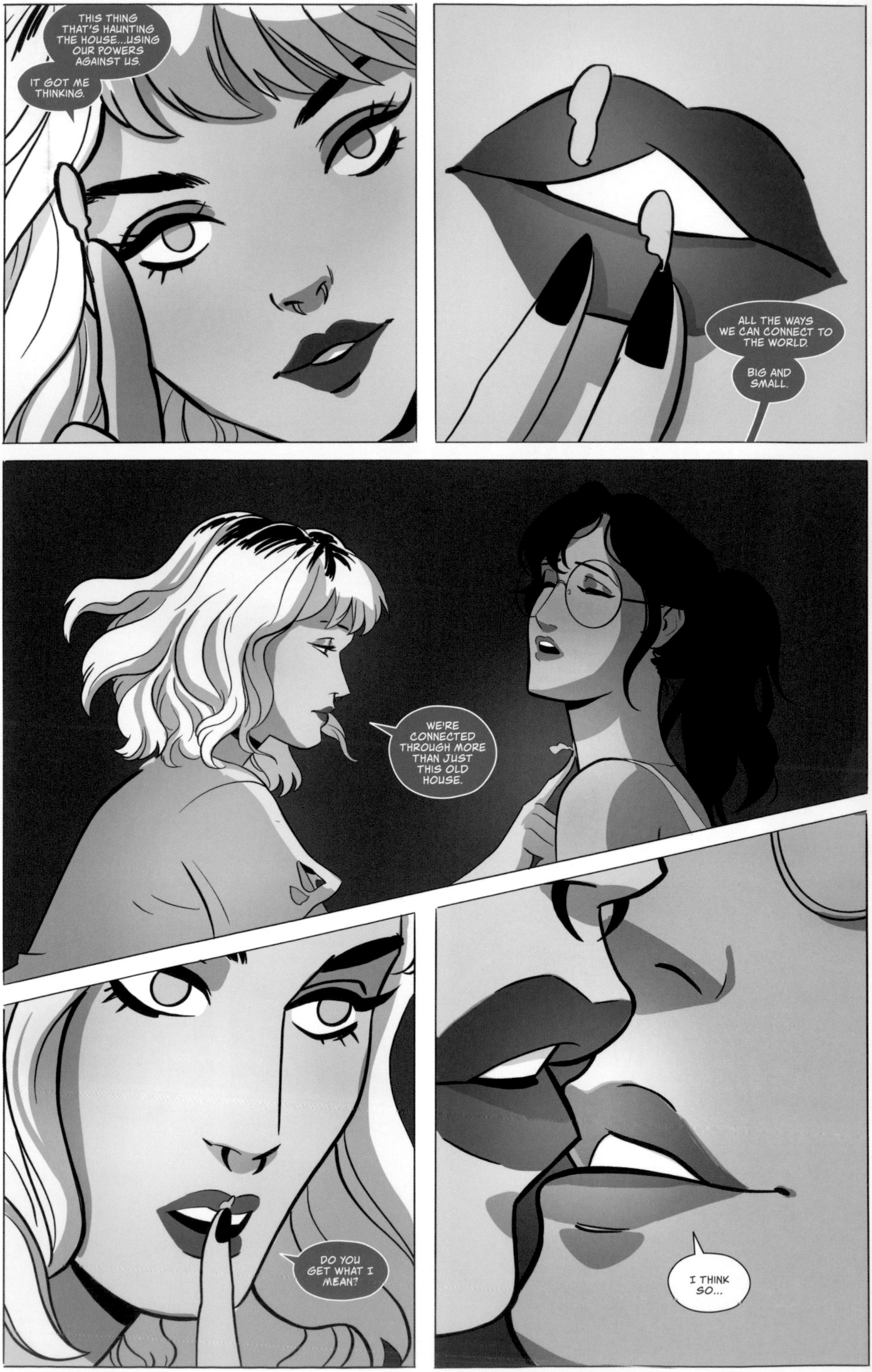
THIS THING THAT'S HAUNTING THE HOUSE...USING OUR POWERS AGAINST US.
IT GOT ME THINKING.
ALL THE WAYS WE CAN CONNECT TO THE WORLD.
BIG AND SMALL.
WE'RE CONNECTED THROUGH MORE THAN JUST THIS OLD HOUSE.
DO YOU GET WHAT I MEAN?
I THINK SO...

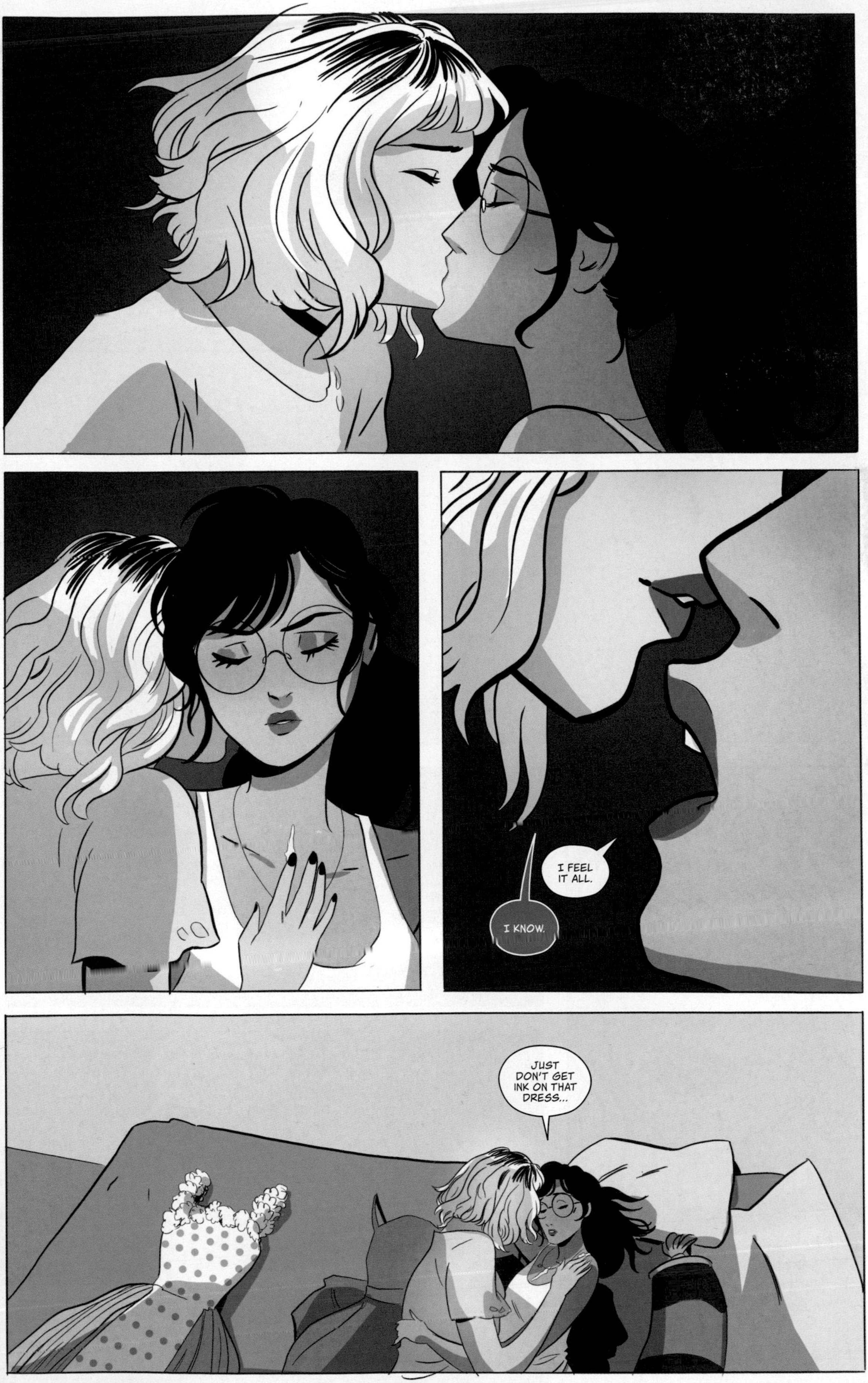
I FEEL IT ALL.
I KNOW.
JUST DON'T GET INK ON THAT DRESS...

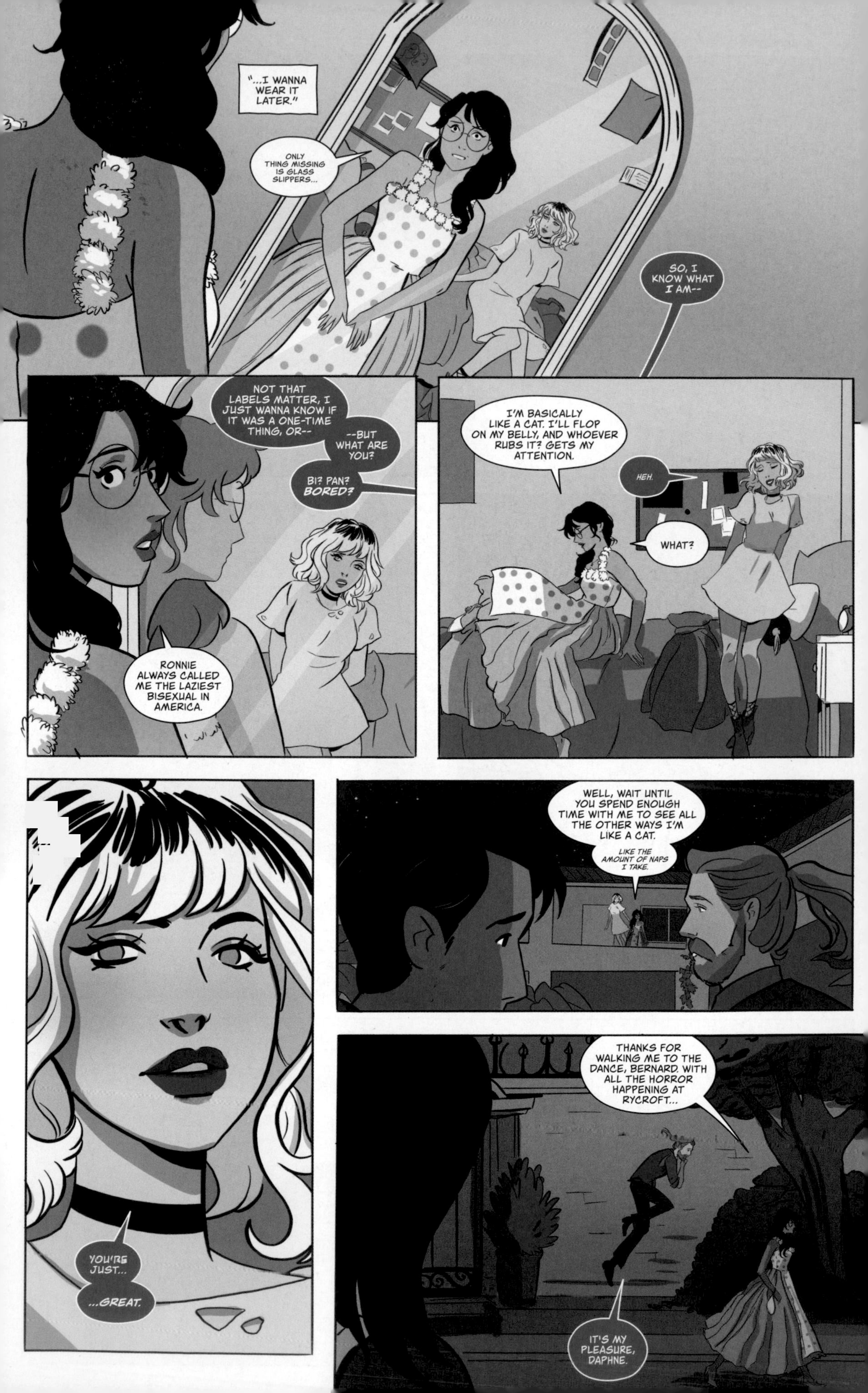
"...I WANNA WEAR IT LATER."
ONLY THING MISSING IS GLASS SLIPPERS...
SO, I KNOW WHAT I AM--
NOT THAT LABELS MATTER, I JUST WANNA KNOW IF IT WAS A ONE-TIME THING, OR--
--BUT WHAT ARE YOU?
BI? PAN? BORED?
RONNIE ALWAYS CALLED ME THE LAZIEST BISEXUAL IN AMERICA.
I'M BASICALLY LIKE A CAT. I'LL FLOP ON MY BELLY, AND WHOEVER RUBS IT? GETS MY ATTENTION.
HEH.
WHAT?
YOU'RE JUST...
...GREAT.
WELL, WAIT UNTIL YOU SPEND ENOUGH TIME WITH ME TO SEE ALL THE OTHER WAYS I'M LIKE A CAT.
LIKE THE AMOUNT OF NAPS I TAKE.
THANKS FOR WALKING ME TO THE DANCE, BERNARD. WITH ALL THE HORROR HAPPENING AT RYCROFT...
IT'S MY PLEASURE, DAPHNE.

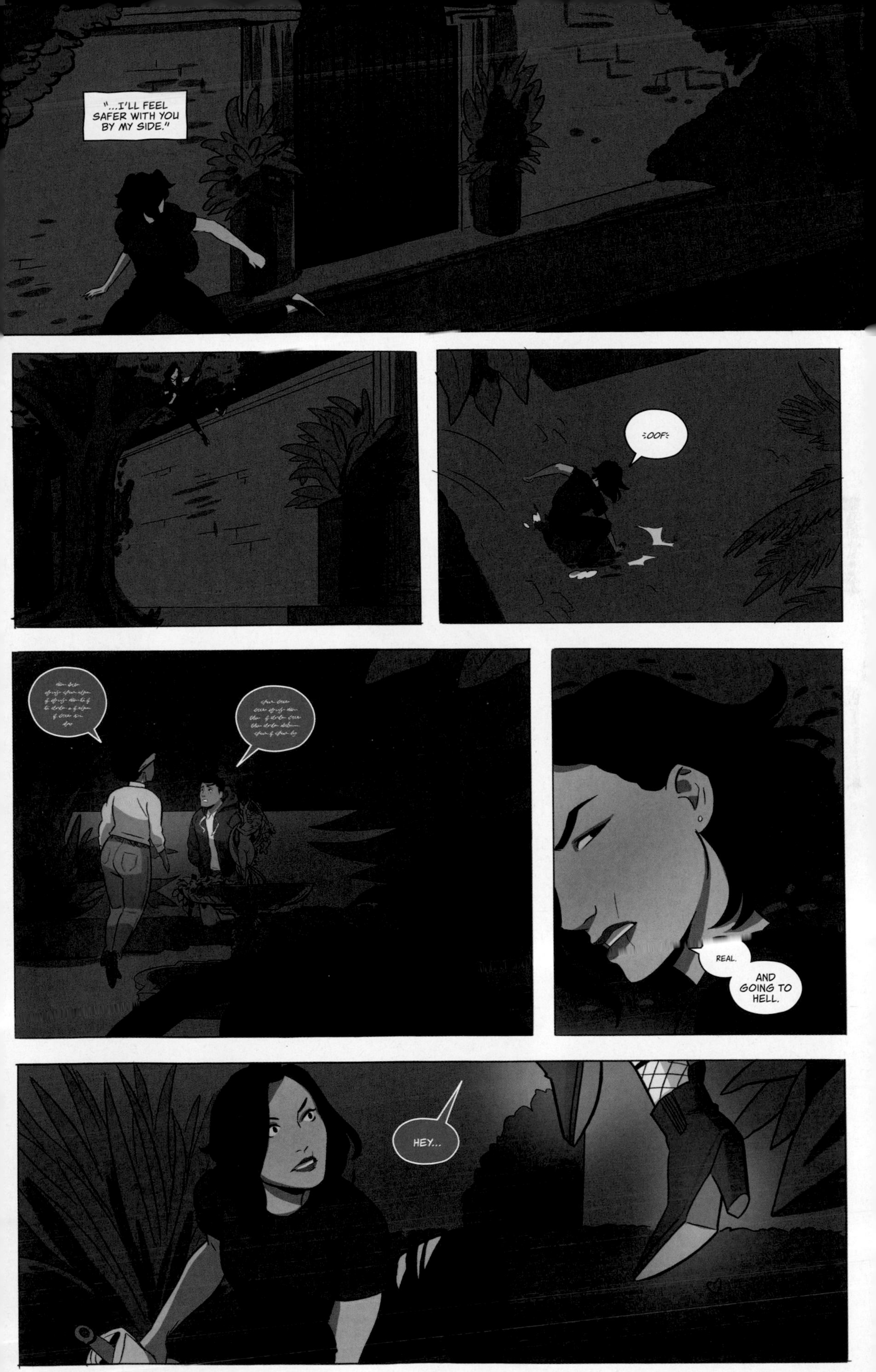
"...I'LL FEEL SAFER WITH YOU BY MY SIDE."
OOF
REAL.
AND GOING TO HELL.
HEY...

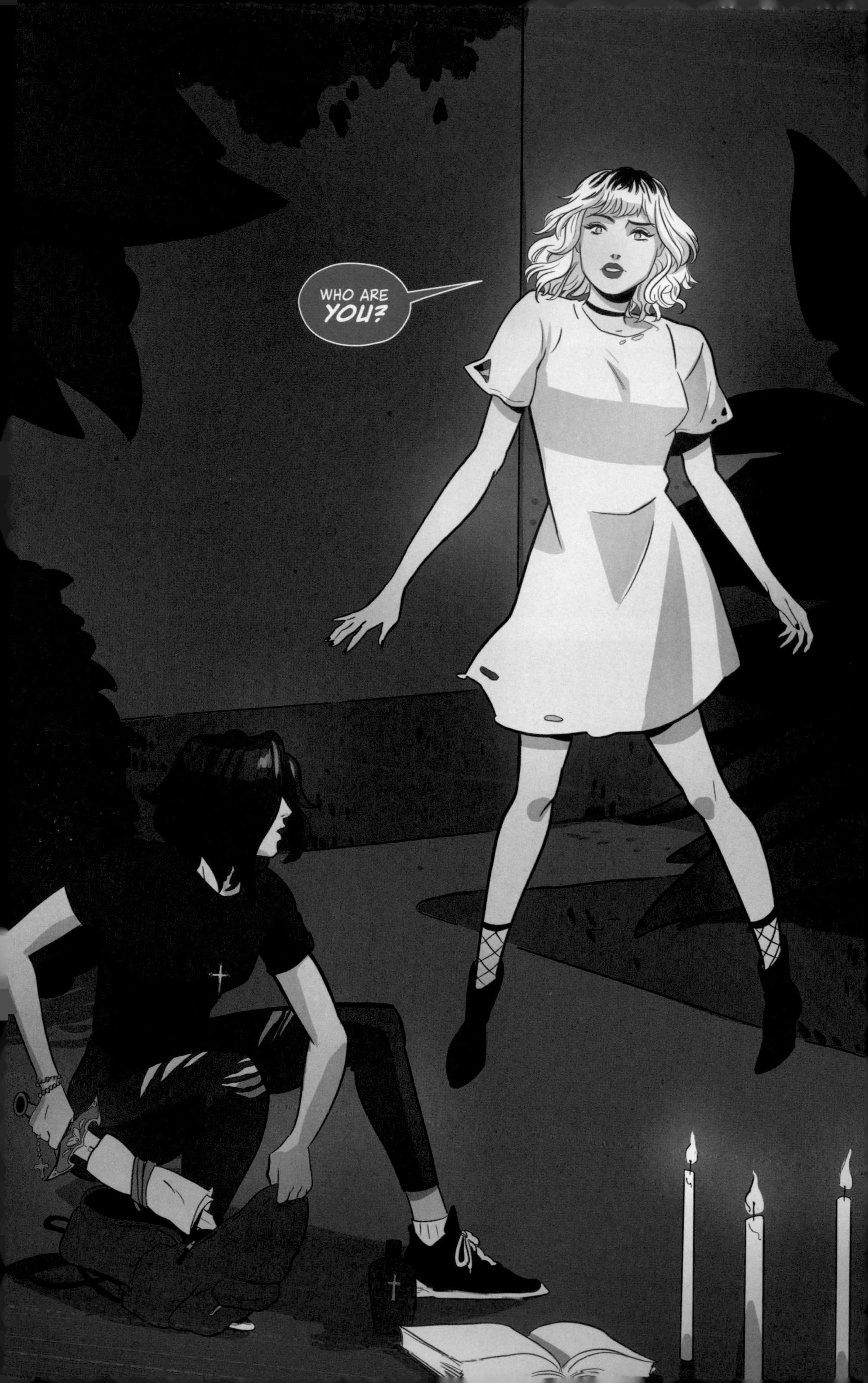
WHO ARE YOU?

Chapter Eleven

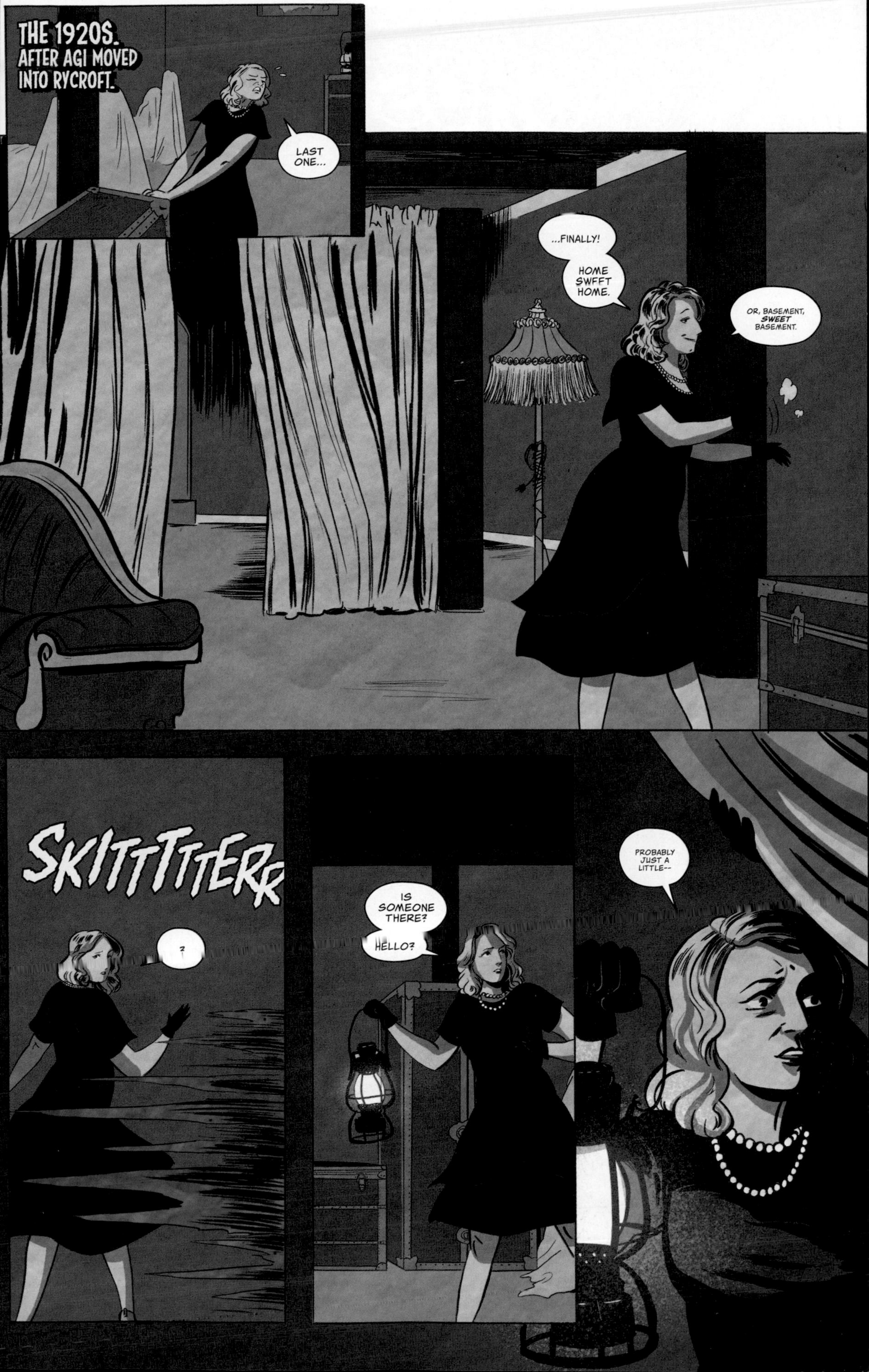
THE 1920S. AFTER AGI MOVED INTO RYCROFT.
LAST ONE...
...FINALLY!
HOME SWFFT HOME.
OR, BASEMENT, *SWEET* BASEMENT.
SKITTTTTERR
?
IS SOMEONE THERE?
HELLO?
PROBABLY JUST A LITTLE--

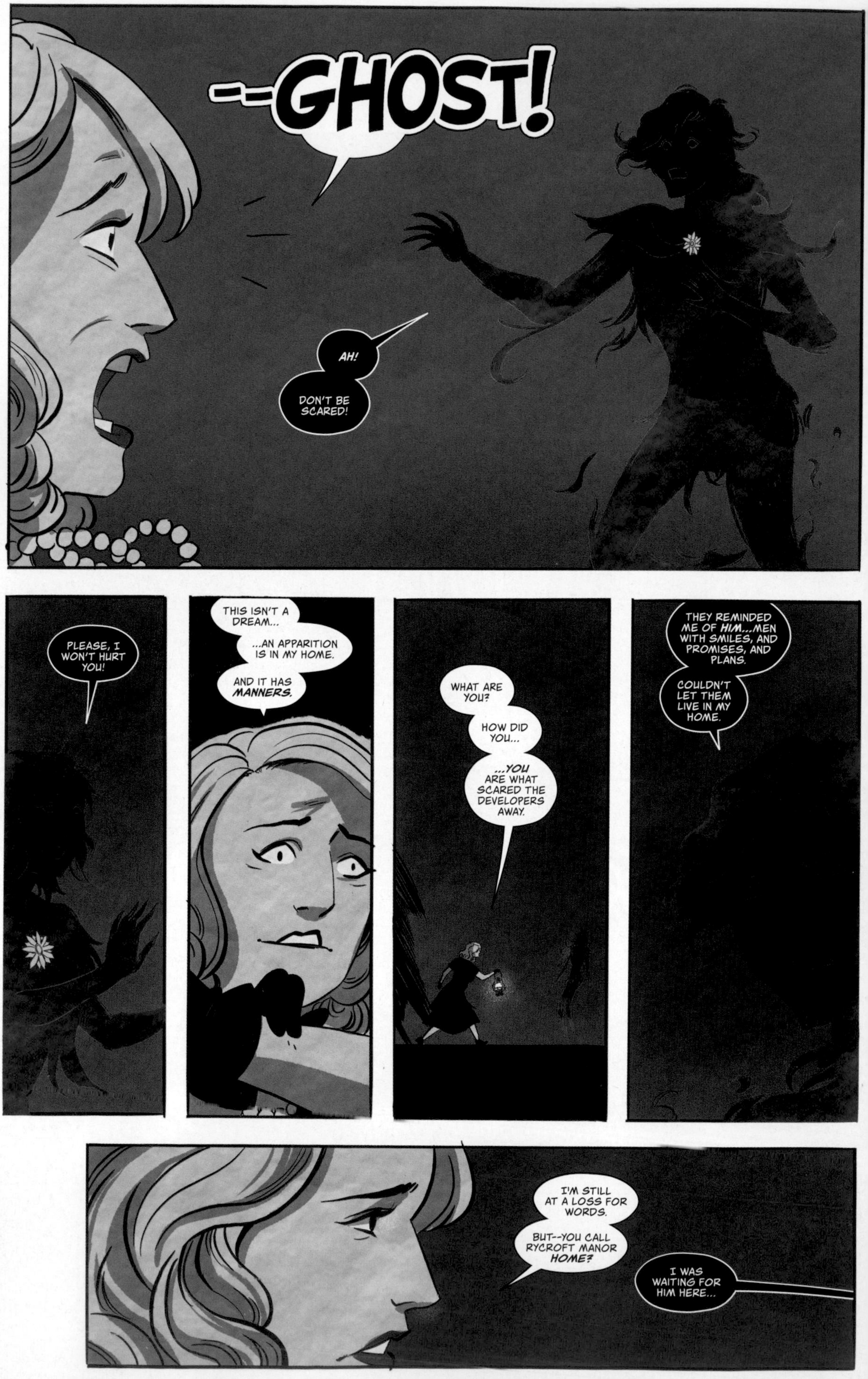

--GHOST!
AH!
DON'T BE SCARED!
PLEASE, I WON'T HURT YOU!
THIS ISN'T A DREAM...
...AN APPARITION IS IN MY HOME.
AND IT HAS MANNERS.
WHAT ARE YOU?
HOW DID YOU...
...YOU ARE WHAT SCARED THE DEVELOPERS AWAY.
THEY REMINDED ME OF HIM...MEN WITH SMILES, AND PROMISES, AND PLANS.
COULDN'T LET THEM LIVE IN MY HOME.
I'M STILL AT A LOSS FOR WORDS.
BUT--YOU CALL RYCROFT MANOR HOME?
I WAS WAITING FOR HIM HERE...

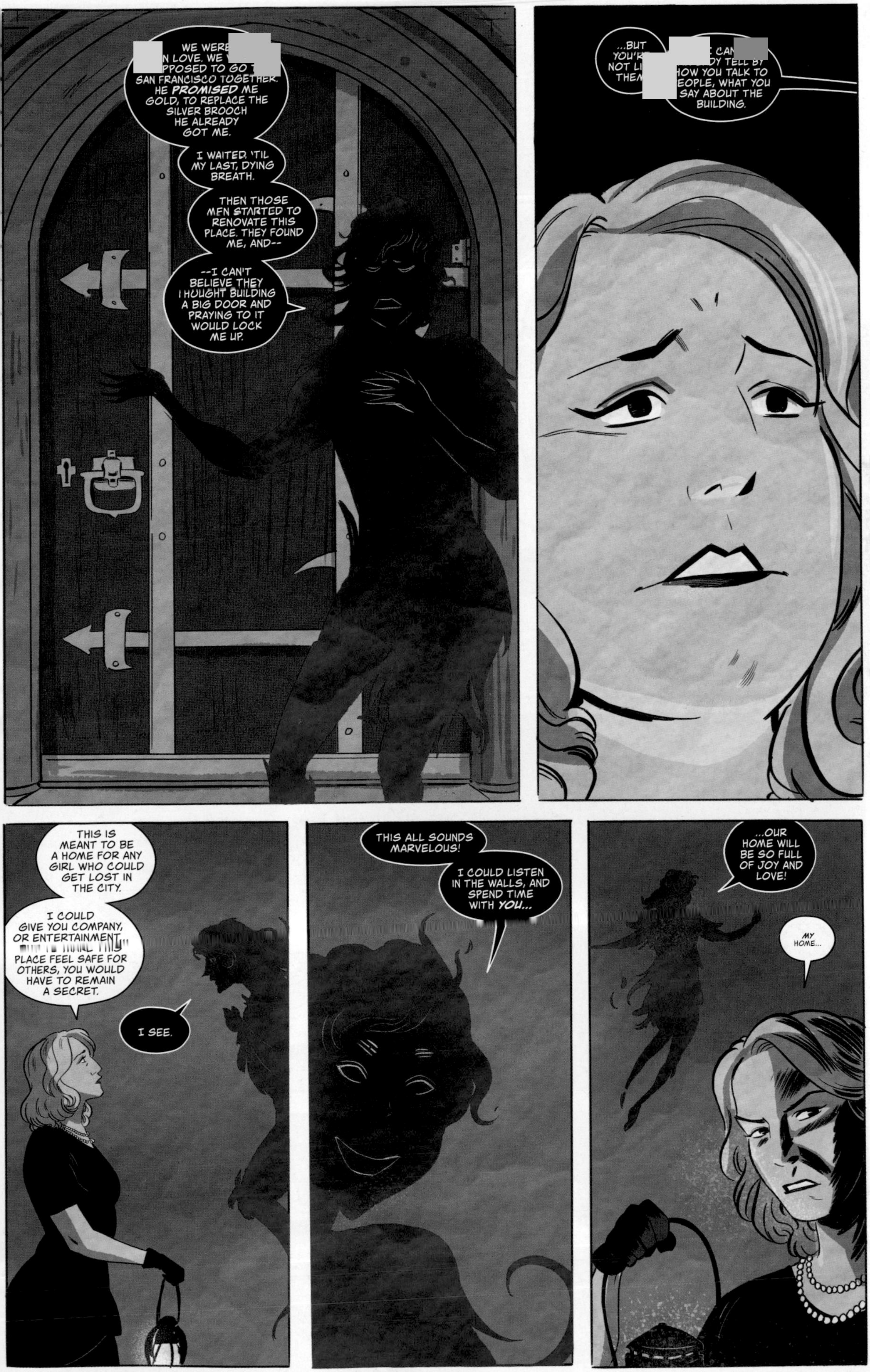
WE WERE
N LOVE. WE
PPOSED TO GO T
SAN FRANCISCO TOGETHER. HE *PROMISED* ME GOLD, TO REPLACE THE SILVER BROOCH HE ALREADY GOT ME.
I WAITED 'TIL MY LAST, DYING BREATH.
THEN THOSE MEN STARTED TO RENOVATE THIS PLACE. THEY FOUND ME, AND--
--I CAN'T BELIEVE THEY THOUGHT BUILDING A BIG DOOR AND PRAYING TO IT WOULD LOCK ME UP.
...BUT YOU'R NOT LI THEM
CAN DY TELL BY HOW YOU TALK TO EOPLE, WHAT YOU SAY ABOUT THE BUILDING.
THIS IS MEANT TO BE A HOME FOR ANY GIRL WHO COULD GET LOST IN THE CITY.
I COULD GIVE YOU COMPANY, OR ENTERTAINMENT. PLACE FEEL SAFE FOR OTHERS, YOU WOULD HAVE TO REMAIN A SECRET.
I SEE.
THIS ALL SOUNDS MARVELOUS!
I COULD LISTEN IN THE WALLS, AND SPEND TIME WITH *YOU...*
...OUR HOME WILL BE SO FULL OF JOY AND LOVE!
MY HOME...

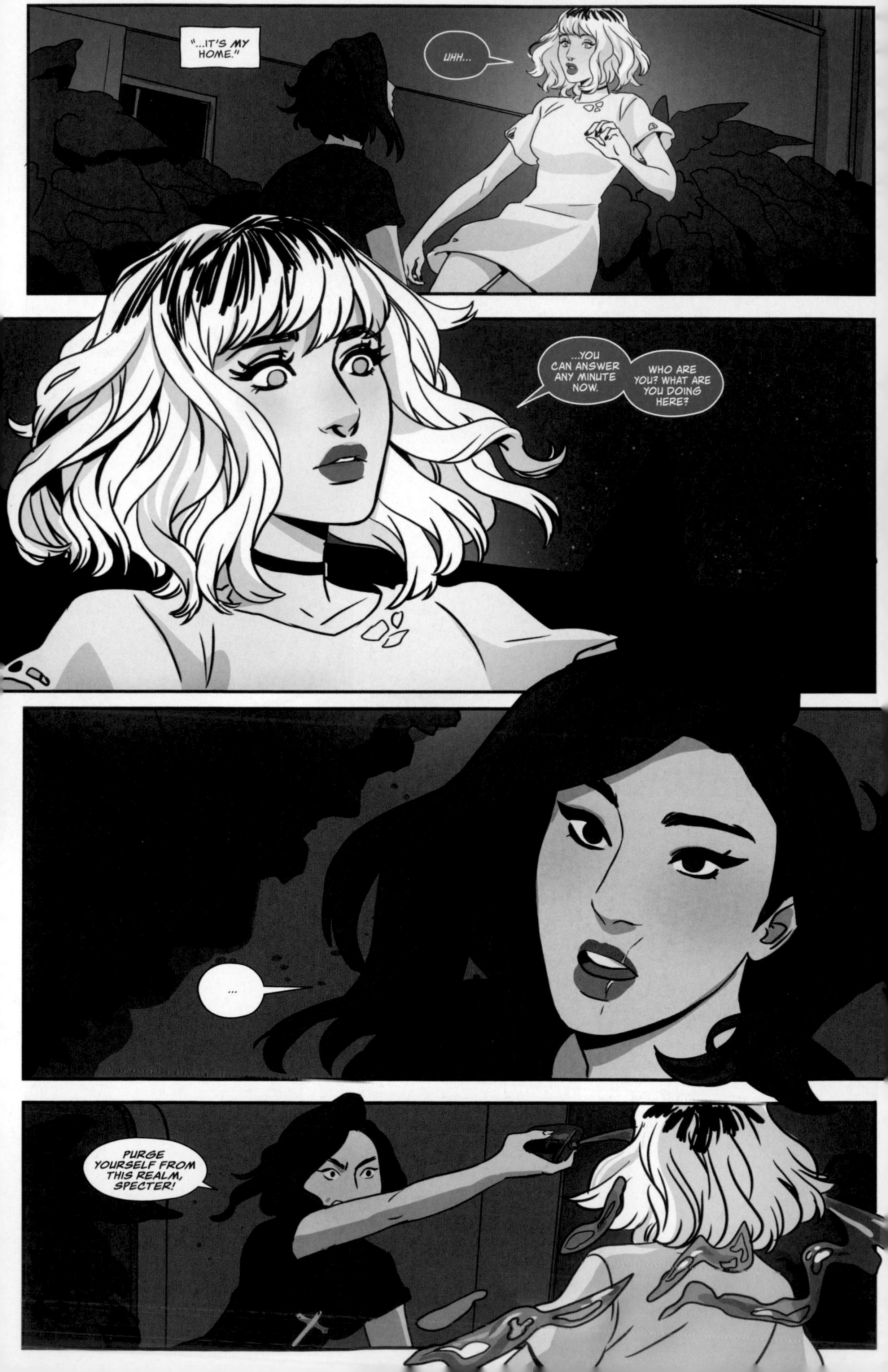
"...IT'S MY HOME."
UHH...
...YOU CAN ANSWER ANY MINUTE NOW.
WHO ARE YOU? WHAT ARE YOU DOING HERE?
...
PURGE YOURSELF FROM THIS REALM, SPECTER!

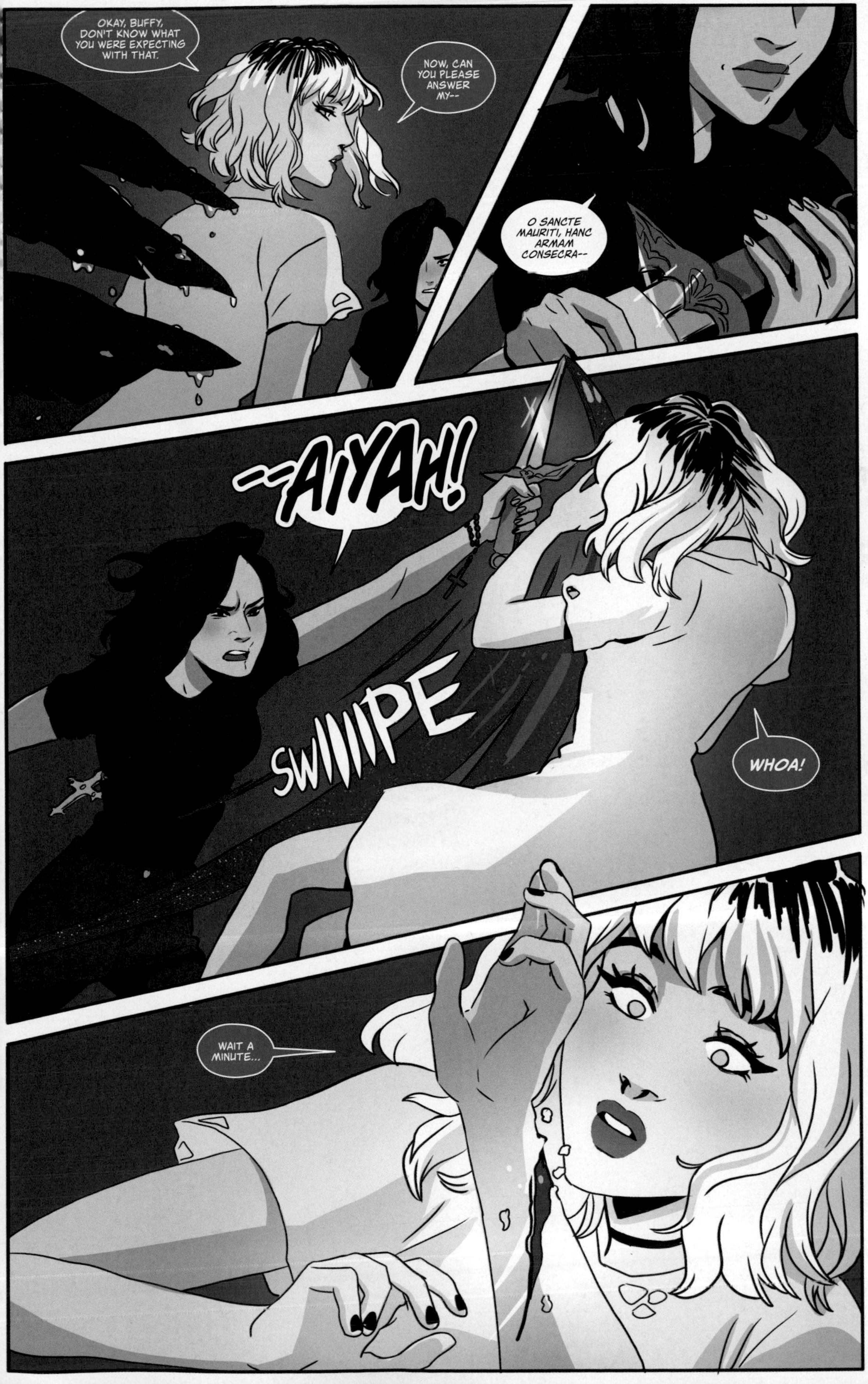
OKAY, BUFFY, DON'T KNOW WHAT YOU WERE EXPECTING WITH THAT.
NOW, CAN YOU PLEASE ANSWER MY--
O SANCTE MAURITI, HANC ARMAM CONSECRA--
--AIYAH!
SWIIIIPE
WHOA!
WAIT A MINUTE...

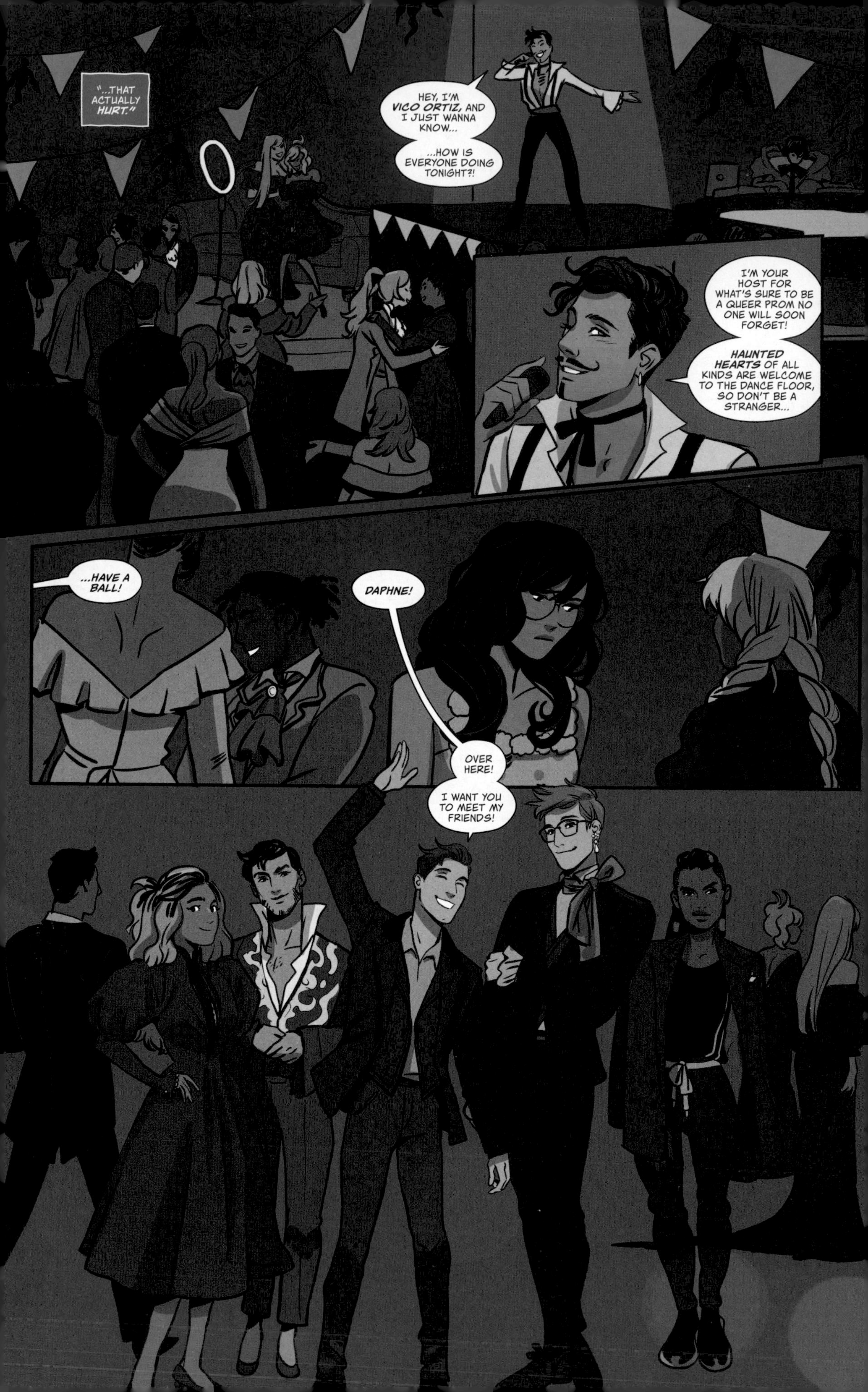
"...THAT ACTUALLY HURT."
HEY, I'M VICO ORTIZ, AND I JUST WANNA KNOW...
...HOW IS EVERYONE DOING TONIGHT?!
I'M YOUR HOST FOR WHAT'S SURE TO BE A QUEER PROM NO ONE WILL SOON FORGET!
HAUNTED HEARTS OF ALL KINDS ARE WELCOME TO THE DANCE FLOOR, SO DON'T BE A STRANGER...
...HAVE A BALL!
DAPHNE!
OVER HERE!
I WANT YOU TO MEET MY FRIENDS!

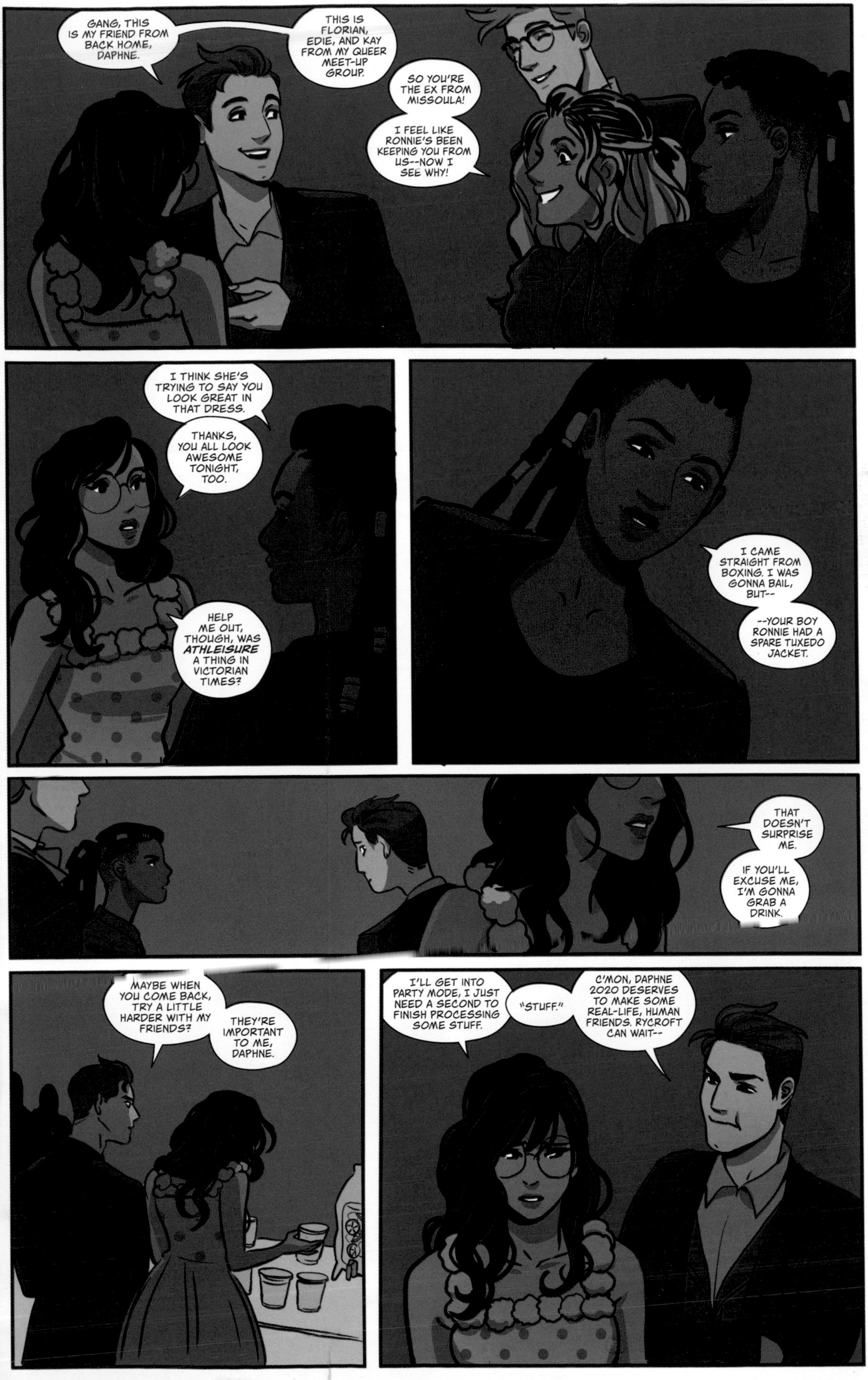
GANG, THIS IS MY FRIEND FROM BACK HOME, DAPHNE.
THIS IS FLORIAN, EDIE, AND KAY FROM MY QUEER MEET-UP GROUP.
SO YOU'RE THE EX FROM MISSOULA!
I FEEL LIKE RONNIE'S BEEN KEEPING YOU FROM US--NOW I SEE WHY!
I THINK SHE'S TRYING TO SAY YOU LOOK GREAT IN THAT DRESS.
THANKS, YOU ALL LOOK AWESOME TONIGHT, TOO.
HELP ME OUT, THOUGH, WAS ATHLEISURE A THING IN VICTORIAN TIMES?
I CAME STRAIGHT FROM BOXING. I WAS GONNA BAIL, BUT--
--YOUR BOY RONNIE HAD A SPARE TUXEDO JACKET.
THAT DOESN'T SURPRISE ME.
IF YOU'LL EXCUSE ME, I'M GONNA GRAB A DRINK.
MAYBE WHEN YOU COME BACK, TRY A LITTLE HARDER WITH MY FRIENDS?
THEY'RE IMPORTANT TO ME, DAPHNE.
I'LL GET INTO PARTY MODE, I JUST NEED A SECOND TO FINISH PROCESSING SOME STUFF.
"STUFF."
C'MON, DAPHNE 2020 DESERVES TO MAKE SOME REAL-LIFE, HUMAN FRIENDS. RYCROFT CAN WAIT--

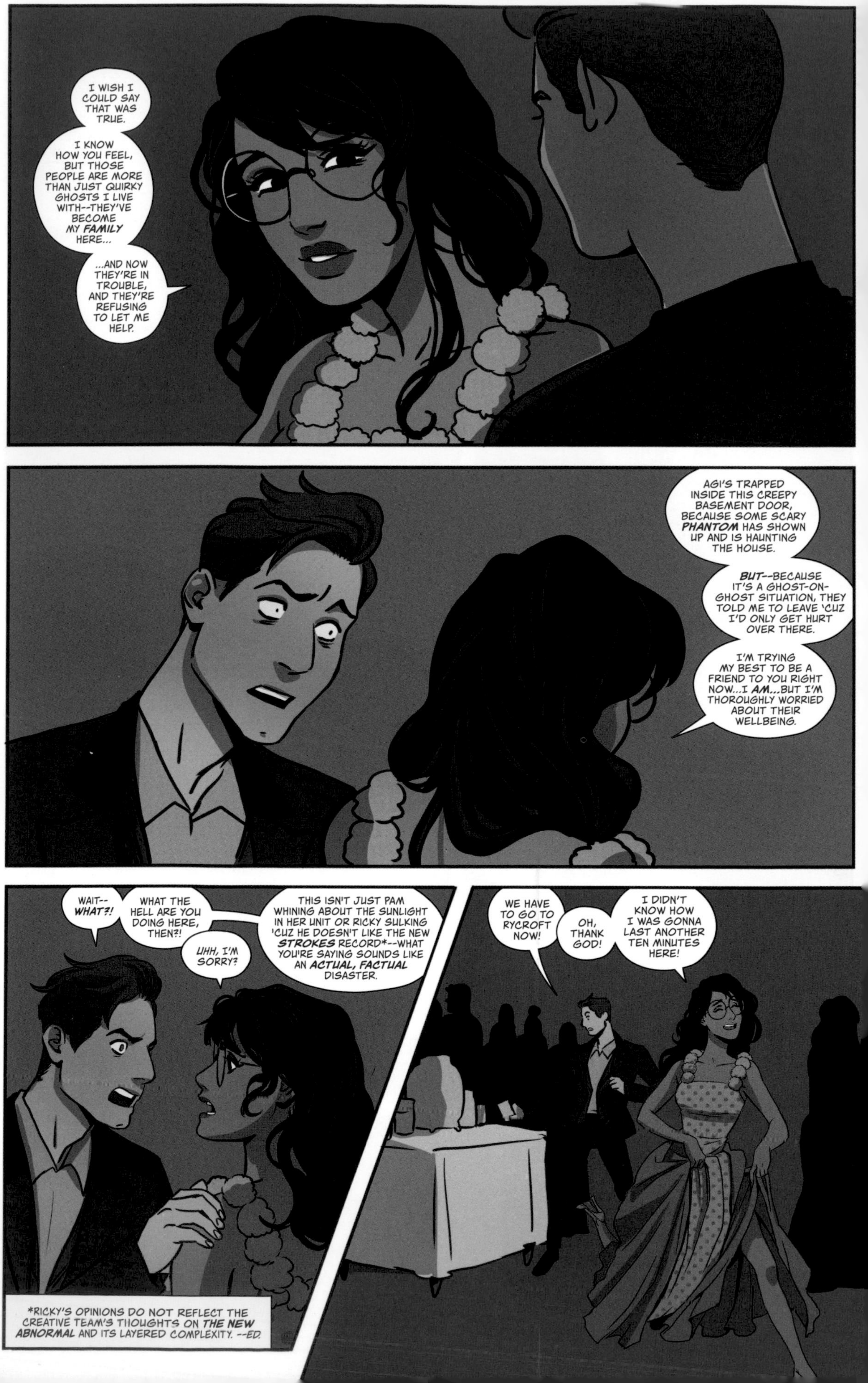

I WISH I COULD SAY THAT WAS TRUE.
I KNOW HOW YOU FEEL, BUT THOSE PEOPLE ARE MORE THAN JUST QUIRKY GHOSTS I LIVE WITH--THEY'VE BECOME MY *FAMILY* HERE...
...AND NOW THEY'RE IN TROUBLE, AND THEY'RE REFUSING TO LET ME HELP.
AGI'S TRAPPED INSIDE THIS CREEPY BASEMENT DOOR, BECAUSE SOME SCARY *PHANTOM* HAS SHOWN UP AND IS HAUNTING THE HOUSE.
BUT--BECAUSE IT'S A GHOST-ON-GHOST SITUATION, THEY TOLD ME TO LEAVE 'CUZ I'D ONLY GET HURT OVER THERE.
I'M TRYING MY BEST TO BE A FRIEND TO YOU RIGHT NOW...I *AM*...BUT I'M THOROUGHLY WORRIED ABOUT THEIR WELLBEING.
WAIT-- *WHAT?!*
WHAT THE HELL ARE YOU DOING HERE, THEN?!
UHH, I'M SORRY?
THIS ISN'T JUST PAM WHINING ABOUT THE SUNLIGHT IN HER UNIT OR RICKY SULKING 'CUZ HE DOESN'T LIKE THE NEW *STROKES* RECORD*--WHAT YOU'RE SAYING SOUNDS LIKE AN *ACTUAL, FACTUAL* DISASTER.
*RICKY'S OPINIONS DO NOT REFLECT THE CREATIVE TEAM'S THOUGHTS ON *THE NEW ABNORMAL* AND ITS LAYERED COMPLEXITY. --ED.
WE HAVE TO GO TO RYCROFT NOW!
OH, THANK GOD!
I DIDN'T KNOW HOW I WAS GONNA LAST ANOTHER TEN MINUTES HERE!

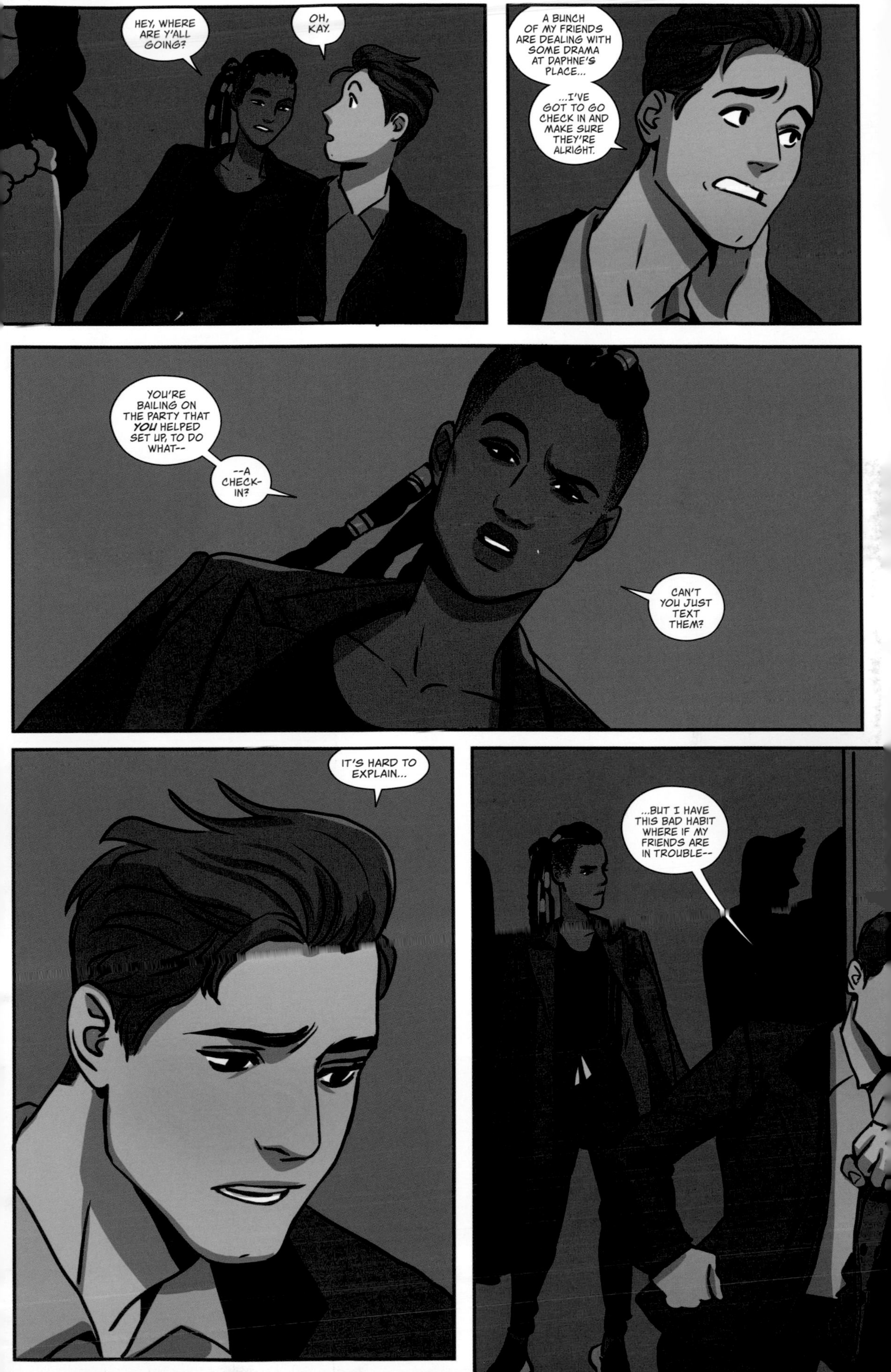
HEY, WHERE ARE Y'ALL GOING?
OH, KAY.
A BUNCH OF MY FRIENDS ARE DEALING WITH SOME DRAMA AT DAPHNE'S PLACE...
...I'VE GOT TO GO CHECK IN AND MAKE SURE THEY'RE ALRIGHT.
YOU'RE BAILING ON THE PARTY THAT *YOU* HELPED SET UP, TO DO WHAT--
--A CHECK-IN?
CAN'T YOU JUST TEXT THEM?
IT'S HARD TO EXPLAIN...
...BUT I HAVE THIS BAD HABIT WHERE IF MY FRIENDS ARE IN TROUBLE--

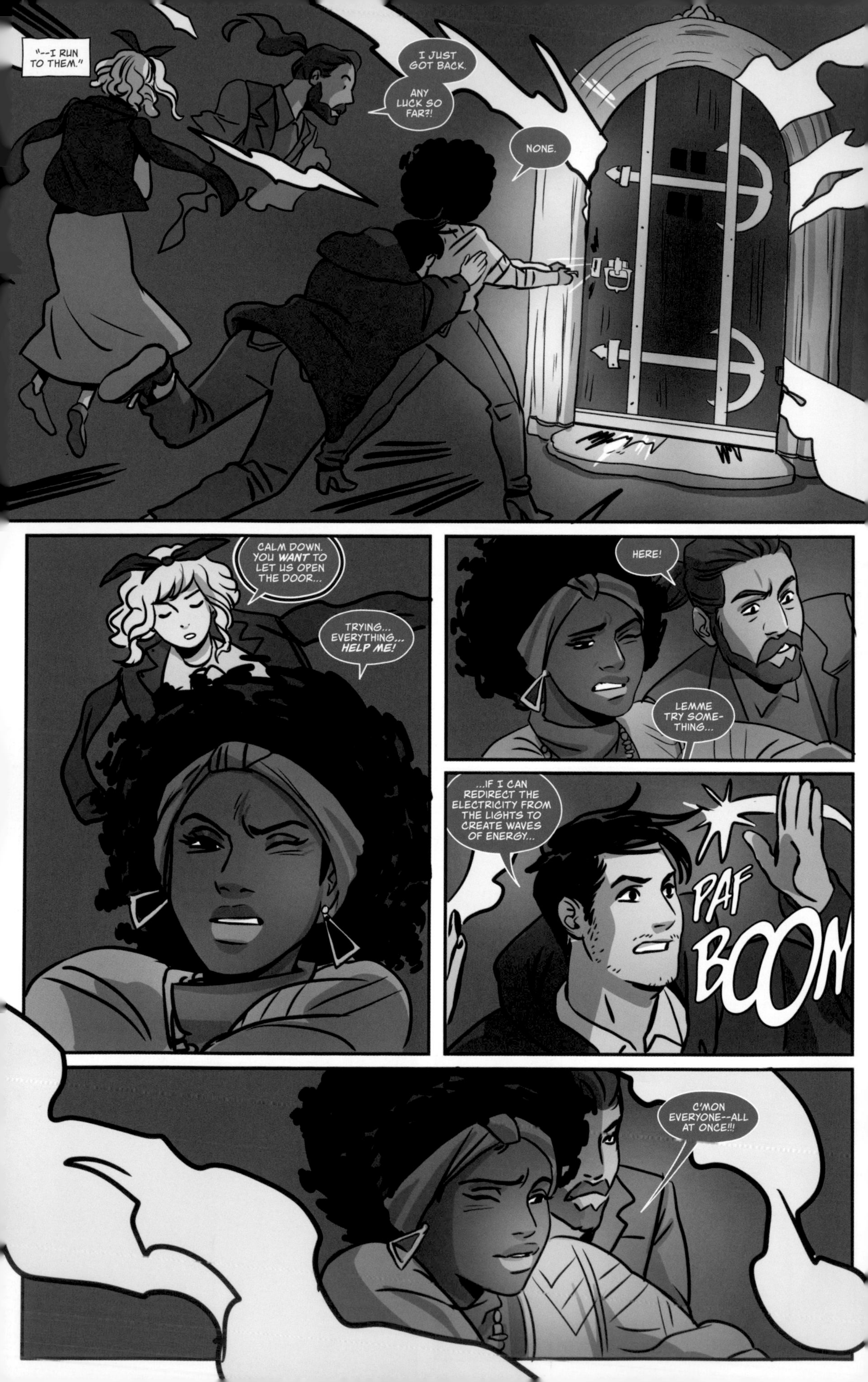
"--I RUN TO THEM."
I JUST GOT BACK.
ANY LUCK SO FAR?!
NONE.
CALM DOWN. YOU *WANT* TO LET US OPEN THE DOOR...
TRYING... EVERYTHING... ***HELP ME!***
HERE!
LEMME TRY SOME-THING...
...IF I CAN REDIRECT THE ELECTRICITY FROM THE LIGHTS TO CREATE WAVES OF ENERGY...
PAF
BOOM
C'MON EVERYONE--ALL AT ONCE!!!

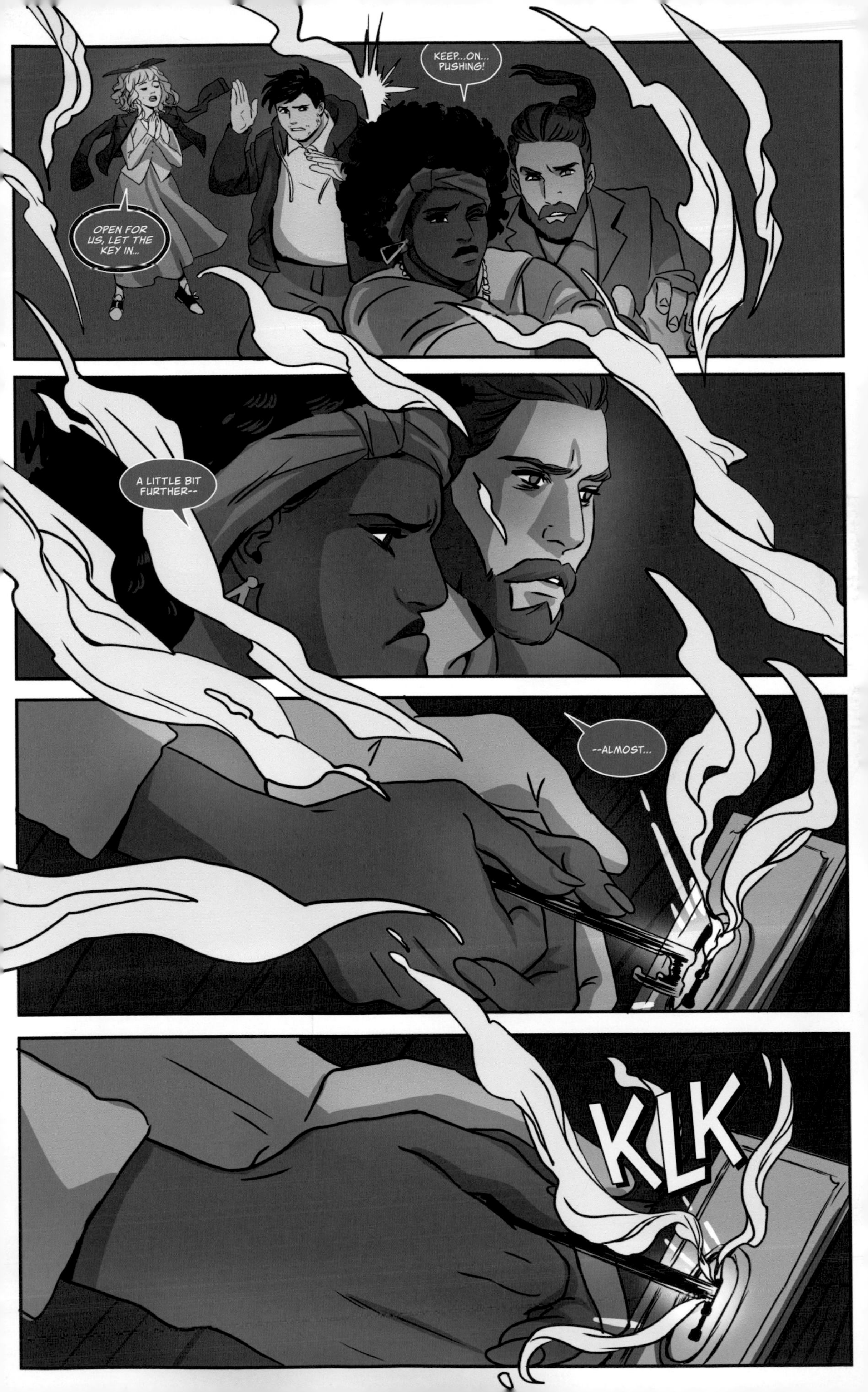
KEEP...ON... PUSHING!
OPEN FOR US, LET THE KEY IN...
A LITTLE BIT FURTHER--
--ALMOST...
KLK

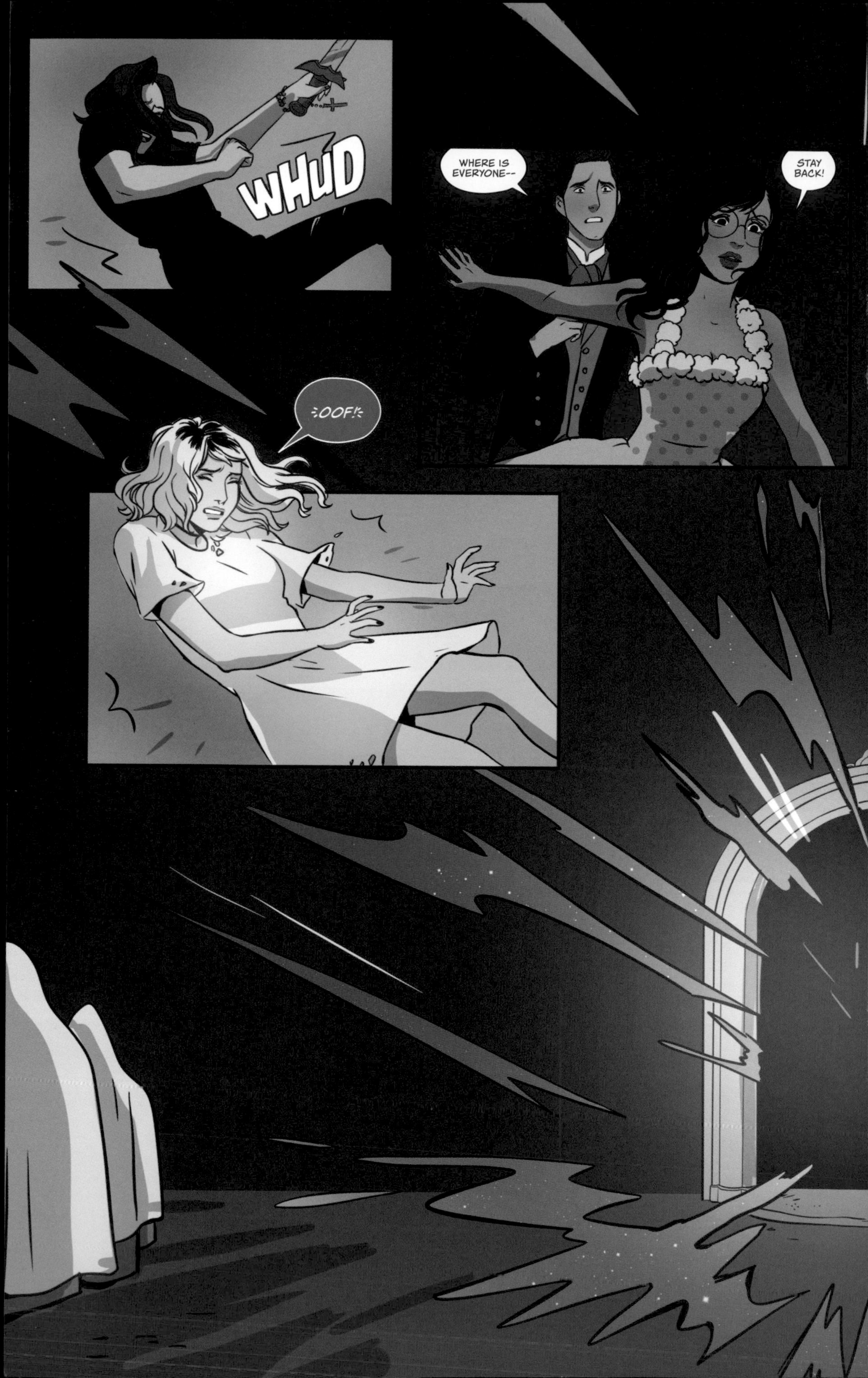
WHUD
WHERE IS EVERYONE--
STAY BACK!
OOF!

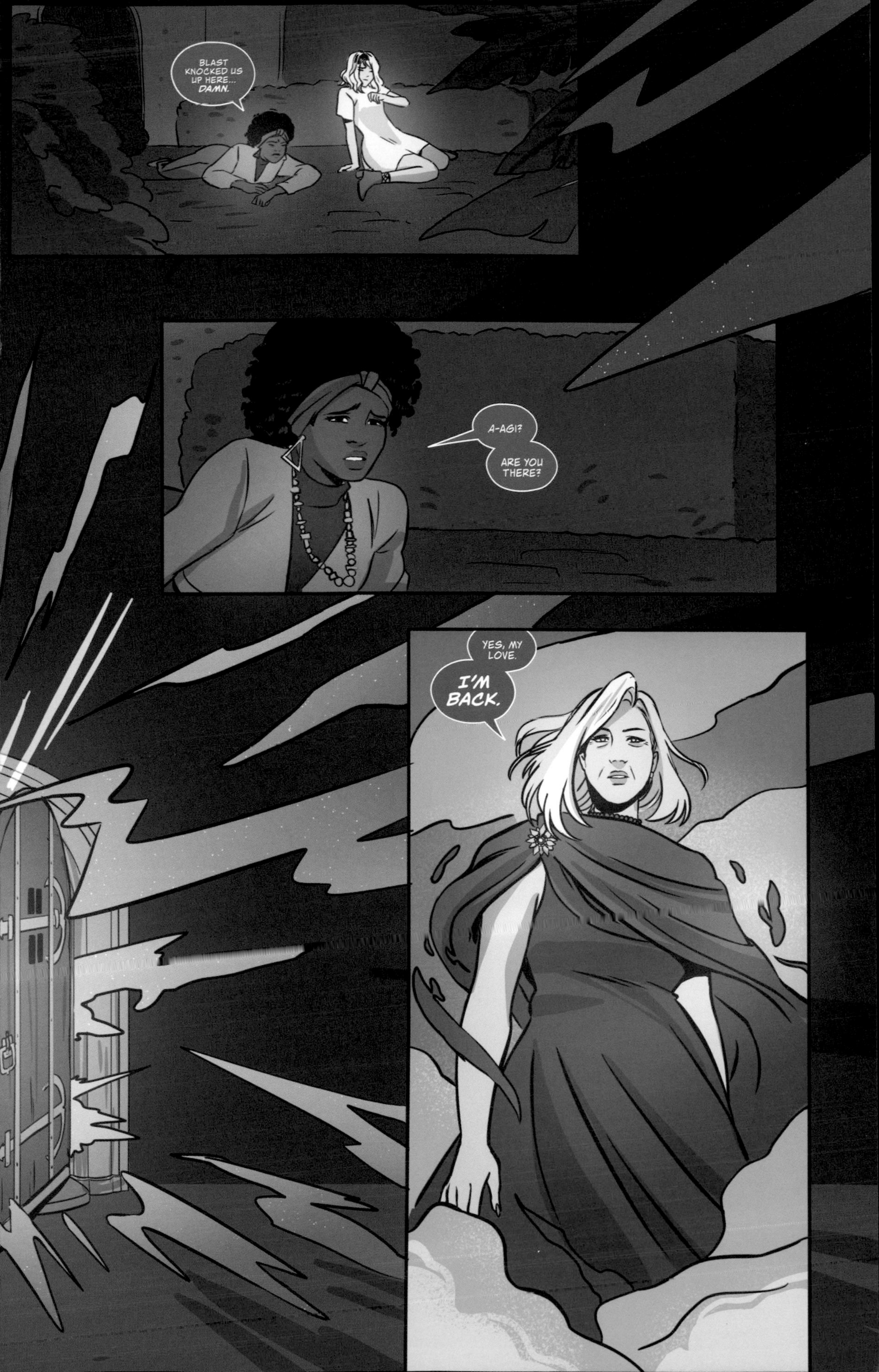
BLAST KNOCKED US UP HERE... DAMN.
A-AGI?
ARE YOU THERE?
YES, MY LOVE.
I'M BACK.

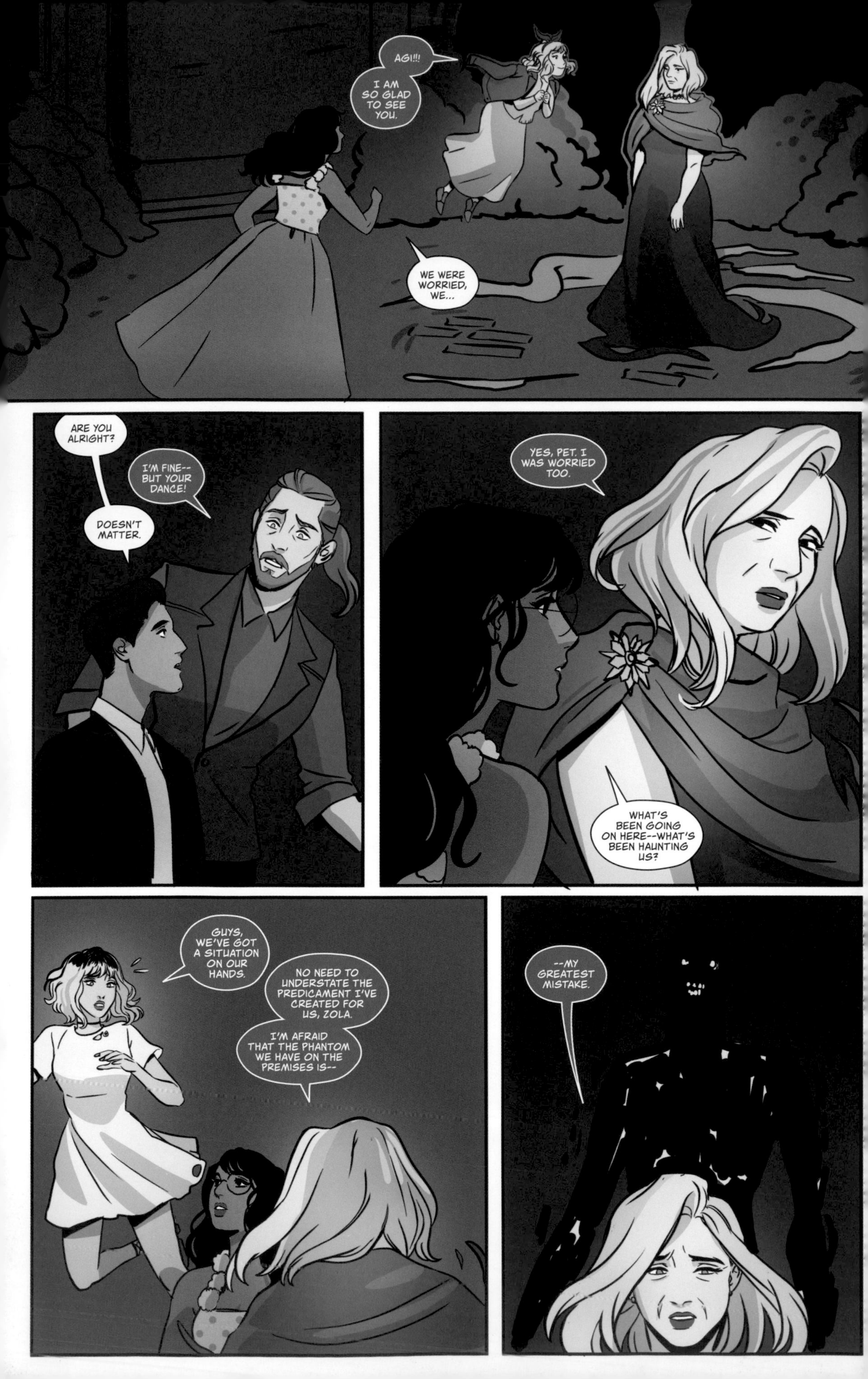
AGI!!!
I AM SO GLAD TO SEE YOU.
WE WERE WORRIED, WE...
ARE YOU ALRIGHT?
I'M FINE--BUT YOUR DANCE!
DOESN'T MATTER.
YES, PET. I WAS WORRIED TOO.
WHAT'S BEEN GOING ON HERE--WHAT'S BEEN HAUNTING US?
GUYS, WE'VE GOT A SITUATION ON OUR HANDS.
NO NEED TO UNDERSTATE THE PREDICAMENT I'VE CREATED FOR US, ZOLA.
I'M AFRAID THAT THE PHANTOM WE HAVE ON THE PREMISES IS--
--MY GREATEST MISTAKE.

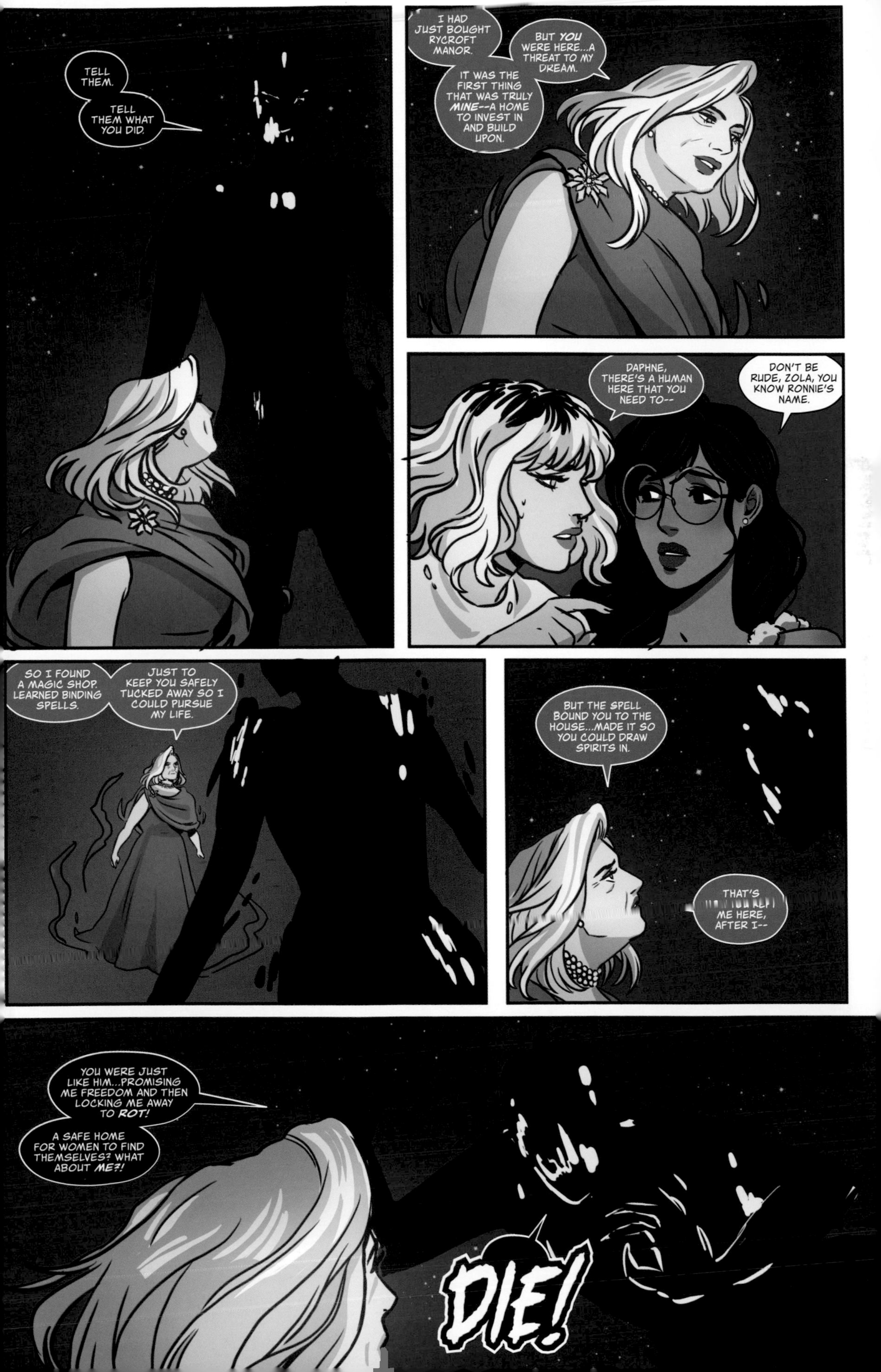
TELL THEM.
TELL THEM WHAT YOU DID.
I HAD JUST BOUGHT RYCROFT MANOR.
IT WAS THE FIRST THING THAT WAS TRULY *MINE*--A HOME TO INVEST IN AND BUILD UPON.
BUT *YOU* WERE HERE...A THREAT TO MY DREAM.
DAPHNE, THERE'S A HUMAN HERE THAT YOU NEED TO--
DON'T BE RUDE, ZOLA, YOU KNOW RONNIE'S NAME.
SO I FOUND A MAGIC SHOP. LEARNED BINDING SPELLS.
JUST TO KEEP YOU SAFELY TUCKED AWAY SO I COULD PURSUE MY LIFE.
BUT THE SPELL BOUND YOU TO THE HOUSE...MADE IT SO YOU COULD DRAW SPIRITS IN.
THAT'S
ME HERE, AFTER I--
YOU WERE JUST LIKE HIM...PROMISING ME FREEDOM AND THEN LOCKING ME AWAY TO *ROT!*
A SAFE HOME FOR WOMEN TO FIND THEMSELVES? WHAT ABOUT *ME?!*
DIE!

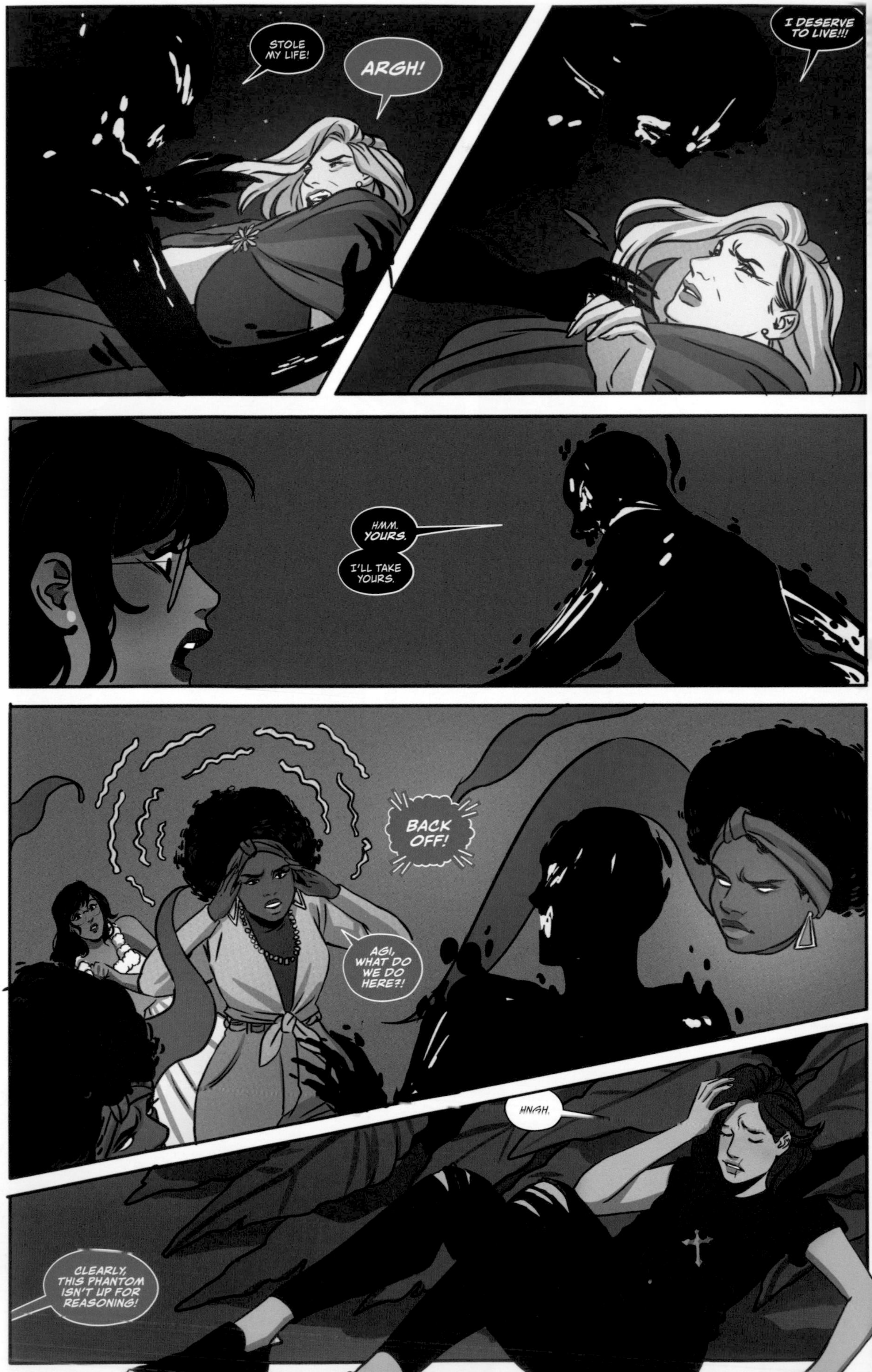
STOLE MY LIFE!
ARGH!
I DESERVE TO LIVE!!!
HMM. YOURS.
I'LL TAKE YOURS.
BACK OFF!
AGI, WHAT DO WE DO HERE?!
HNGH.
CLEARLY, THIS PHANTOM ISN'T UP FOR REASONING!

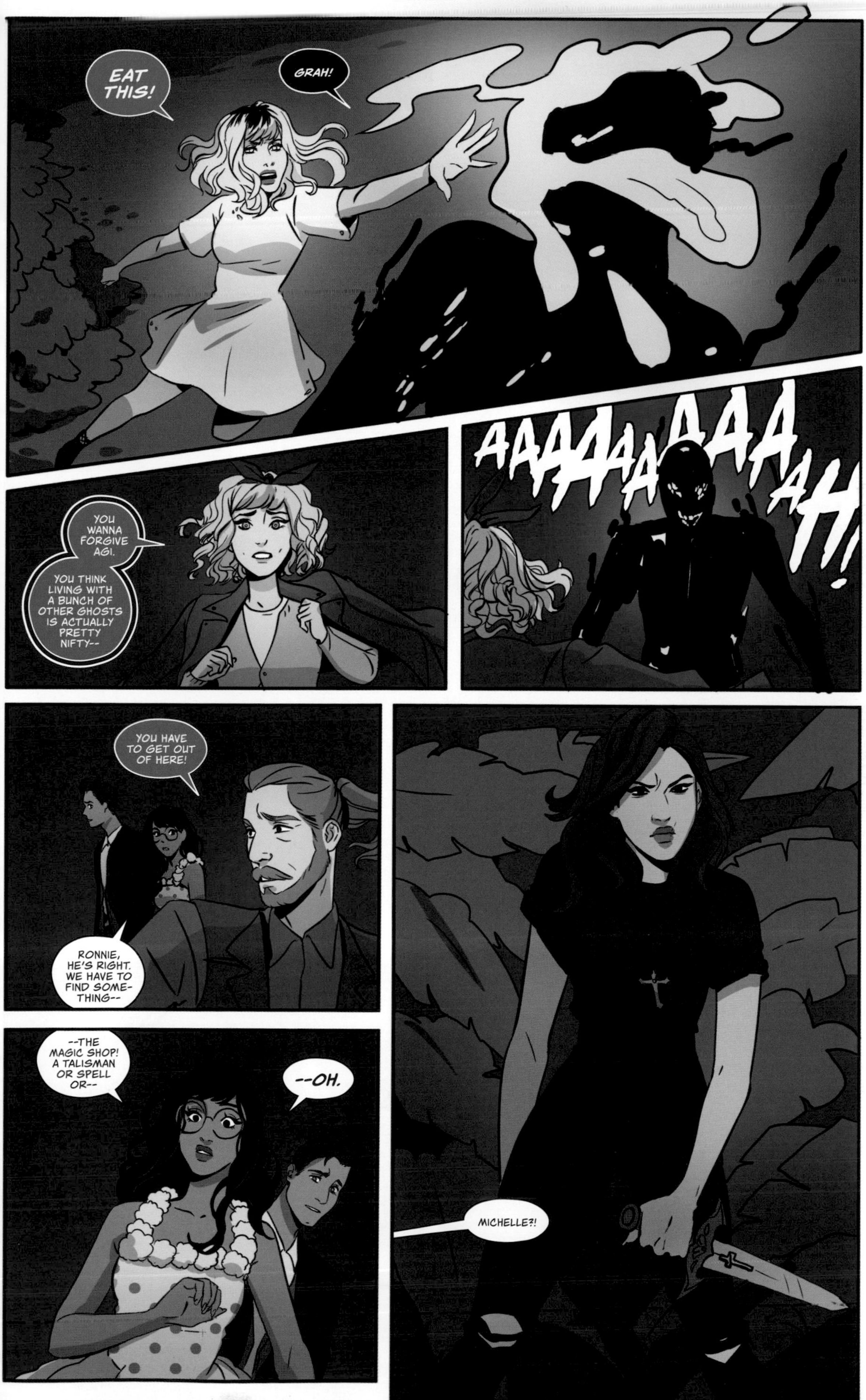

EAT THIS!
GRAH!
YOU WANNA FORGIVE AGI.
YOU THINK LIVING WITH A BUNCH OF OTHER GHOSTS IS ACTUALLY PRETTY NIFTY--
AAAAAAAAAAAH!!
YOU HAVE TO GET OUT OF HERE!
RONNIE, HE'S RIGHT. WE HAVE TO FIND SOME-THING--
--THE MAGIC SHOP! A TALISMAN OR SPELL OR--
--OH.
MICHELLE?!

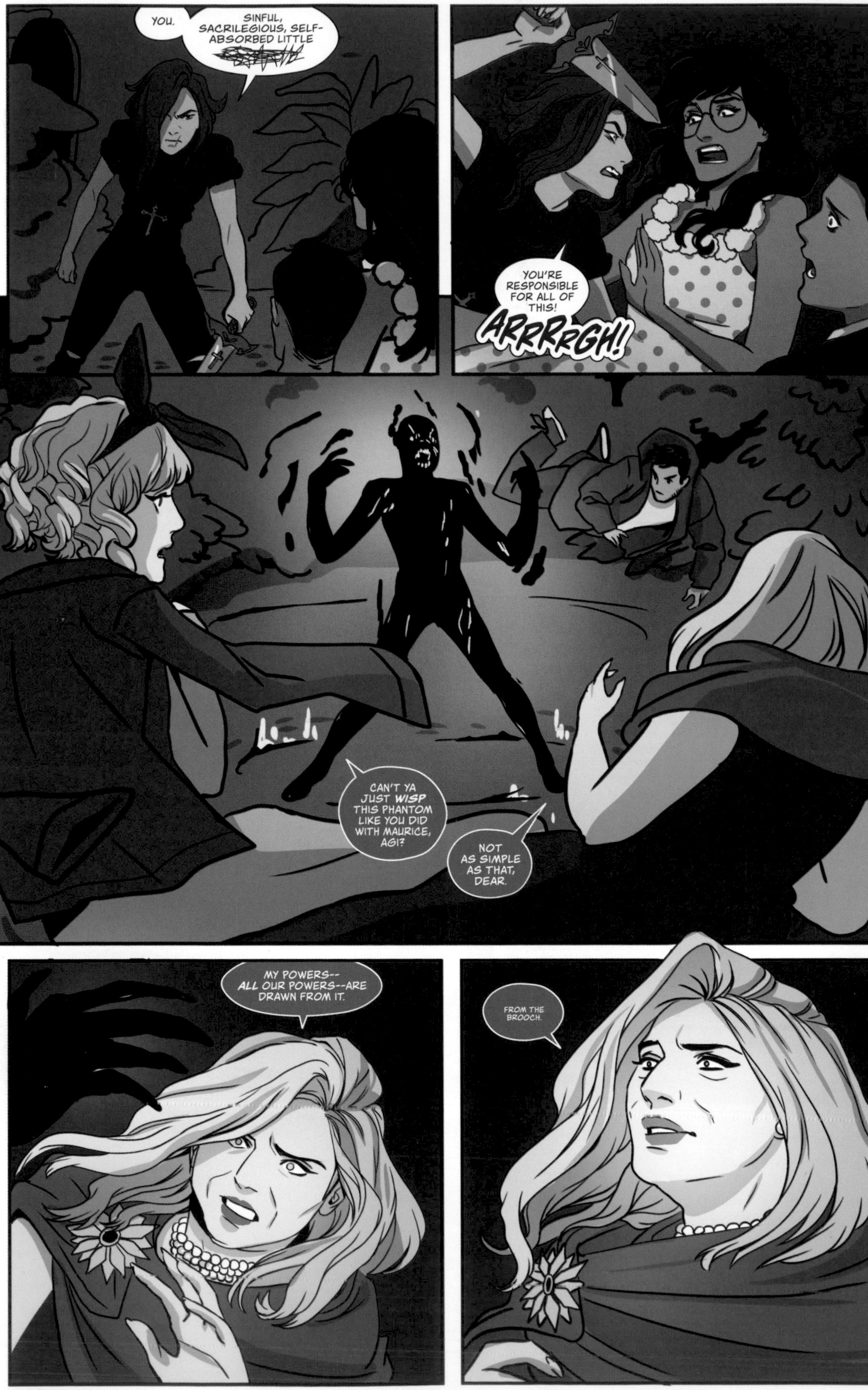

YOU.
SINFUL, SACRILEGIOUS, SELF-ABSORBED LITTLE
YOU'RE RESPONSIBLE FOR ALL OF THIS!
ARRRRGH!
CAN'T YA JUST WISP THIS PHANTOM LIKE YOU DID WITH MAURICE, AGI?
NOT AS SIMPLE AS THAT, DEAR.
MY POWERS-- ALL OUR POWERS--ARE DRAWN FROM IT.
FROM THE BROOCH.

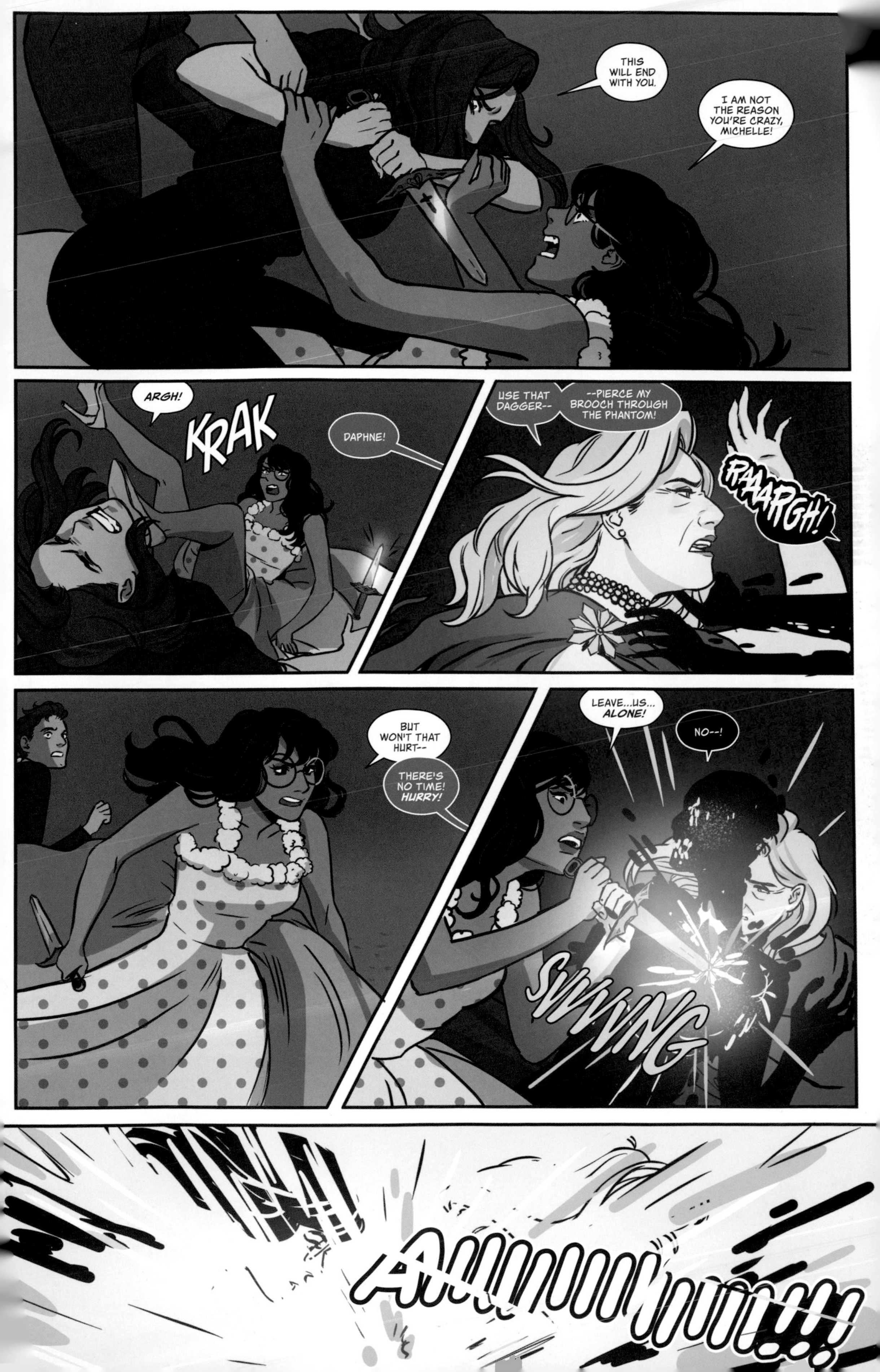
THIS WILL END WITH YOU.
I AM NOT THE REASON YOU'RE CRAZY, MICHELLE!
ARGH!
KRAK
DAPHNE!
USE THAT DAGGER--
--PIERCE MY BROOCH THROUGH THE PHANTOM!
RAAARGH!
BUT WON'T THAT HURT--
THERE'S NO TIME! HURRY!
LEAVE...US... ALONE!
NO--!
SWING

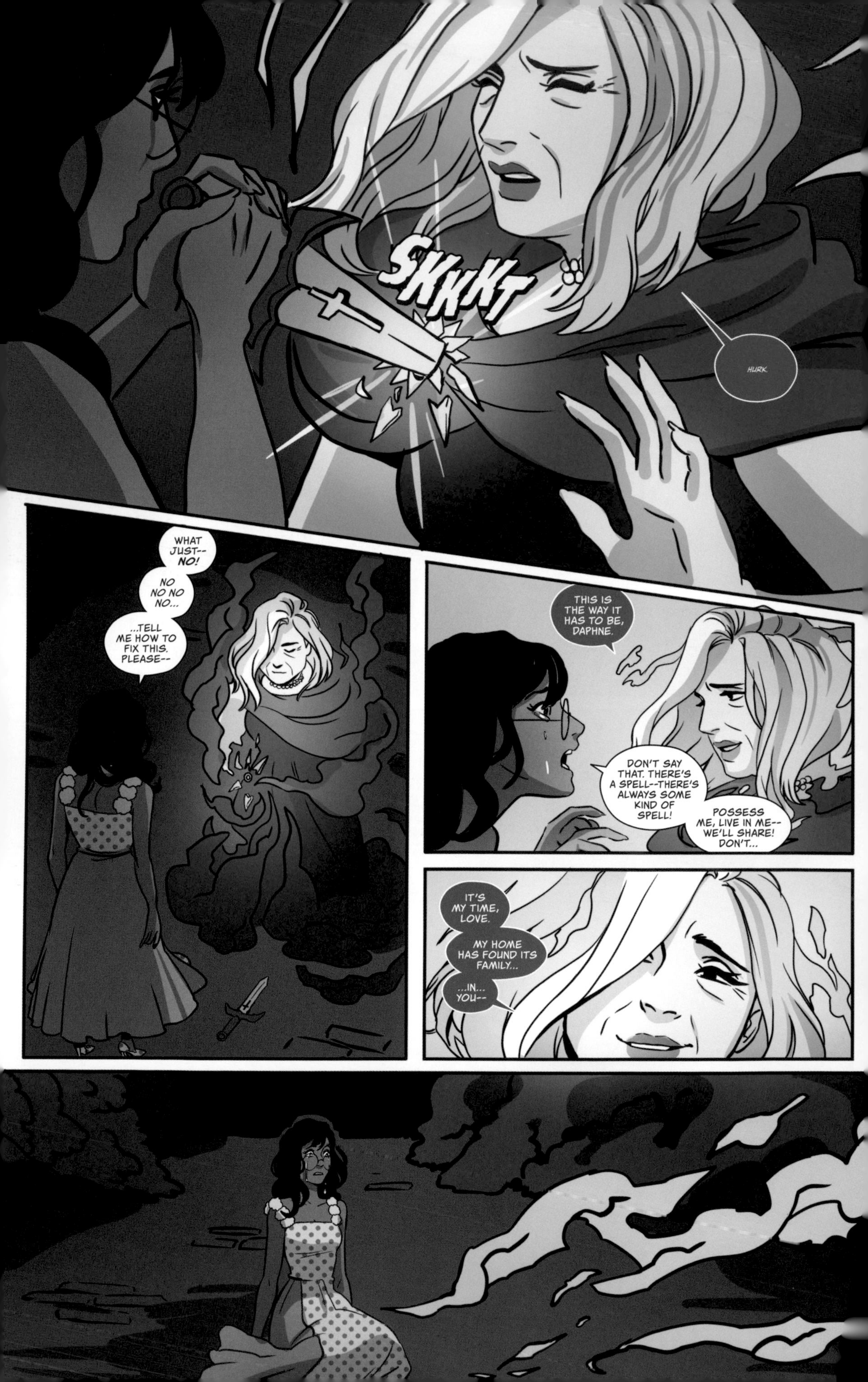
SKKKT
HURK.
WHAT JUST-- NO!
NO NO NO NO...
...TELL ME HOW TO FIX THIS. PLEASE--
THIS IS THE WAY IT HAS TO BE, DAPHNE.
DON'T SAY THAT. THERE'S A SPELL--THERE'S ALWAYS SOME KIND OF SPELL!
POSSESS ME, LIVE IN ME-- WE'LL SHARE! DON'T...
IT'S MY TIME, LOVE.
MY HOME HAS FOUND ITS FAMILY...
...IN... YOU--

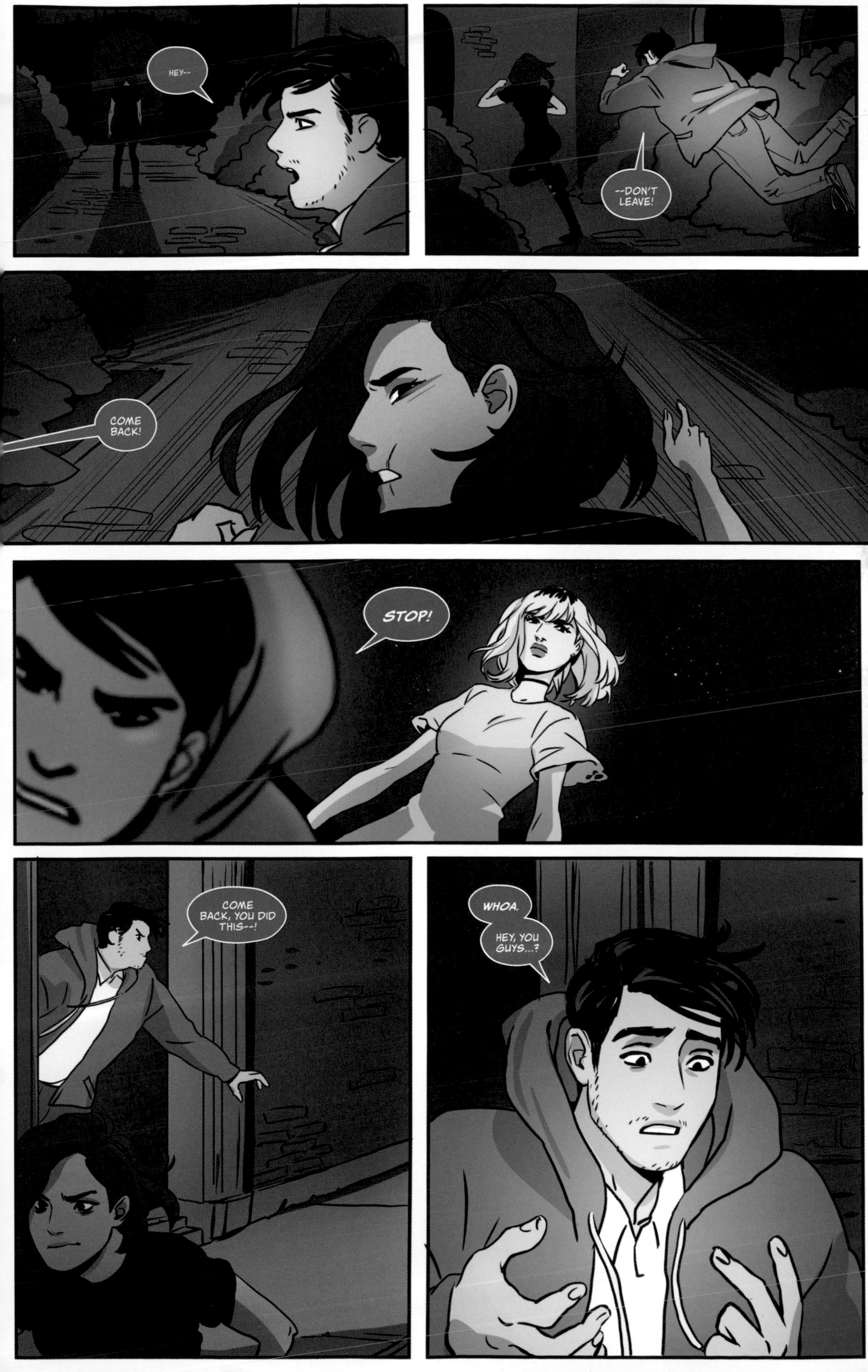
HEY--
--DON'T LEAVE!
COME BACK!
STOP!
COME BACK, YOU DID THIS--!
WHOA.
HEY, YOU GUYS...?

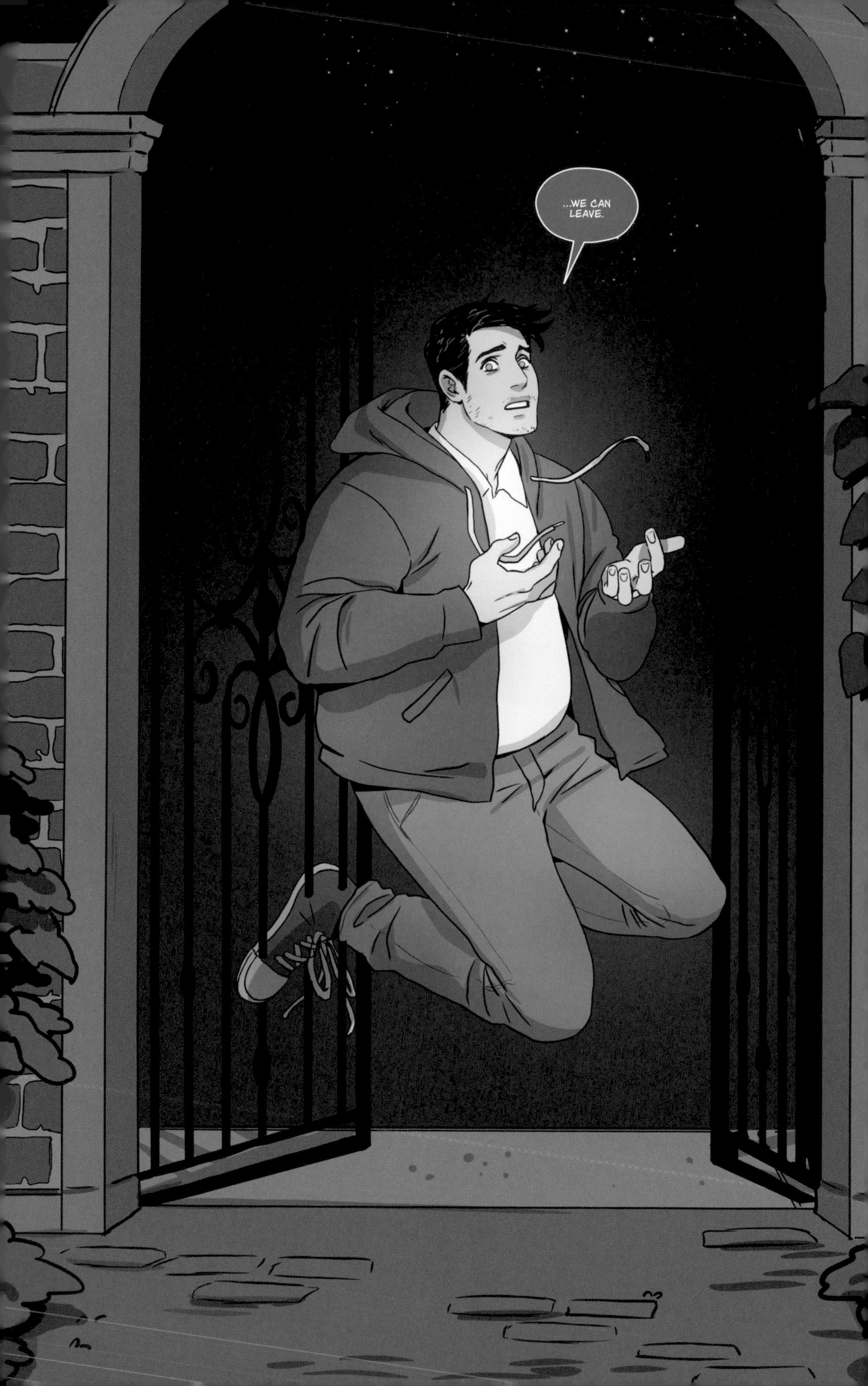
...WE CAN LEAVE.

Chapter Twelve

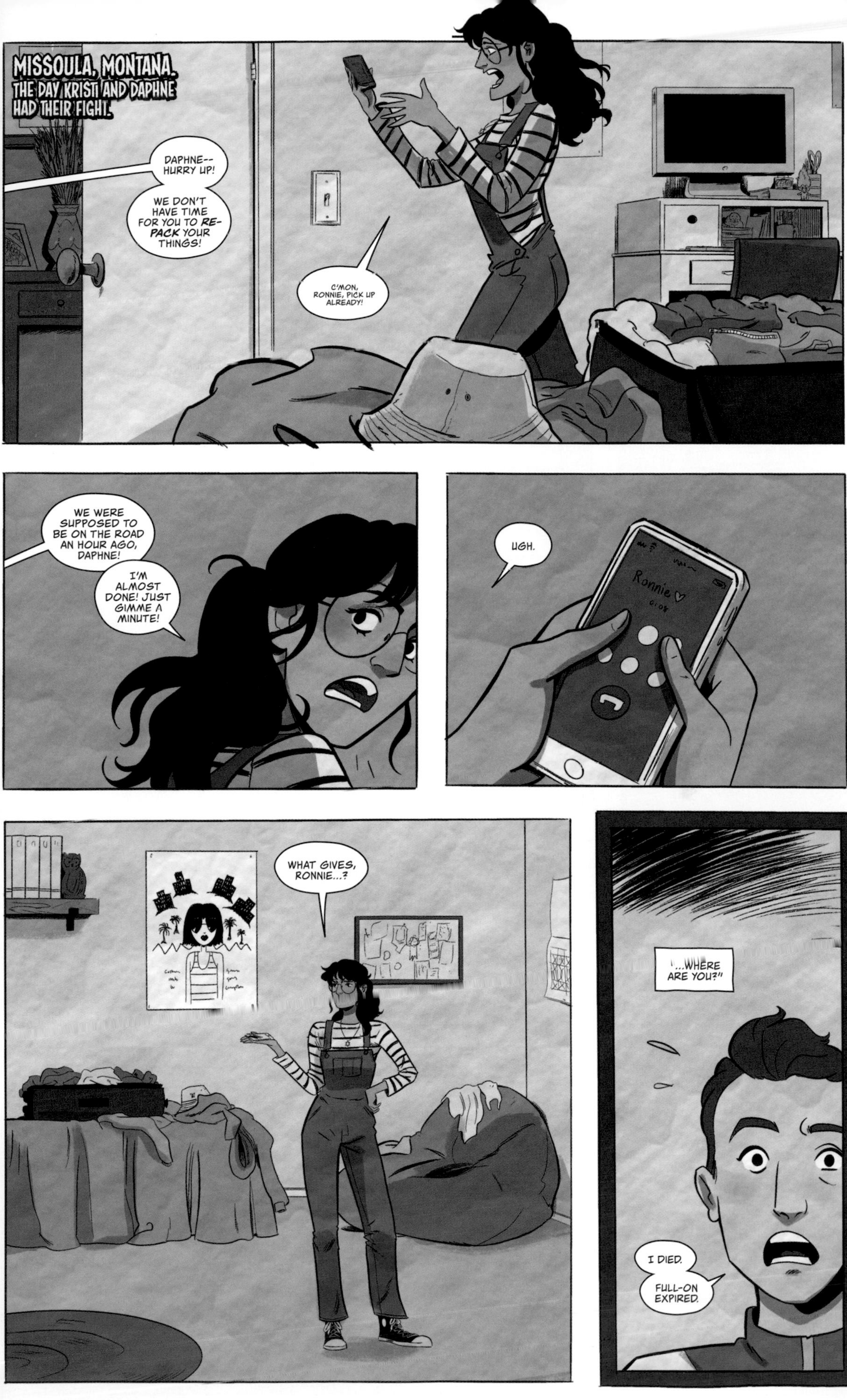
MISSOULA, MONTANA.
THE DAY KRISTI AND DAPHNE HAD THEIR FIGHT.
DAPHNE-- HURRY UP!
WE DON'T HAVE TIME FOR YOU TO RE-PACK YOUR THINGS!
C'MON, RONNIE, PICK UP ALREADY!
WE WERE SUPPOSED TO BE ON THE ROAD AN HOUR AGO, DAPHNE!
I'M ALMOST DONE! JUST GIMME A MINUTE!
UGH.
Ronnie ♡
WHAT GIVES, RONNIE...?
"...WHERE ARE YOU?"
I DIED.
FULL-ON EXPIRED.

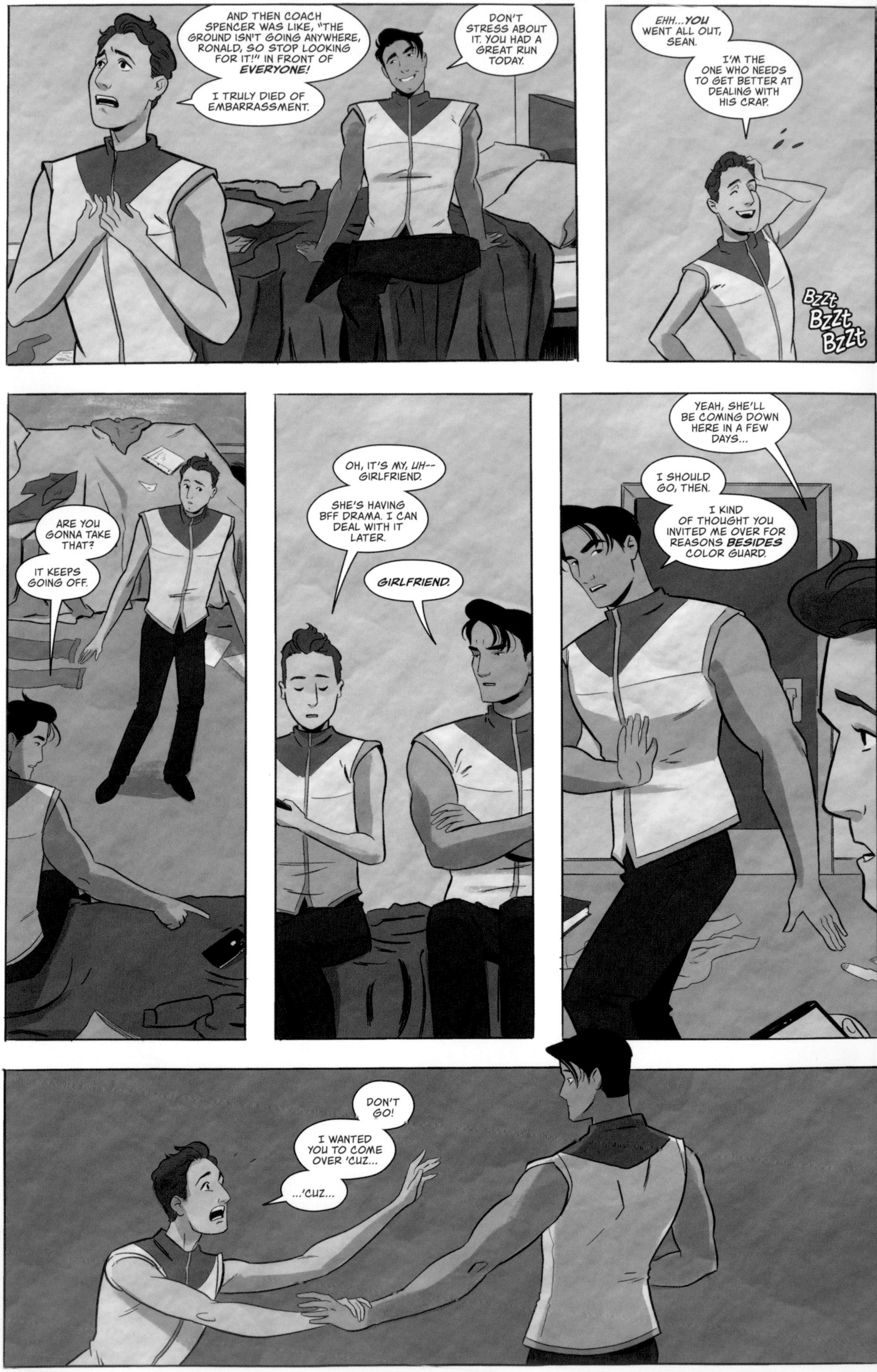
AND THEN COACH SPENCER WAS LIKE, "THE GROUND ISN'T GOING ANYWHERE, RONALD, SO STOP LOOKING FOR IT!" IN FRONT OF EVERYONE!
I TRULY DIED OF EMBARRASSMENT.
DON'T STRESS ABOUT IT. YOU HAD A GREAT RUN TODAY.
EHH...YOU WENT ALL OUT, SEAN.
I'M THE ONE WHO NEEDS TO GET BETTER AT DEALING WITH HIS CRAP.
BZZT BZZT BZZT
ARE YOU GONNA TAKE THAT?
IT KEEPS GOING OFF.
OH, IT'S MY, UH-- GIRLFRIEND.
SHE'S HAVING BFF DRAMA. I CAN DEAL WITH IT LATER.
GIRLFRIEND.
YEAH, SHE'LL BE COMING DOWN HERE IN A FEW DAYS...
I SHOULD GO, THEN.
I KIND OF THOUGHT YOU INVITED ME OVER FOR REASONS BESIDES COLOR GUARD.
DON'T GO!
I WANTED YOU TO COME OVER 'CUZ...
...'CUZ...

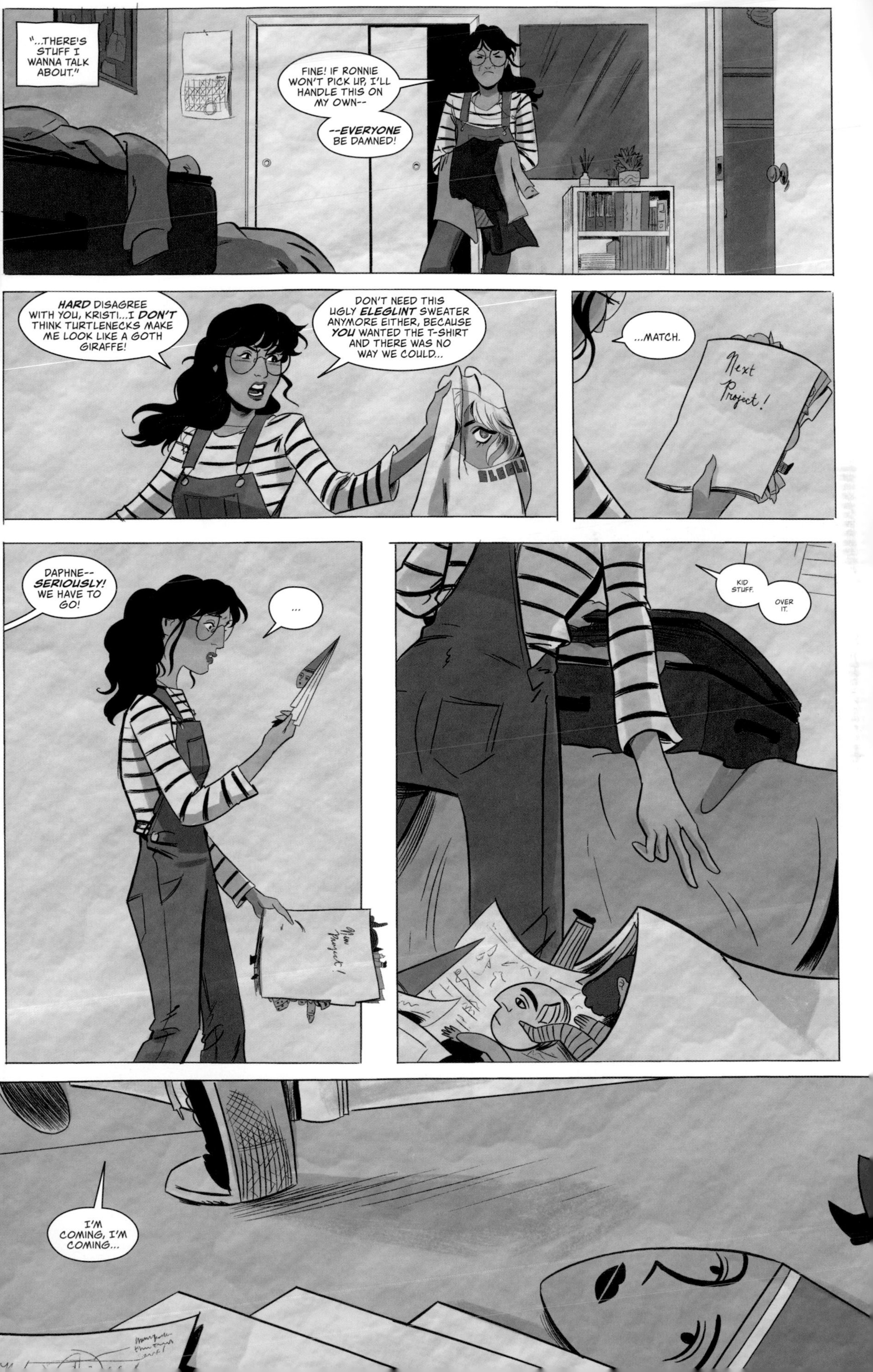
"...THERE'S STUFF I WANNA TALK ABOUT."
FINE! IF RONNIE WON'T PICK UP, I'LL HANDLE THIS ON MY OWN--
--EVERYONE BE DAMNED!
HARD DISAGREE WITH YOU, KRISTI...I DON'T THINK TURTLENECKS MAKE ME LOOK LIKE A GOTH GIRAFFE!
DON'T NEED THIS UGLY ELEGLINT SWEATER ANYMORE EITHER, BECAUSE YOU WANTED THE T-SHIRT AND THERE WAS NO WAY WE COULD...
...MATCH.
Next Project!
DAPHNE-- SERIOUSLY! WE HAVE TO GO!
...
KID STUFF.
OVER IT.
I'M COMING, I'M COMING...

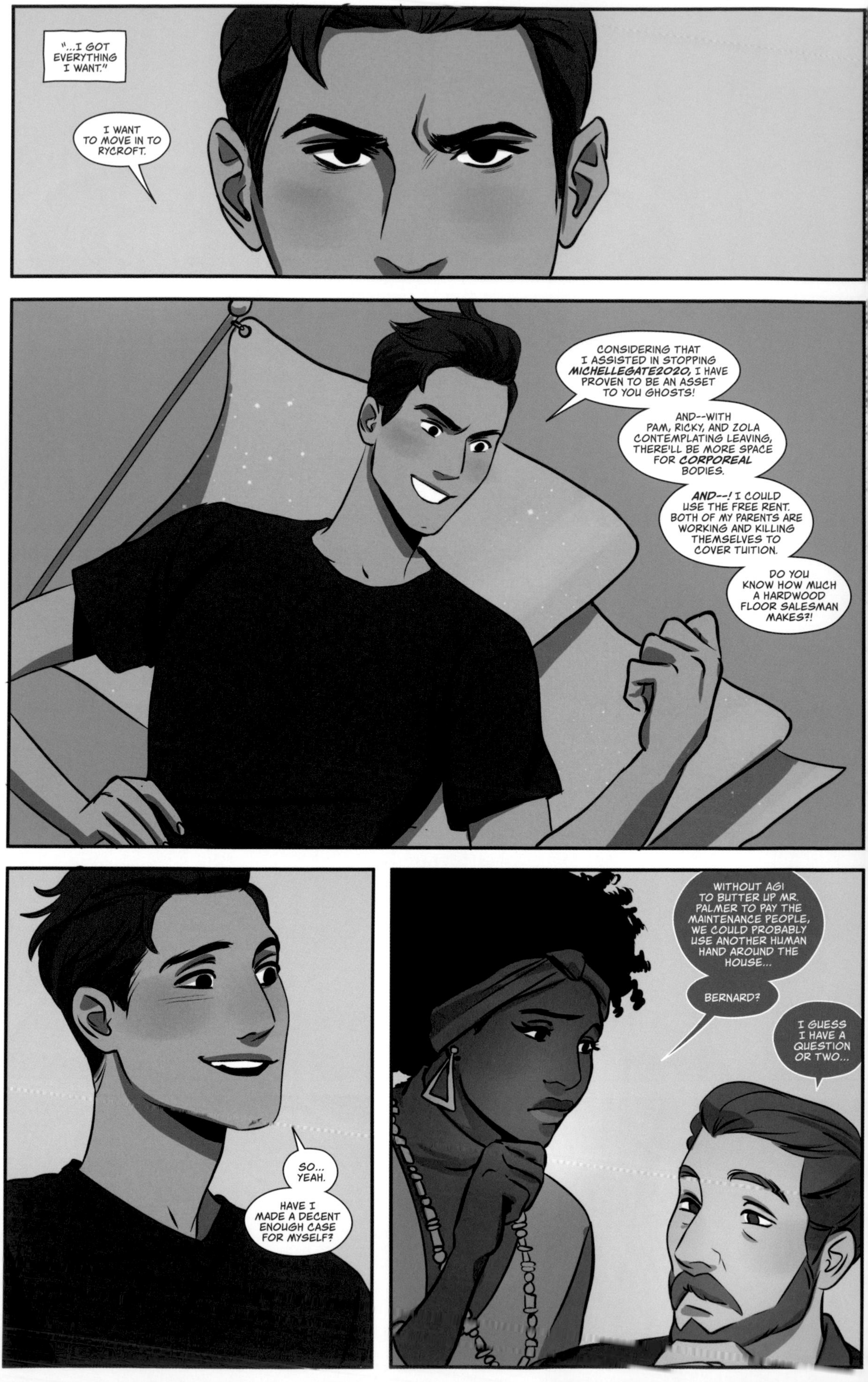
"...I GOT EVERYTHING I WANT."
I WANT TO MOVE IN TO RYCROFT.
CONSIDERING THAT I ASSISTED IN STOPPING MICHELLEGATE2020, I HAVE PROVEN TO BE AN ASSET TO YOU GHOSTS!
AND--WITH PAM, RICKY, AND ZOLA CONTEMPLATING LEAVING, THERE'LL BE MORE SPACE FOR CORPOREAL BODIES.
AND--! I COULD USE THE FREE RENT. BOTH OF MY PARENTS ARE WORKING AND KILLING THEMSELVES TO COVER TUITION.
DO YOU KNOW HOW MUCH A HARDWOOD FLOOR SALESMAN MAKES?!
SO... YEAH.
HAVE I MADE A DECENT ENOUGH CASE FOR MYSELF?
WITHOUT AGI TO BUTTER UP MR. PALMER TO PAY THE MAINTENANCE PEOPLE, WE COULD PROBABLY USE ANOTHER HUMAN HAND AROUND THE HOUSE...
BERNARD?
I GUESS I HAVE A QUESTION OR TWO...

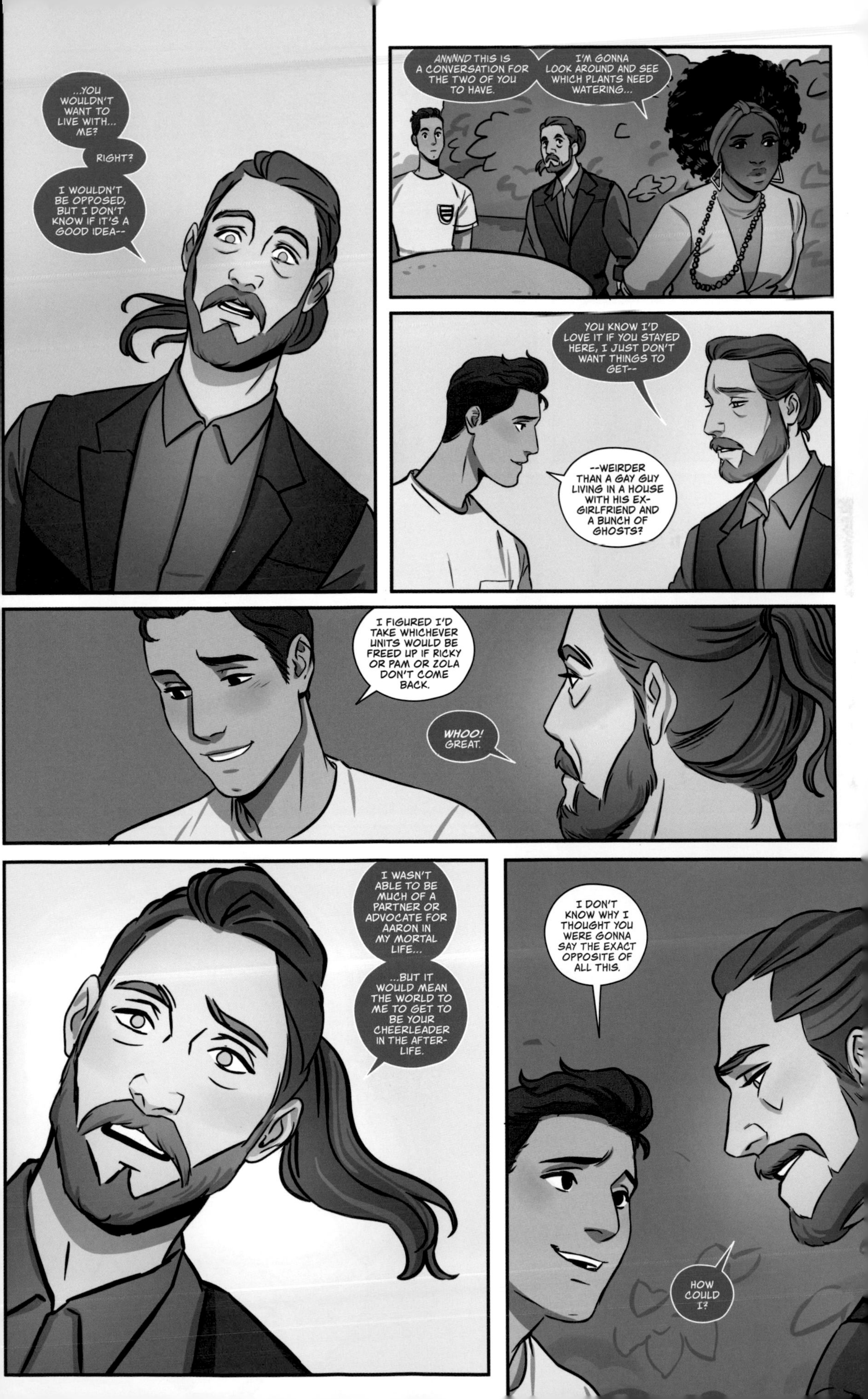
...YOU WOULDN'T WANT TO LIVE WITH... ME?
RIGHT?
I WOULDN'T BE OPPOSED, BUT I DON'T KNOW IF IT'S A GOOD IDEA--
ANNNND THIS IS A CONVERSATION FOR THE TWO OF YOU TO HAVE.
I'M GONNA LOOK AROUND AND SEE WHICH PLANTS NEED WATERING...
YOU KNOW I'D LOVE IT IF YOU STAYED HERE, I JUST DON'T WANT THINGS TO GET--
--WEIRDER THAN A GAY GUY LIVING IN A HOUSE WITH HIS EX-GIRLFRIEND AND A BUNCH OF GHOSTS?
I FIGURED I'D TAKE WHICHEVER UNITS WOULD BE FREED UP IF RICKY OR PAM OR ZOLA DON'T COME BACK.
WHOO! GREAT.
I WASN'T ABLE TO BE MUCH OF A PARTNER OR ADVOCATE FOR AARON IN MY MORTAL LIFE...
...BUT IT WOULD MEAN THE WORLD TO ME TO GET TO BE YOUR CHEERLEADER IN THE AFTER-LIFE.
I DON'T KNOW WHY I THOUGHT YOU WERE GONNA SAY THE EXACT OPPOSITE OF ALL THIS.
HOW COULD I?

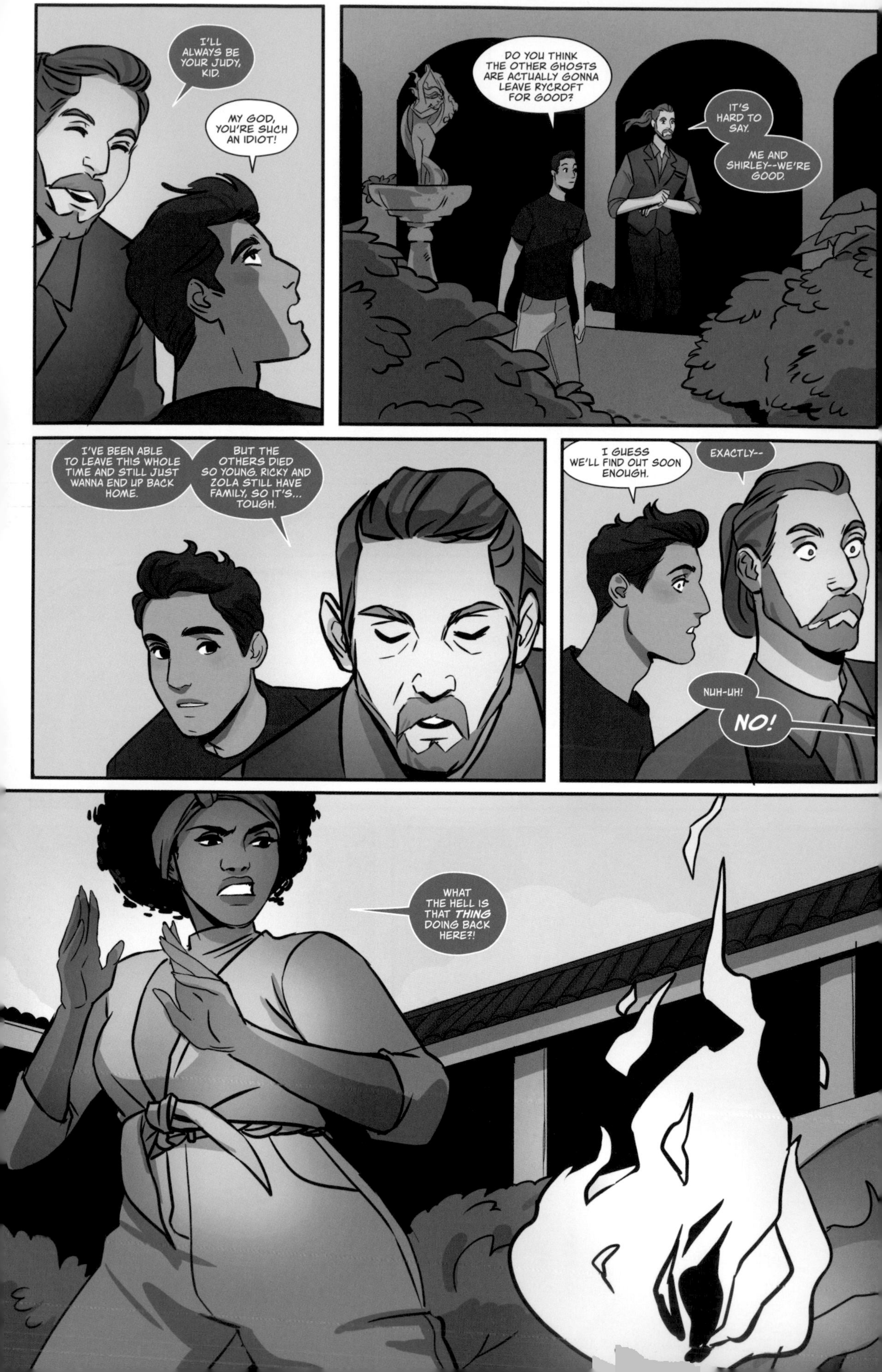
I'LL ALWAYS BE YOUR JUDY, KID.
MY GOD, YOU'RE SUCH AN IDIOT!
DO YOU THINK THE OTHER GHOSTS ARE ACTUALLY GONNA LEAVE RYCROFT FOR GOOD?
IT'S HARD TO SAY.
ME AND SHIRLEY--WE'RE GOOD.
I'VE BEEN ABLE TO LEAVE THIS WHOLE TIME AND STILL JUST WANNA END UP BACK HOME.
BUT THE OTHERS DIED SO YOUNG. RICKY AND ZOLA STILL HAVE FAMILY, SO IT'S... TOUGH.
I GUESS WE'LL FIND OUT SOON ENOUGH.
EXACTLY--
NUH-UH!
NO!
WHAT THE HELL IS THAT *THING* DOING BACK HERE?!

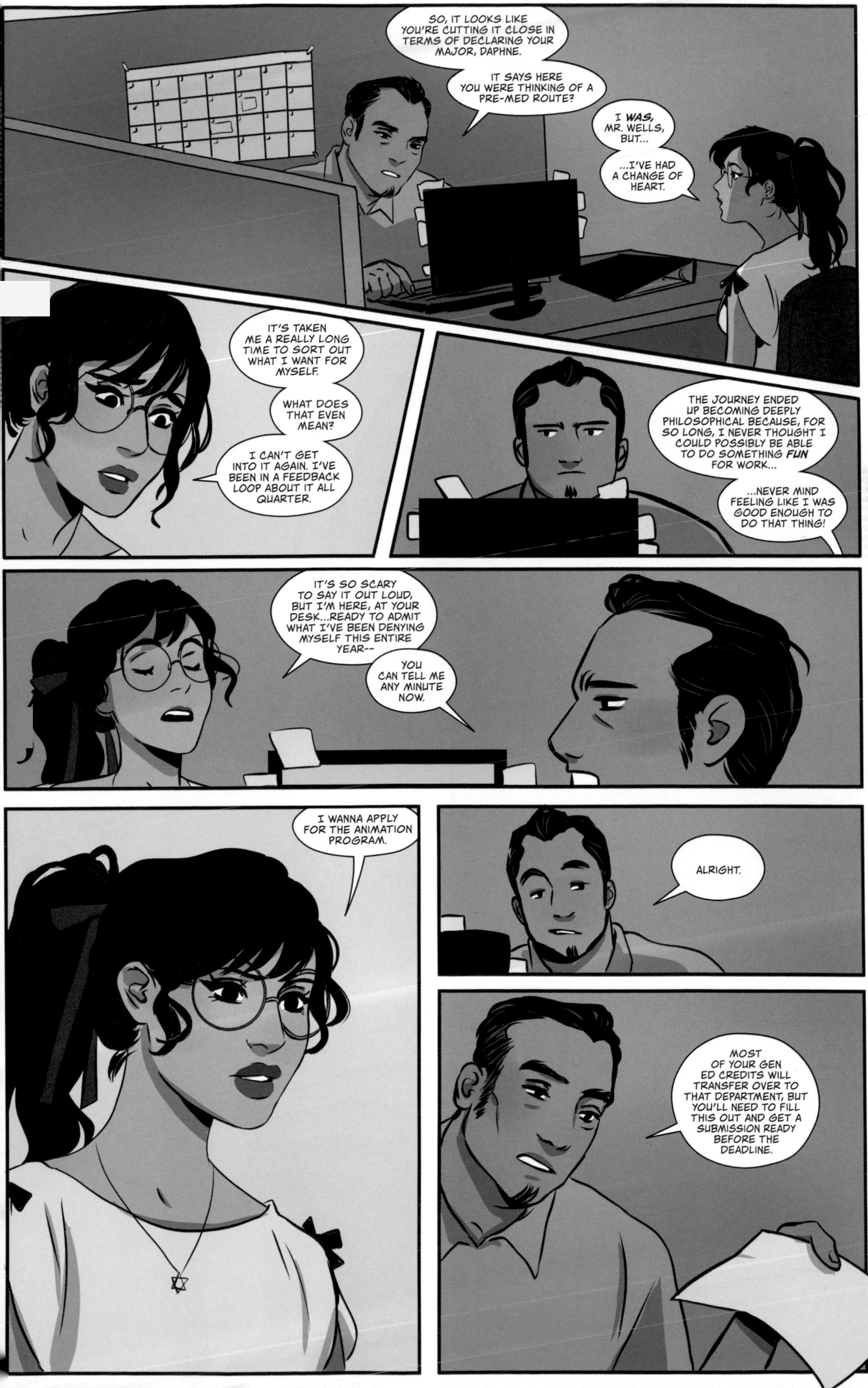
SO, IT LOOKS LIKE YOU'RE CUTTING IT CLOSE IN TERMS OF DECLARING YOUR MAJOR, DAPHNE.
IT SAYS HERE YOU WERE THINKING OF A PRE-MED ROUTE?
I WAS, MR. WELLS, BUT...
...I'VE HAD A CHANGE OF HEART.
IT'S TAKEN ME A REALLY LONG TIME TO SORT OUT WHAT I WANT FOR MYSELF.
WHAT DOES THAT EVEN MEAN?
I CAN'T GET INTO IT AGAIN. I'VE BEEN IN A FEEDBACK LOOP ABOUT IT ALL QUARTER.
THE JOURNEY ENDED UP BECOMING DEEPLY PHILOSOPHICAL BECAUSE, FOR SO LONG, I NEVER THOUGHT I COULD POSSIBLY BE ABLE TO DO SOMETHING FUN FOR WORK...
...NEVER MIND FEELING LIKE I WAS GOOD ENOUGH TO DO THAT THING!
IT'S SO SCARY TO SAY IT OUT LOUD, BUT I'M HERE, AT YOUR DESK...READY TO ADMIT WHAT I'VE BEEN DENYING MYSELF THIS ENTIRE YEAR--
YOU CAN TELL ME ANY MINUTE NOW.
I WANNA APPLY FOR THE ANIMATION PROGRAM.
ALRIGHT.
MOST OF YOUR GEN ED CREDITS WILL TRANSFER OVER TO THAT DEPARTMENT, BUT YOU'LL NEED TO FILL THIS OUT AND GET A SUBMISSION READY BEFORE THE DEADLINE.

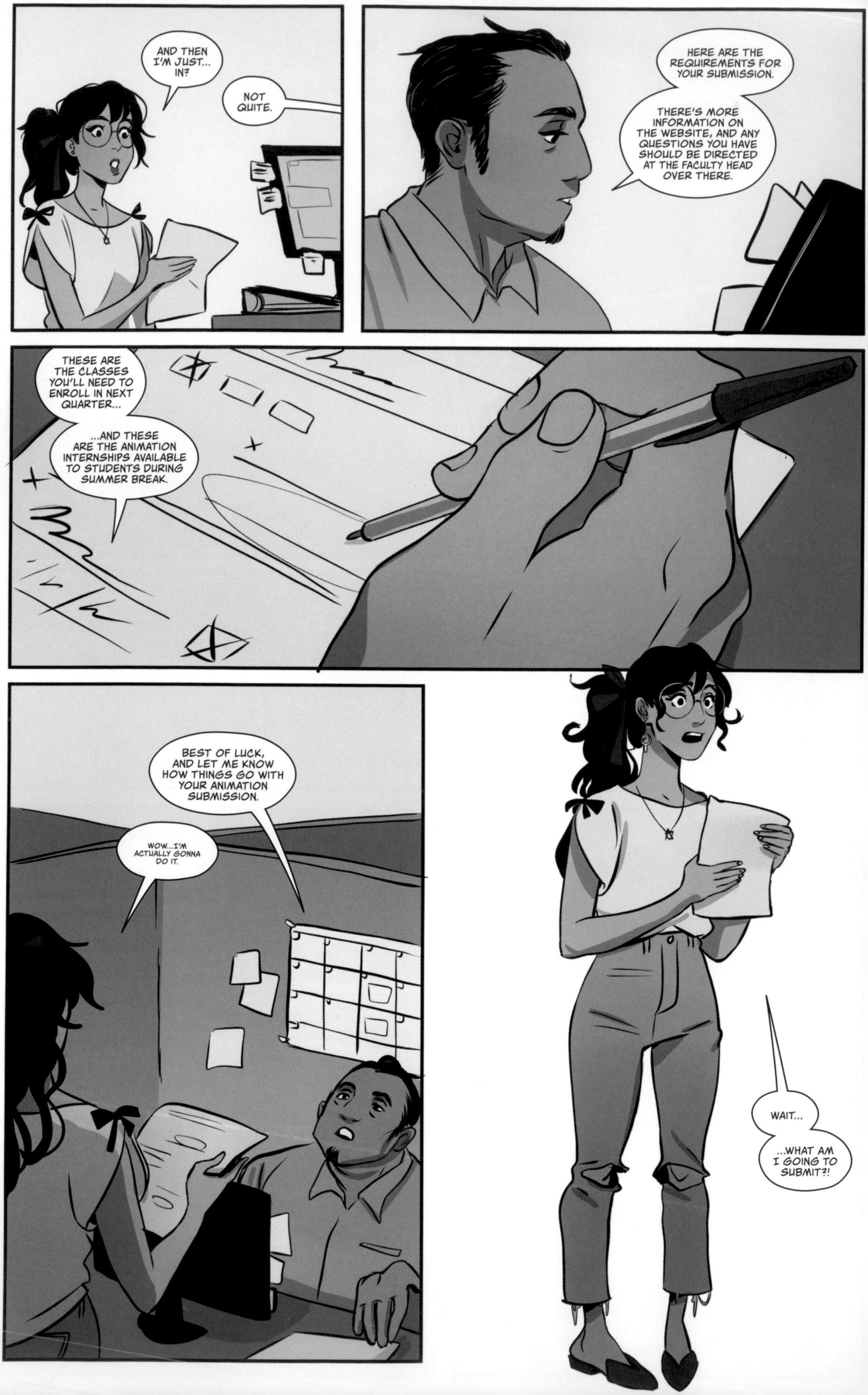
AND THEN I'M JUST... IN?
NOT QUITE.
HERE ARE THE REQUIREMENTS FOR YOUR SUBMISSION.
THERE'S MORE INFORMATION ON THE WEBSITE, AND ANY QUESTIONS YOU HAVE SHOULD BE DIRECTED AT THE FACULTY HEAD OVER THERE.
THESE ARE THE CLASSES YOU'LL NEED TO ENROLL IN NEXT QUARTER...
...AND THESE ARE THE ANIMATION INTERNSHIPS AVAILABLE TO STUDENTS DURING SUMMER BREAK.
BEST OF LUCK, AND LET ME KNOW HOW THINGS GO WITH YOUR ANIMATION SUBMISSION.
WOW...I'M ACTUALLY GONNA DO IT.
WAIT...
...WHAT AM I GOING TO SUBMIT?!

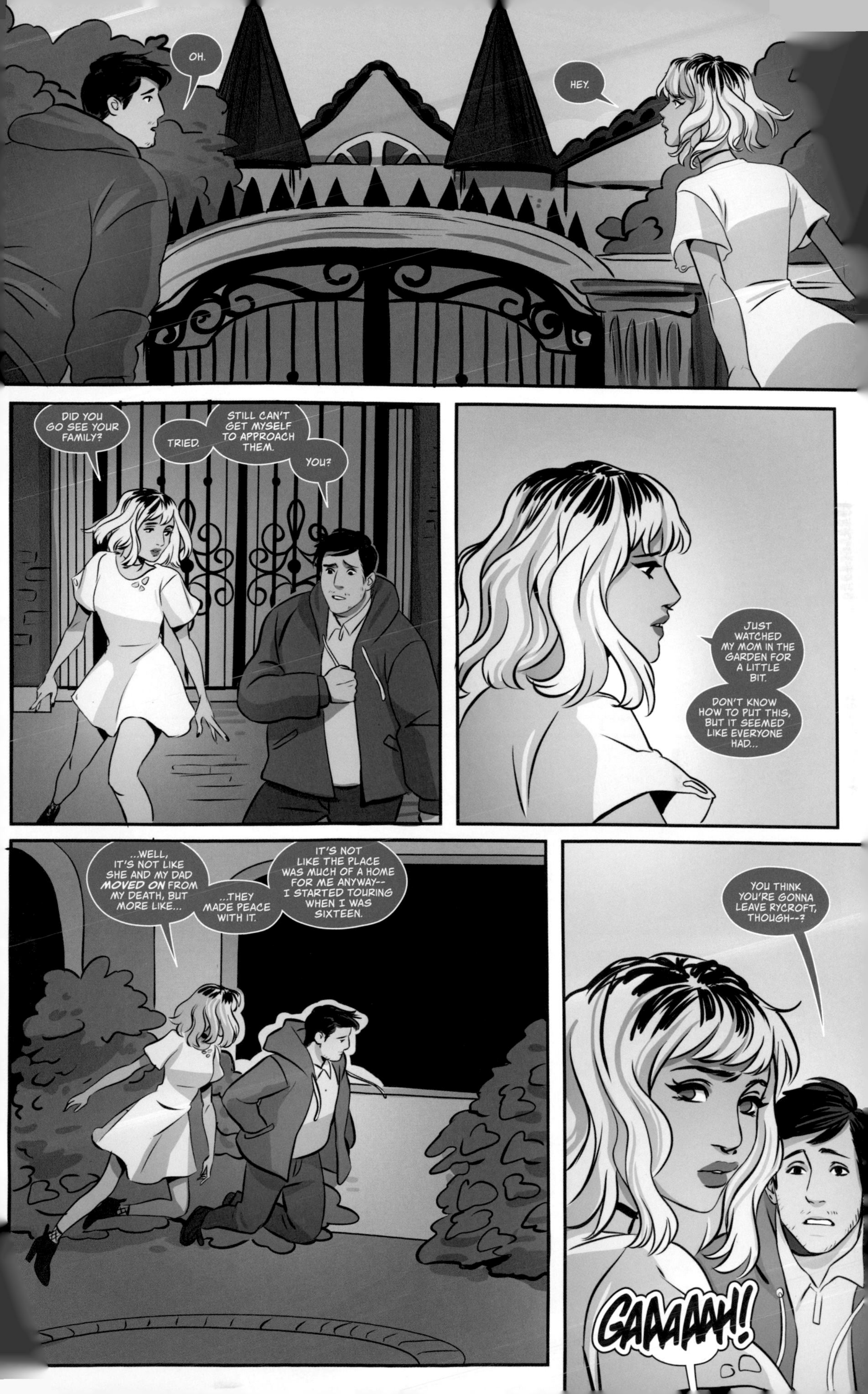
OH.
HEY.
DID YOU GO SEE YOUR FAMILY?
TRIED.
STILL CAN'T GET MYSELF TO APPROACH THEM.
YOU?
JUST WATCHED MY MOM IN THE GARDEN FOR A LITTLE BIT.
DON'T KNOW HOW TO PUT THIS, BUT IT SEEMED LIKE EVERYONE HAD...
...WELL, IT'S NOT LIKE SHE AND MY DAD MOVED ON FROM MY DEATH, BUT MORE LIKE...
...THEY MADE PEACE WITH IT.
IT'S NOT LIKE THE PLACE WAS MUCH OF A HOME FOR ME ANYWAY-- I STARTED TOURING WHEN I WAS SIXTEEN.
YOU THINK YOU'RE GONNA LEAVE RYCROFT, THOUGH--?
GAAAAAH!!

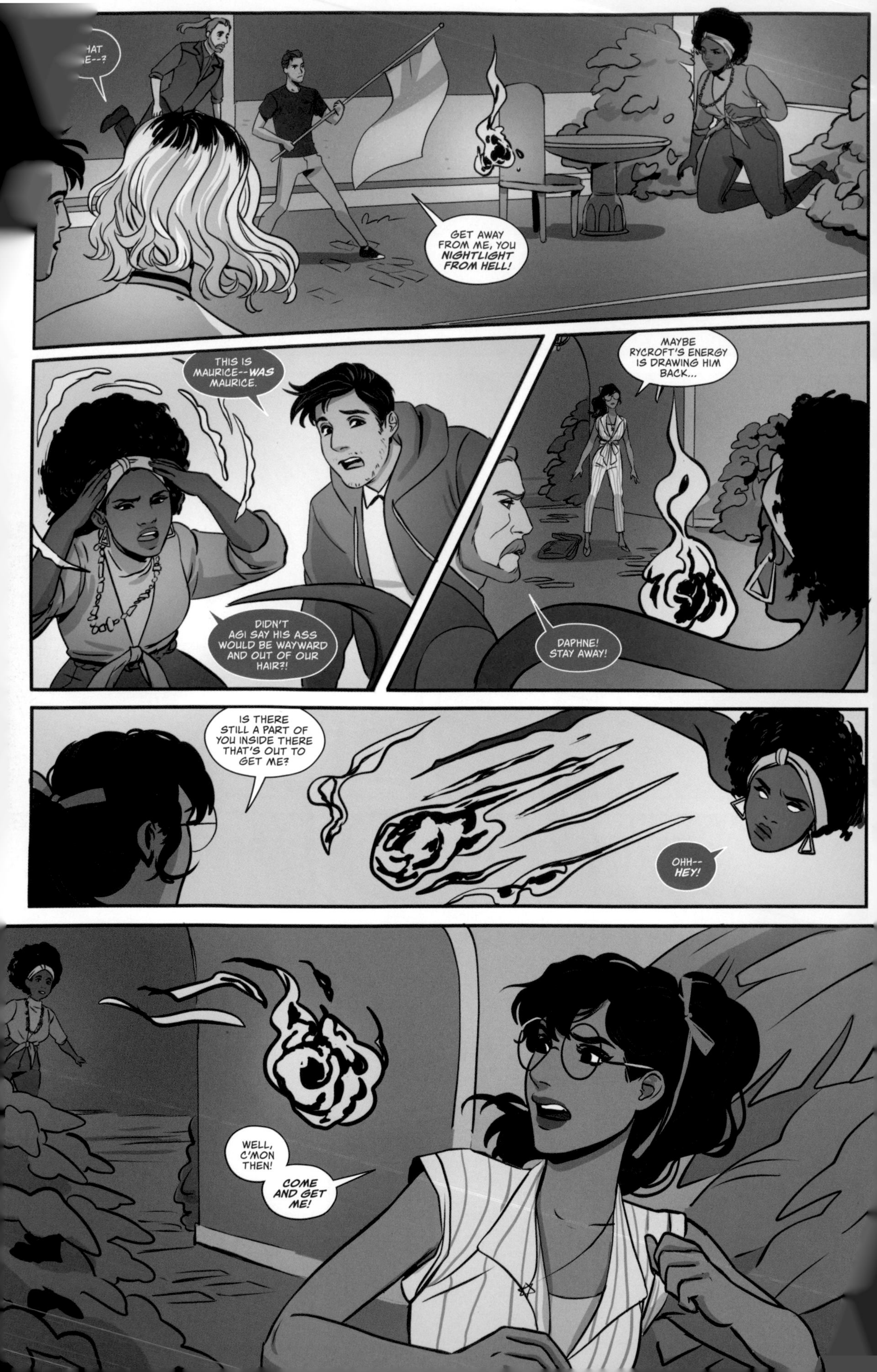
GET AWAY FROM ME, YOU NIGHTLIGHT FROM HELL!
THIS IS MAURICE--WAS MAURICE.
DIDN'T AGI SAY HIS ASS WOULD BE WAYWARD AND OUT OF OUR HAIR?!
MAYBE RYCROFT'S ENERGY IS DRAWING HIM BACK...
DAPHNE! STAY AWAY!
IS THERE STILL A PART OF YOU INSIDE THERE THAT'S OUT TO GET ME?
OHH-- HEY!
WELL, C'MON THEN!
COME AND GET ME!

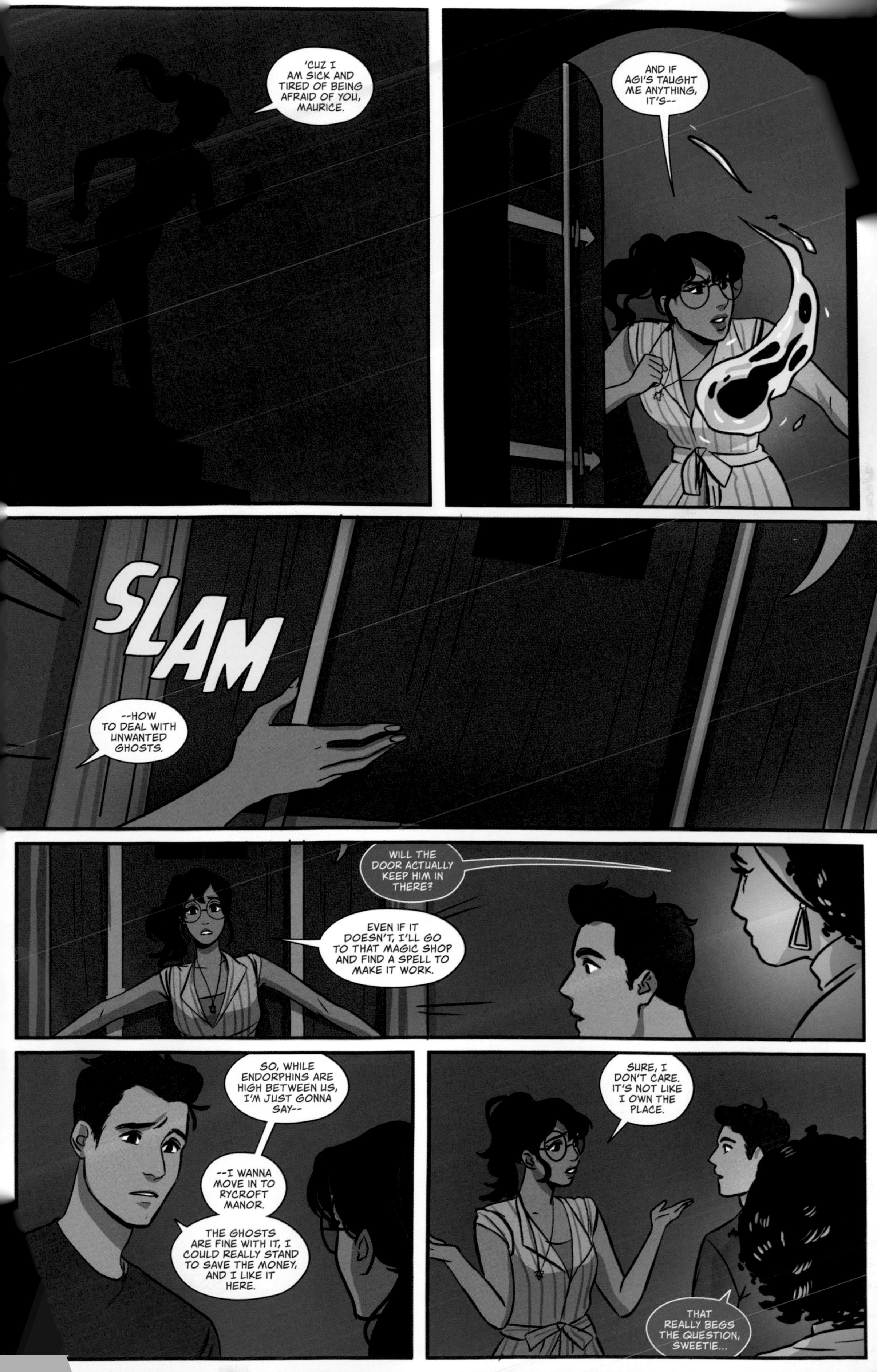
'CUZ I AM SICK AND TIRED OF BEING AFRAID OF YOU, MAURICE.
AND IF AGI'S TAUGHT ME ANYTHING, IT'S--
SLAM
--HOW TO DEAL WITH UNWANTED GHOSTS.
WILL THE DOOR ACTUALLY KEEP HIM IN THERE?
EVEN IF IT DOESN'T, I'LL GO TO THAT MAGIC SHOP AND FIND A SPELL TO MAKE IT WORK.
SO, WHILE ENDORPHINS ARE HIGH BETWEEN US, I'M JUST GONNA SAY--
--I WANNA MOVE IN TO RYCROFT MANOR.
THE GHOSTS ARE FINE WITH IT, I COULD REALLY STAND TO SAVE THE MONEY, AND I LIKE IT HERE.
SURE, I DON'T CARE. IT'S NOT LIKE I OWN THE PLACE.
THAT REALLY BEGS THE QUESTION, SWEETIE...

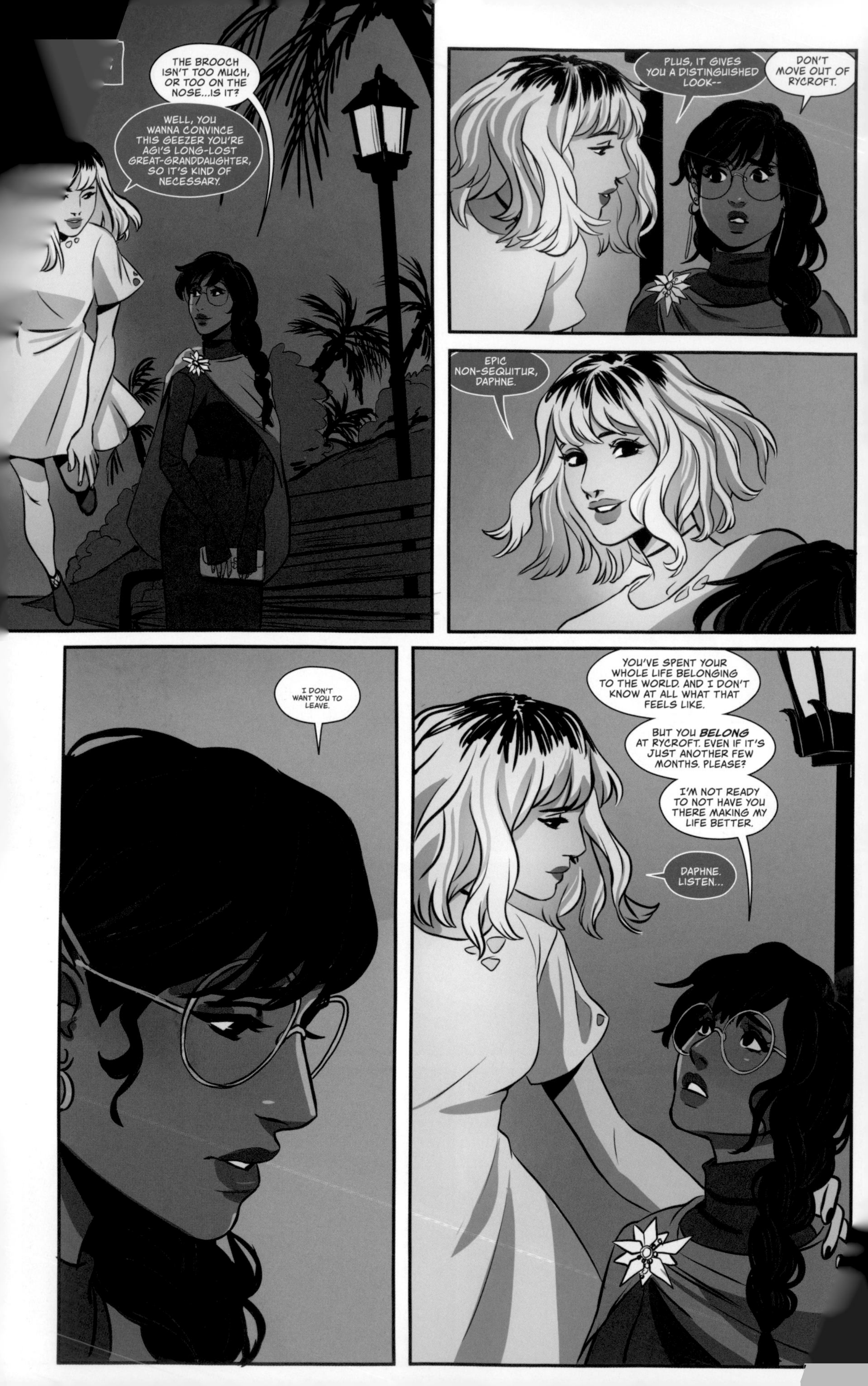
THE BROOCH ISN'T TOO MUCH, OR TOO ON THE NOSE...IS IT?
WELL, YOU WANNA CONVINCE THIS GEEZER YOU'RE AGI'S LONG-LOST GREAT-GRANDDAUGHTER, SO IT'S KIND OF NECESSARY.
PLUS, IT GIVES YOU A DISTINGUISHED LOOK--
DON'T MOVE OUT OF RYCROFT.
EPIC NON-SEQUITUR, DAPHNE.
I DON'T WANT YOU TO LEAVE.
YOU'VE SPENT YOUR WHOLE LIFE BELONGING TO THE WORLD. AND I DON'T KNOW AT ALL WHAT THAT FEELS LIKE.
BUT YOU *BELONG* AT RYCROFT. EVEN IF IT'S JUST ANOTHER FEW MONTHS. PLEASE?
I'M NOT READY TO NOT HAVE YOU THERE MAKING MY LIFE BETTER.
DAPHNE. LISTEN...

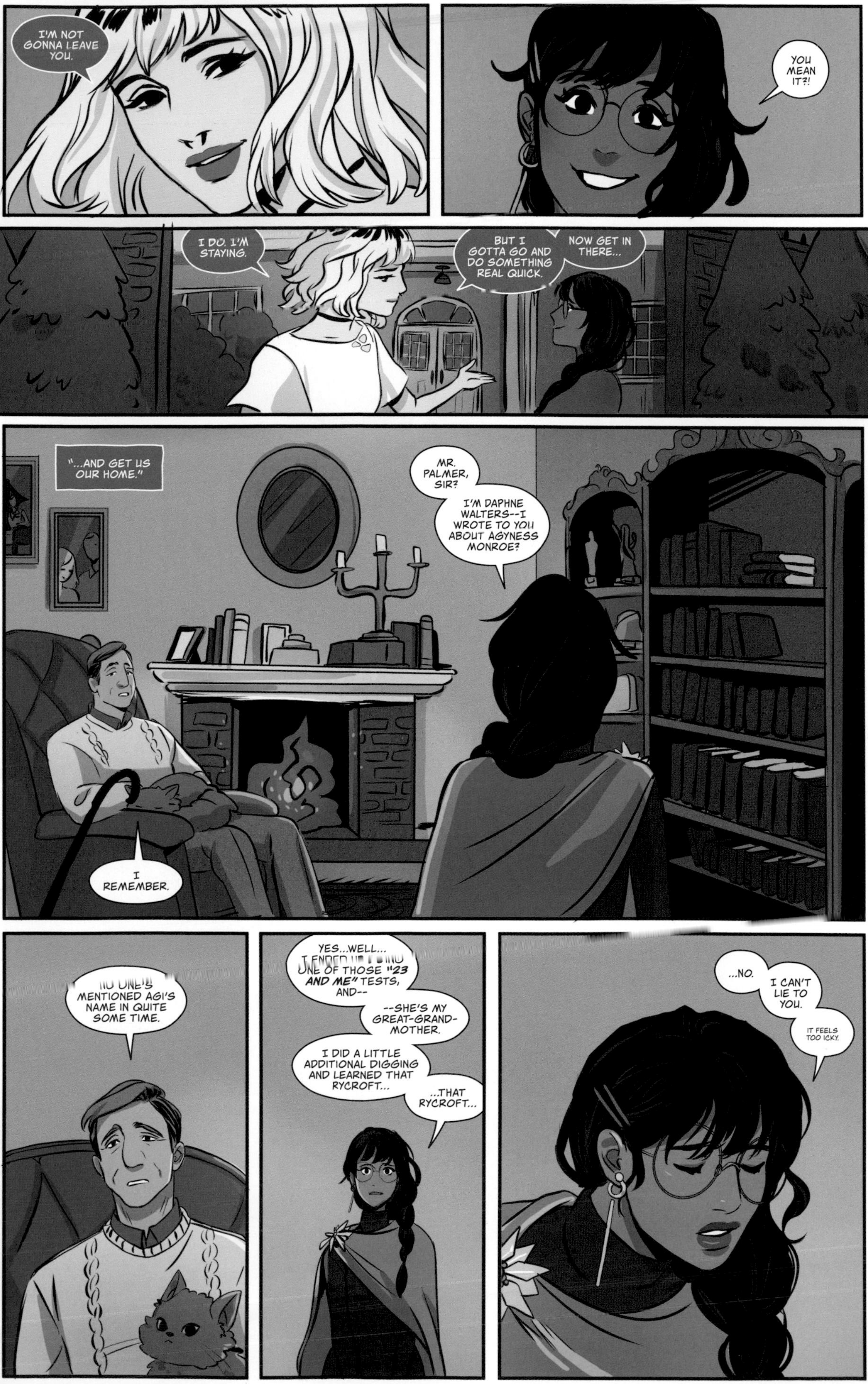
I'M NOT GONNA LEAVE YOU.
YOU MEAN IT?!
I DO. I'M STAYING.
BUT I GOTTA GO AND DO SOMETHING REAL QUICK.
NOW GET IN THERE...
"...AND GET US OUR HOME."
MR. PALMER, SIR?
I'M DAPHNE WALTERS--I WROTE TO YOU ABOUT AGYNESS MONROE?
I REMEMBER.
NO ONE'S MENTIONED AGI'S NAME IN QUITE SOME TIME.
YES...WELL...
ONE OF THOSE "23 AND ME" TESTS, AND--
--SHE'S MY GREAT-GRAND-MOTHER.
I DID A LITTLE ADDITIONAL DIGGING AND LEARNED THAT RYCROFT...
...THAT RYCROFT...
...NO.
I CAN'T LIE TO YOU.
IT FEELS TOO ICKY.

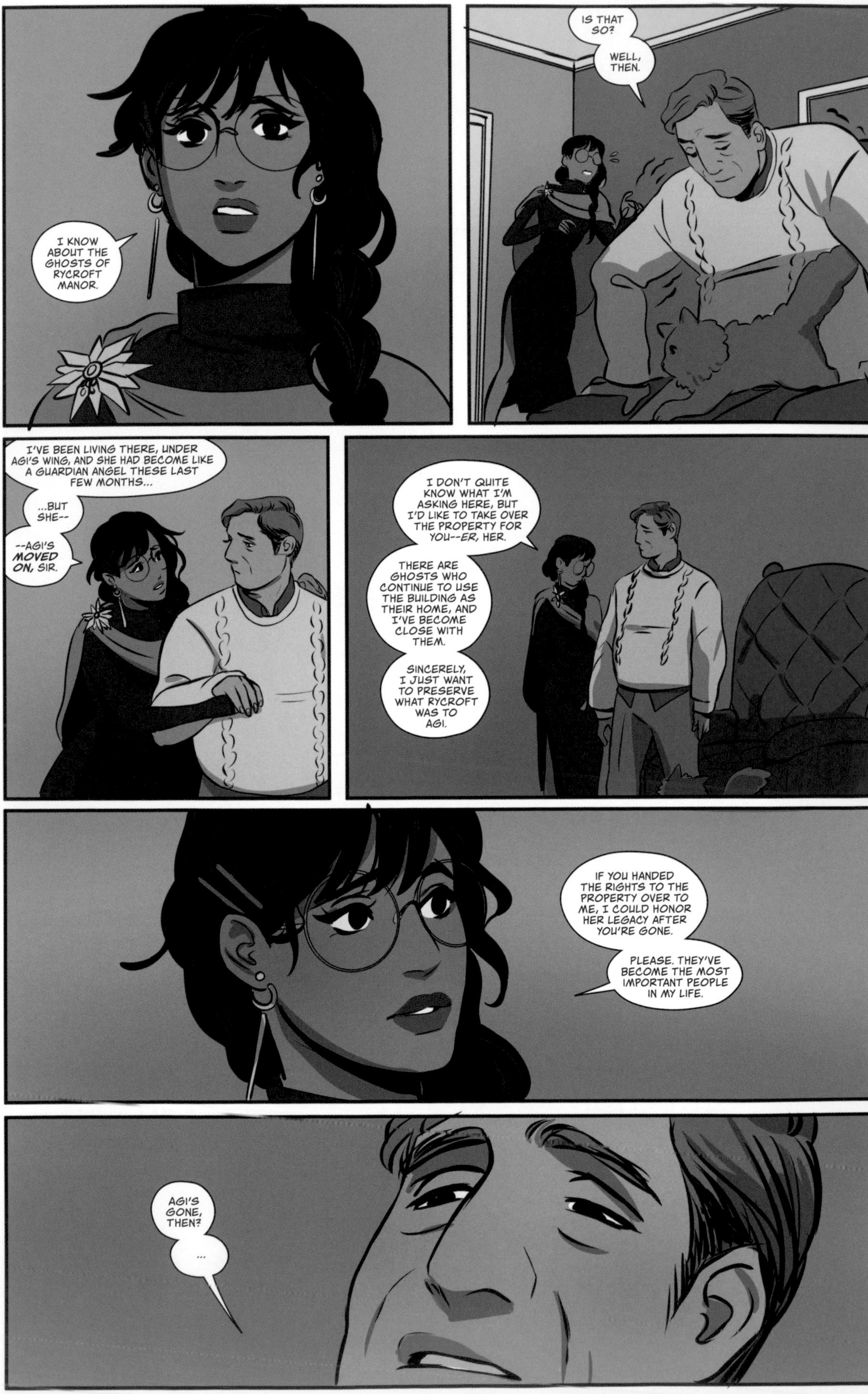
I KNOW ABOUT THE GHOSTS OF RYCROFT MANOR.
IS THAT SO?
WELL, THEN.
I'VE BEEN LIVING THERE, UNDER AGI'S WING, AND SHE HAD BECOME LIKE A GUARDIAN ANGEL THESE LAST FEW MONTHS...
...BUT SHE--
--AGI'S **MOVED ON,** SIR.
I DON'T QUITE KNOW WHAT I'M ASKING HERE, BUT I'D LIKE TO TAKE OVER THE PROPERTY FOR YOU--*ER*, HER.
THERE ARE GHOSTS WHO CONTINUE TO USE THE BUILDING AS THEIR HOME, AND I'VE BECOME CLOSE WITH THEM.
SINCERELY, I JUST WANT TO PRESERVE WHAT RYCROFT WAS TO AGI.
IF YOU HANDED THE RIGHTS TO THE PROPERTY OVER TO ME, I COULD HONOR HER LEGACY AFTER YOU'RE GONE.
PLEASE. THEY'VE BECOME THE MOST IMPORTANT PEOPLE IN MY LIFE.
AGI'S GONE, THEN?
...

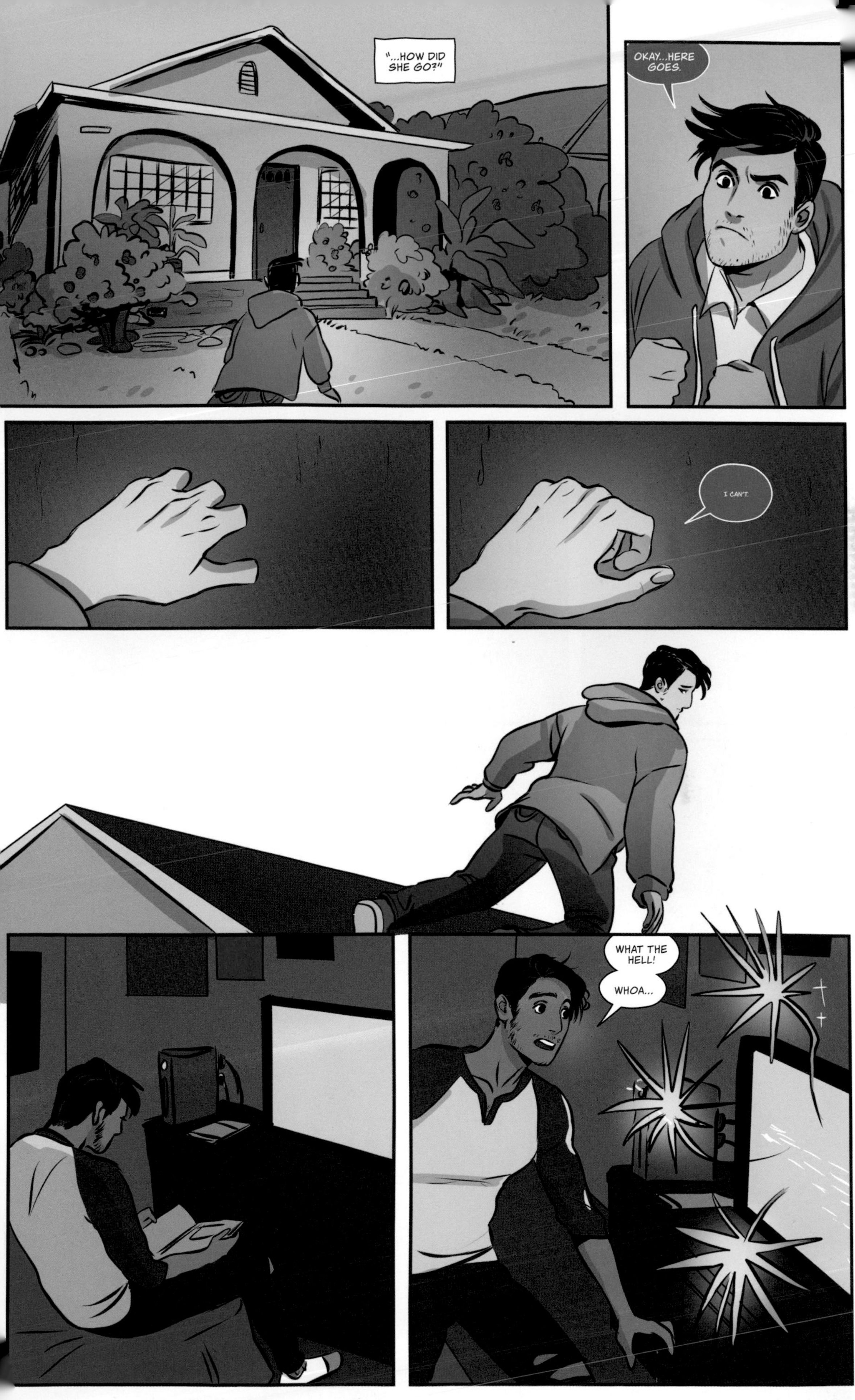
"...HOW DID SHE GO?"
OKAY...HERE GOES.
I CAN'T.
WHAT THE HELL!
WHOA...

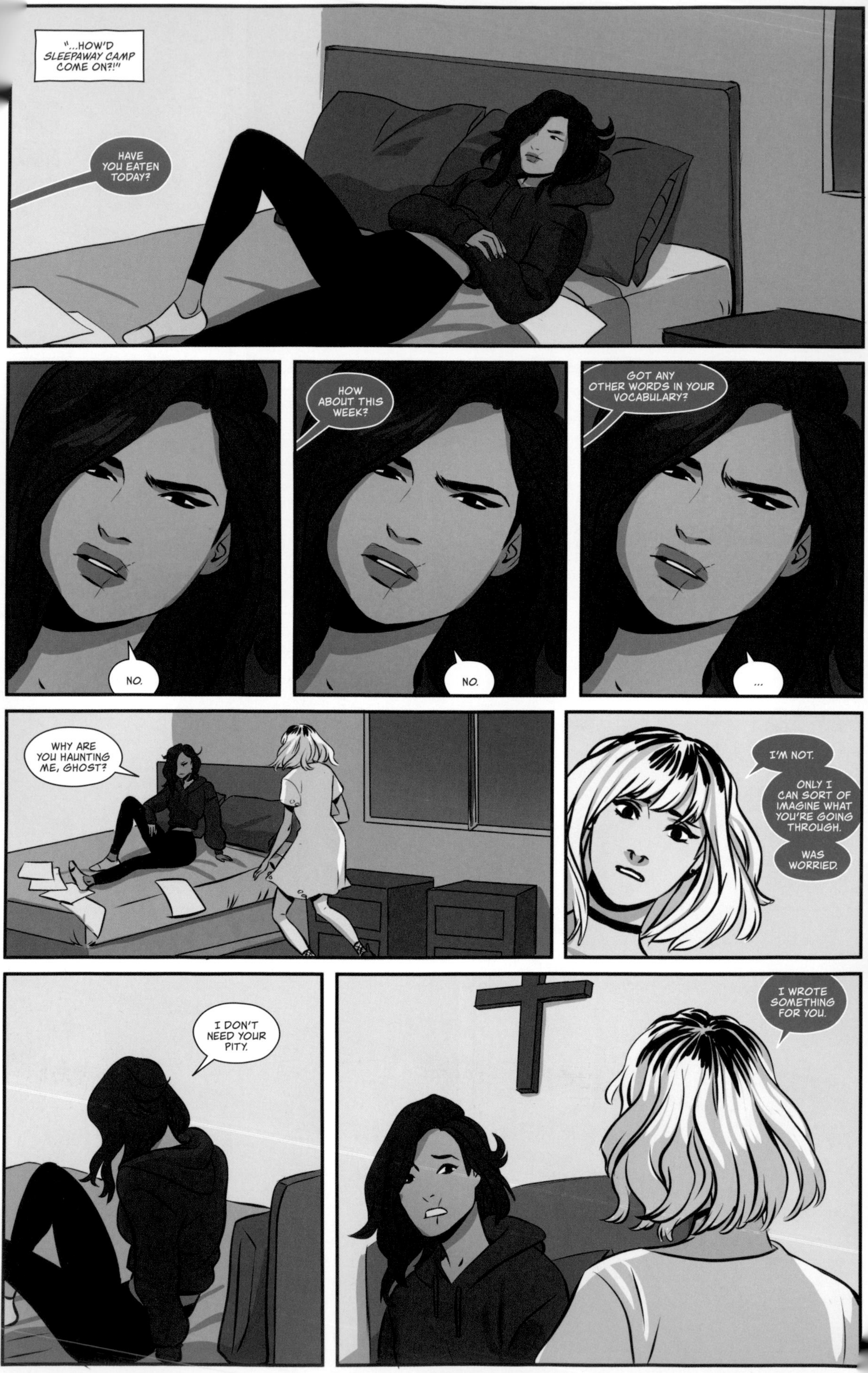
"...HOW'D SLEEPAWAY CAMP COME ON?!"
HAVE YOU EATEN TODAY?
NO.
HOW ABOUT THIS WEEK?
NO.
GOT ANY OTHER WORDS IN YOUR VOCABULARY?
...
WHY ARE YOU HAUNTING ME, GHOST?
I'M NOT.
ONLY I CAN SORT OF IMAGINE WHAT YOU'RE GOING THROUGH.
WAS WORRIED.
I DON'T NEED YOUR PITY.
I WROTE SOMETHING FOR YOU.

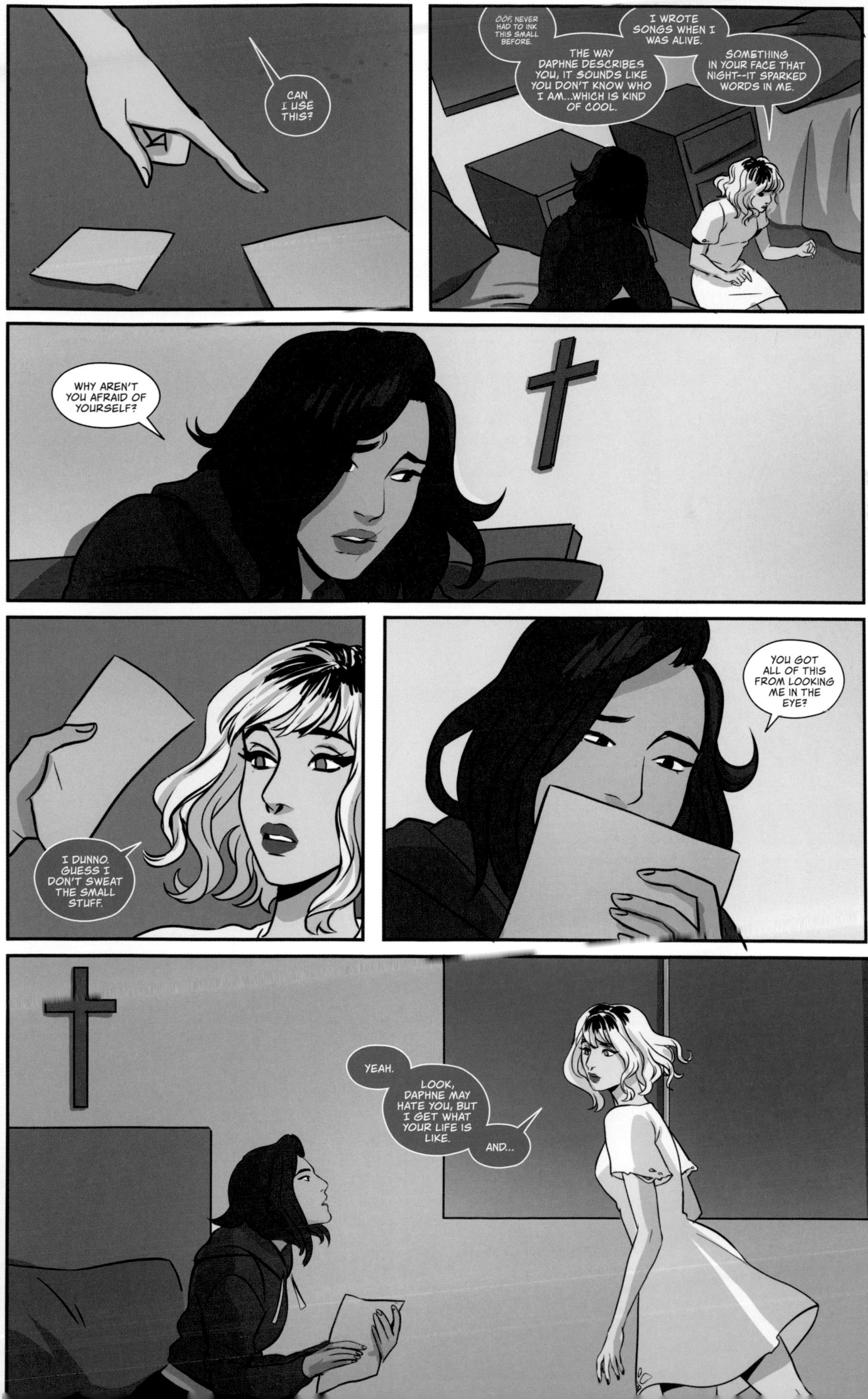
CAN I USE THIS?
OOF, NEVER HAD TO INK THIS SMALL BEFORE.
I WROTE SONGS WHEN I WAS ALIVE.
THE WAY DAPHNE DESCRIBES YOU, IT SOUNDS LIKE YOU DON'T KNOW WHO I AM...WHICH IS KIND OF COOL.
SOMETHING IN YOUR FACE THAT NIGHT--IT SPARKED WORDS IN ME.
WHY AREN'T YOU AFRAID OF YOURSELF?
I DUNNO. GUESS I DON'T SWEAT THE SMALL STUFF.
YOU GOT ALL OF THIS FROM LOOKING ME IN THE EYE?
YEAH.
LOOK, DAPHNE MAY HATE YOU, BUT I GET WHAT YOUR LIFE IS LIKE.
AND...

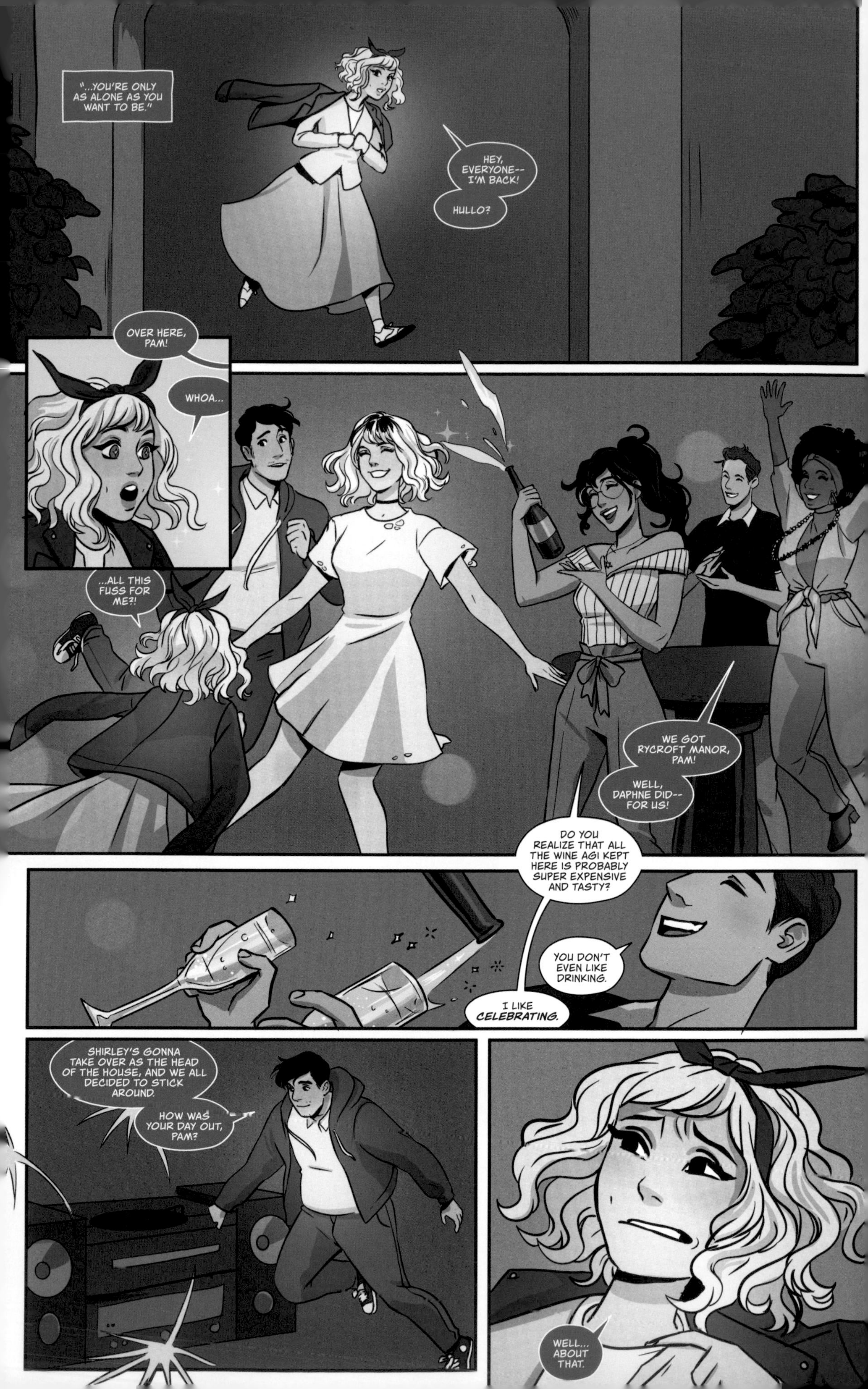
"...YOU'RE ONLY AS ALONE AS YOU WANT TO BE."
HEY, EVERYONE-- I'M BACK!
HULLO?
OVER HERE, PAM!
WHOA...
...ALL THIS FUSS FOR ME?!
WE GOT RYCROFT MANOR, PAM!
WELL, DAPHNE DID-- FOR US!
DO YOU REALIZE THAT ALL THE WINE AGI KEPT HERE IS PROBABLY SUPER EXPENSIVE AND TASTY?
YOU DON'T EVEN LIKE DRINKING.
I LIKE *CELEBRATING.*
SHIRLEY'S GONNA TAKE OVER AS THE HEAD OF THE HOUSE, AND WE ALL DECIDED TO STICK AROUND.
HOW WAS YOUR DAY OUT, PAM?
WELL... ABOUT THAT.

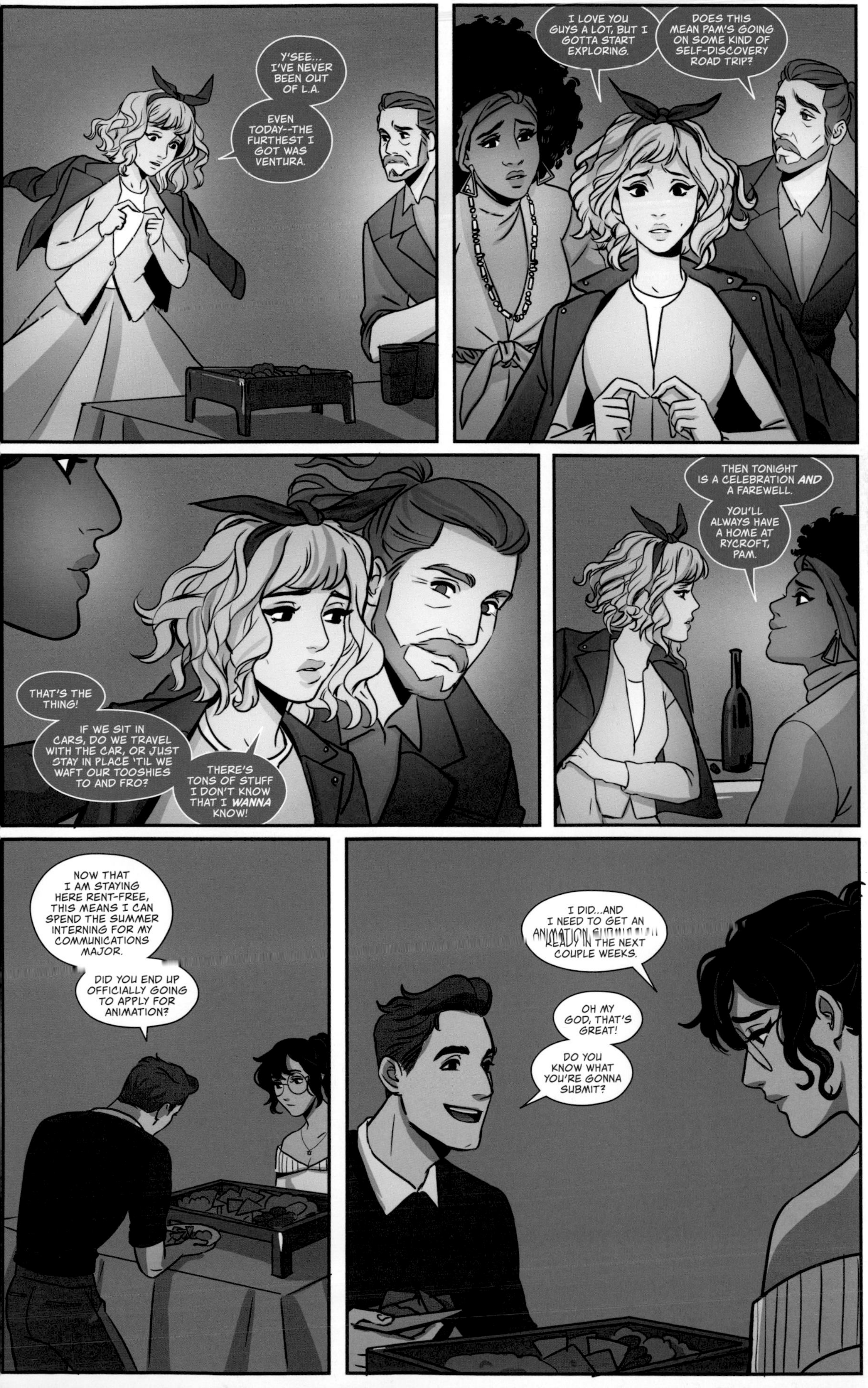

Y'SEE... I'VE NEVER BEEN OUT OF L.A.
EVEN TODAY--THE FURTHEST I GOT WAS VENTURA.
I LOVE YOU GUYS A LOT, BUT I GOTTA START EXPLORING.
DOES THIS MEAN PAM'S GOING ON SOME KIND OF SELF-DISCOVERY ROAD TRIP?
THAT'S THE THING!
IF WE SIT IN CARS, DO WE TRAVEL WITH THE CAR, OR JUST STAY IN PLACE 'TIL WE WAFT OUR TOOSHIES TO AND FRO?
THERE'S TONS OF STUFF I DON'T KNOW THAT I *WANNA* KNOW!
THEN TONIGHT IS A CELEBRATION **AND** A FAREWELL.
YOU'LL ALWAYS HAVE A HOME AT RYCROFT, PAM.
NOW THAT I AM STAYING HERE RENT-FREE, THIS MEANS I CAN SPEND THE SUMMER INTERNING FOR MY COMMUNICATIONS MAJOR.
DID YOU END UP OFFICIALLY GOING TO APPLY FOR ANIMATION?
I DID...AND I NEED TO GET AN ANIMATION SUBMISSION READY IN THE NEXT COUPLE WEEKS.
OH MY GOD, THAT'S GREAT!
DO YOU KNOW WHAT YOU'RE GONNA SUBMIT?

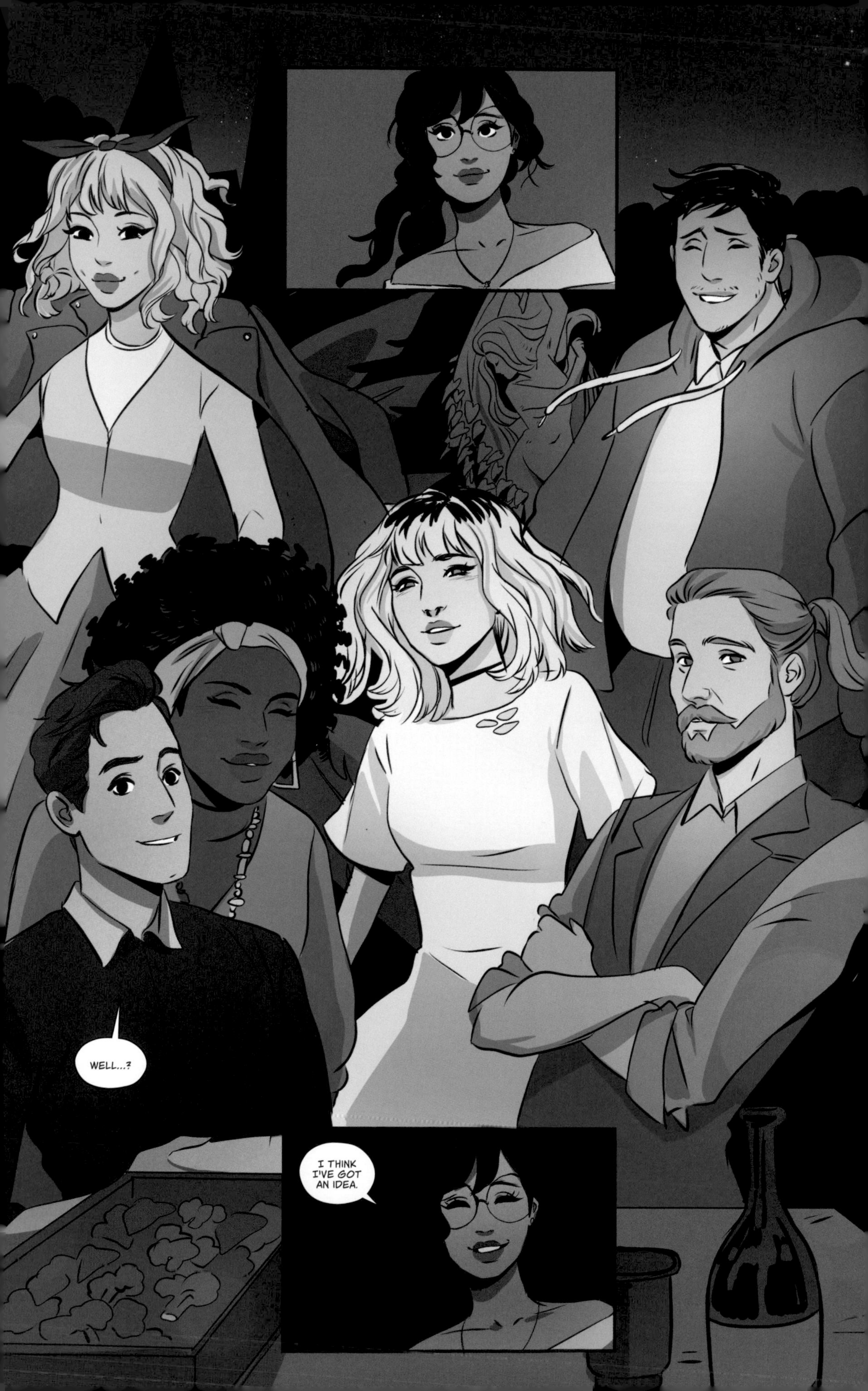
WELL...?
I THINK I'VE GOT AN IDEA.

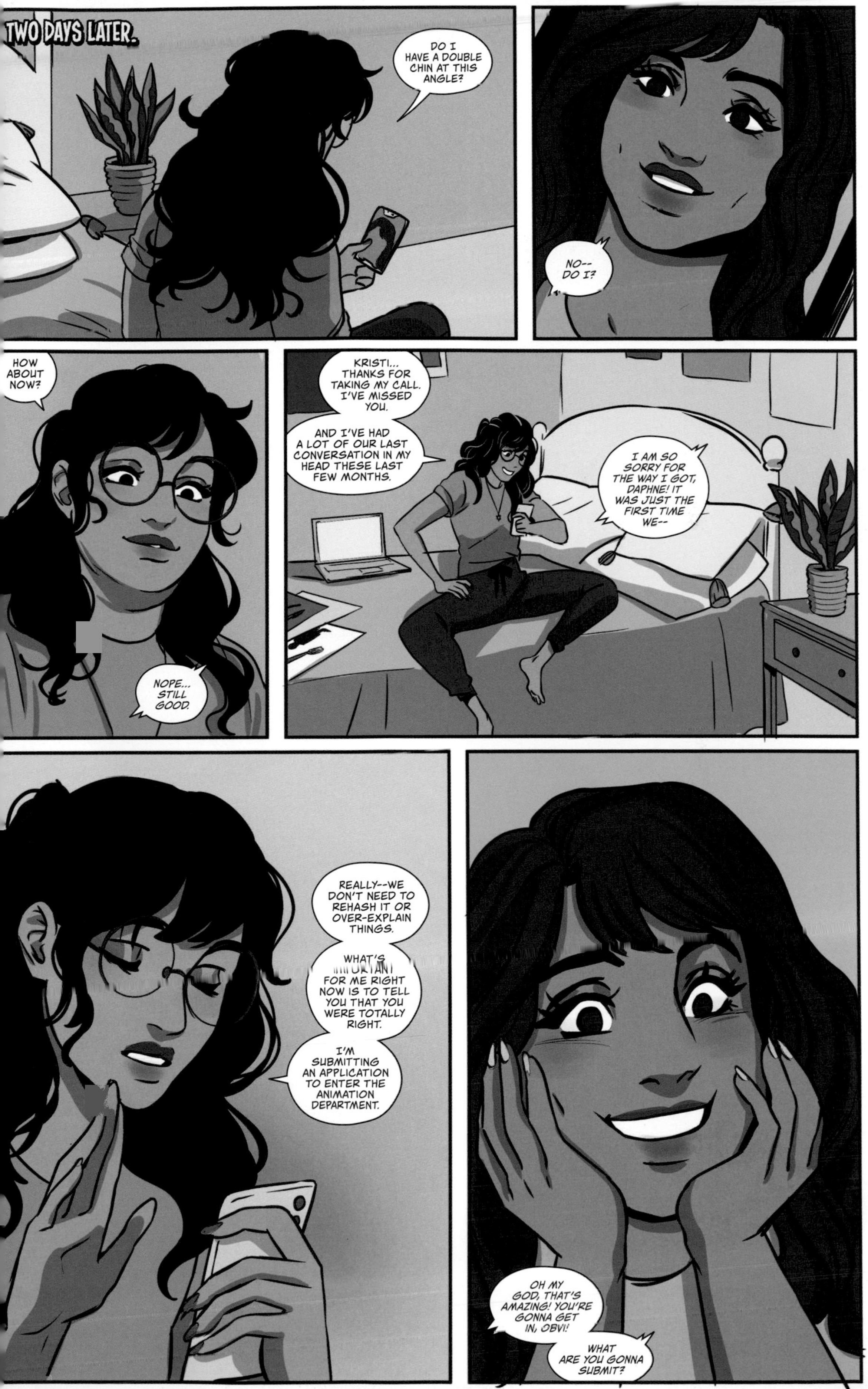
TWO DAYS LATER.
DO I HAVE A DOUBLE CHIN AT THIS ANGLE?
NO-- DO I?
HOW ABOUT NOW?
NOPE... STILL GOOD.
KRISTI... THANKS FOR TAKING MY CALL. I'VE MISSED YOU.
AND I'VE HAD A LOT OF OUR LAST CONVERSATION IN MY HEAD THESE LAST FEW MONTHS.
I AM SO SORRY FOR THE WAY I GOT, DAPHNE! IT WAS JUST THE FIRST TIME WE--
REALLY--WE DON'T NEED TO REHASH IT OR OVER-EXPLAIN THINGS.
WHAT'S IMPORTANT FOR ME RIGHT NOW IS TO TELL YOU THAT YOU WERE TOTALLY RIGHT.
I'M SUBMITTING AN APPLICATION TO ENTER THE ANIMATION DEPARTMENT.
OH MY GOD, THAT'S AMAZING! YOU'RE GONNA GET IN, OBVI!
WHAT ARE YOU GONNA SUBMIT?

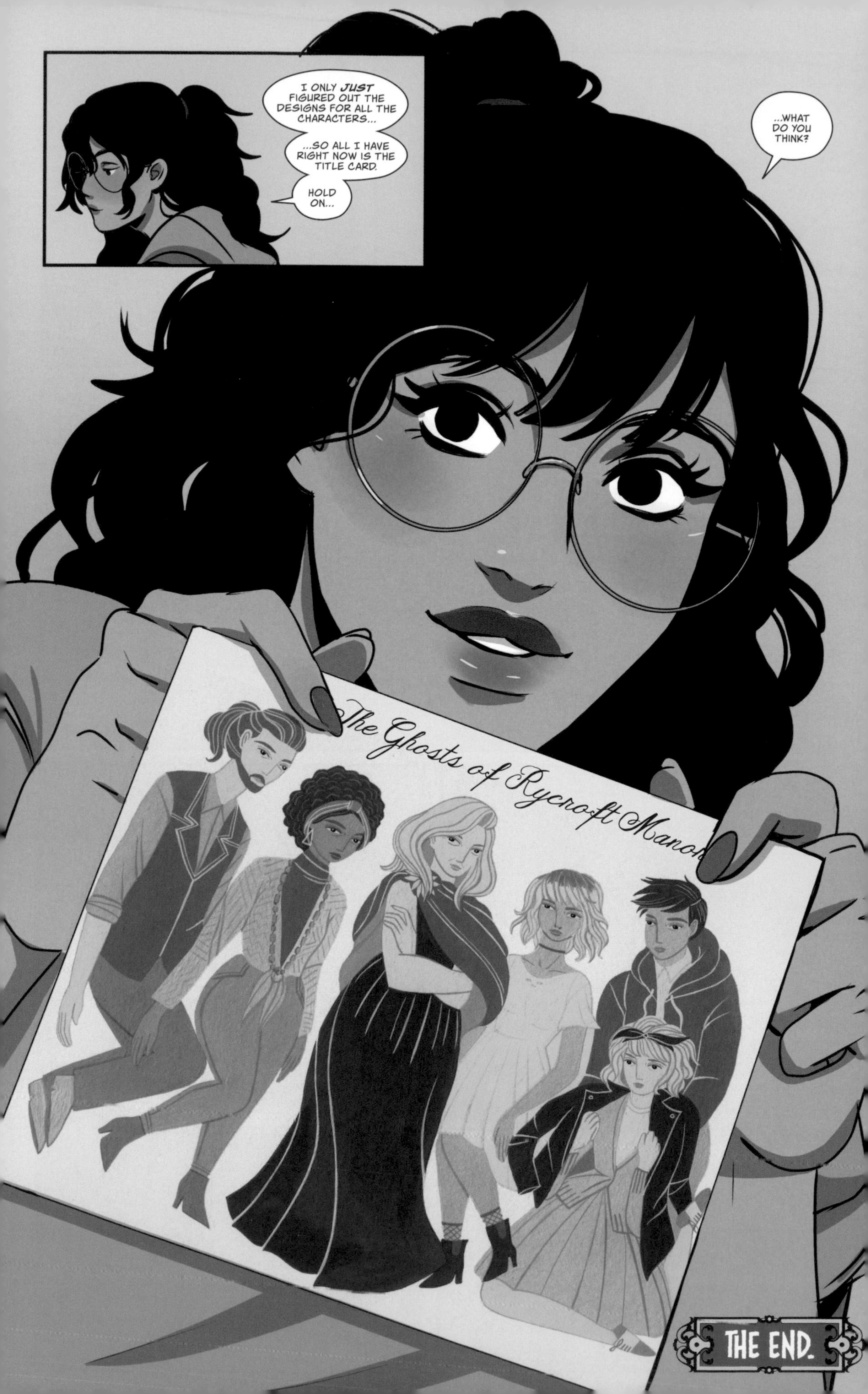
I ONLY JUST FIGURED OUT THE DESIGNS FOR ALL THE CHARACTERS...
...SO ALL I HAVE RIGHT NOW IS THE TITLE CARD.
HOLD ON...
...WHAT DO YOU THINK?
The Ghosts of Rycroft Manor
THE END.

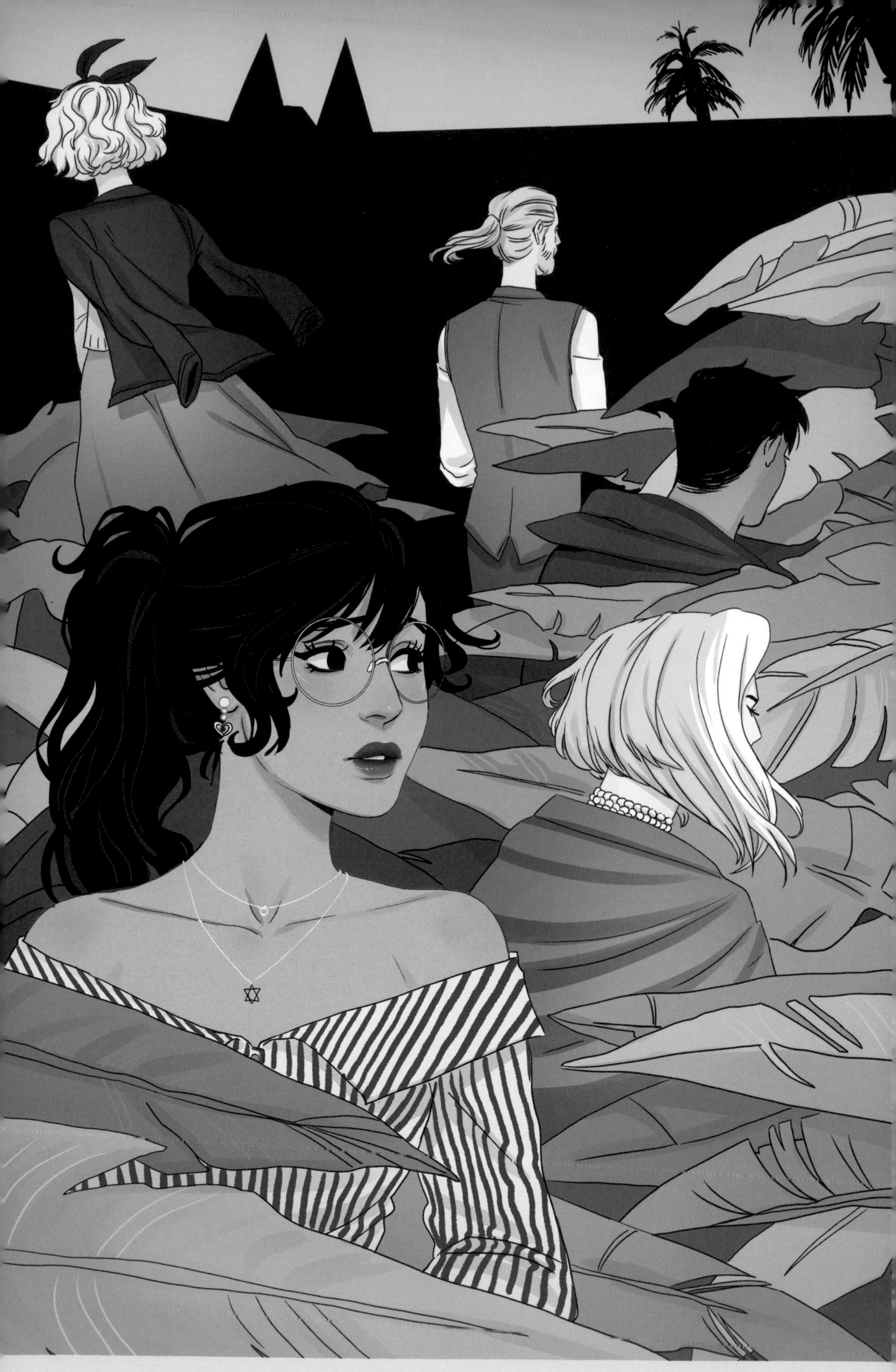

Issue Nine Main Cover by **Siobhan Keenan**

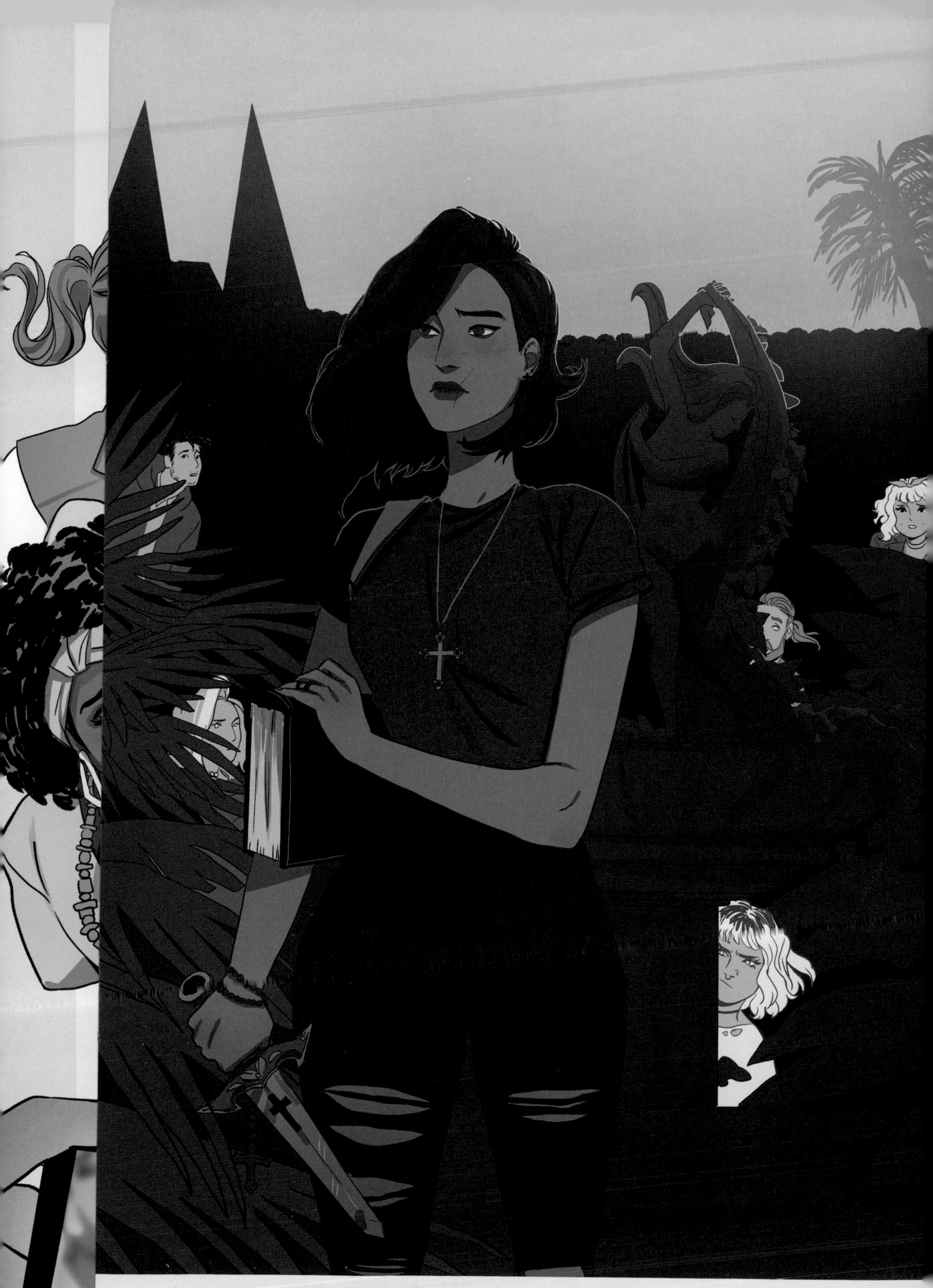

Issue Ten Main Cover by **Siobhan Keenan**

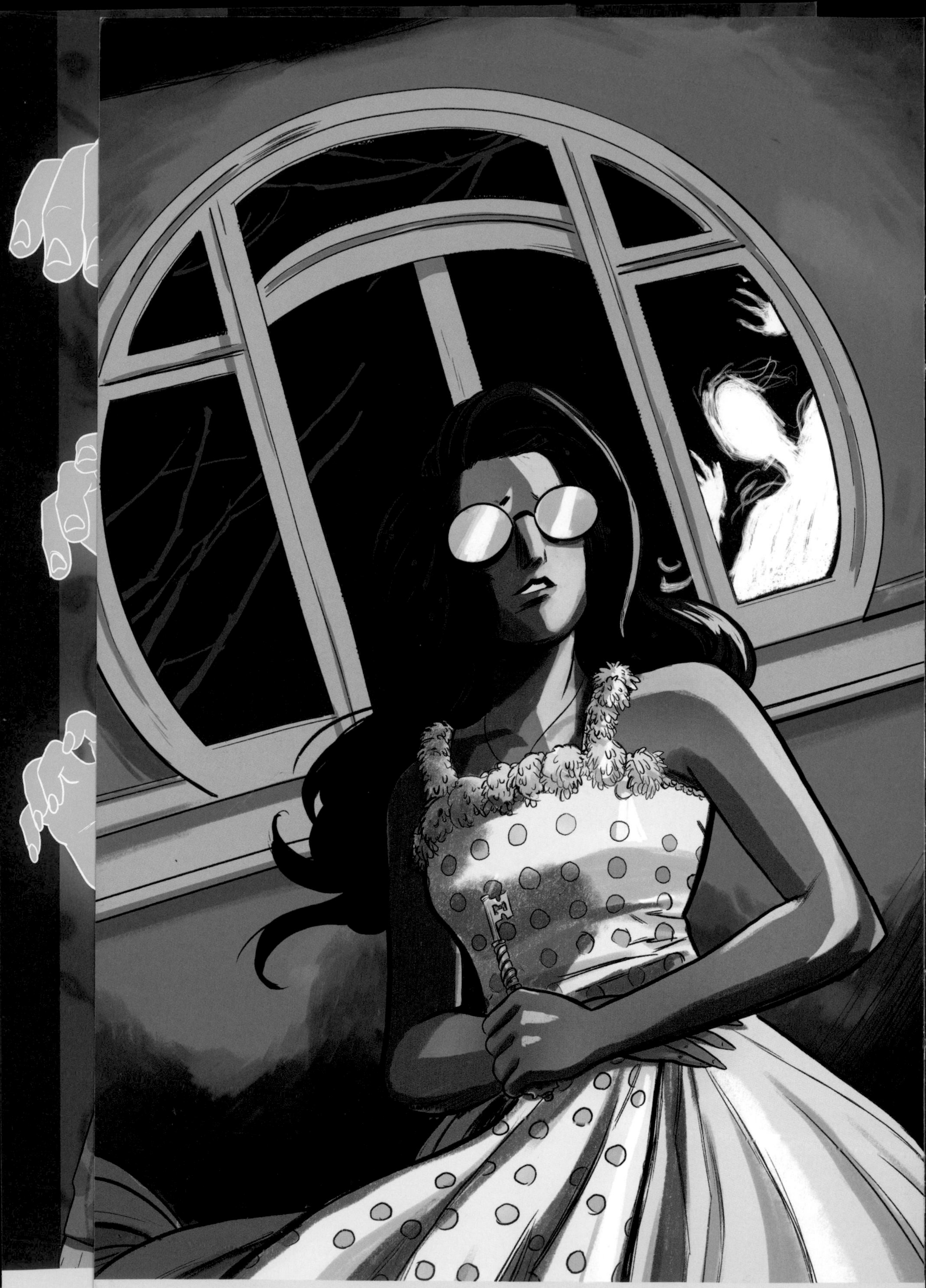

Issue Eleven Variant Cover by **Sina Grace** with Colors by **Cathy Le**

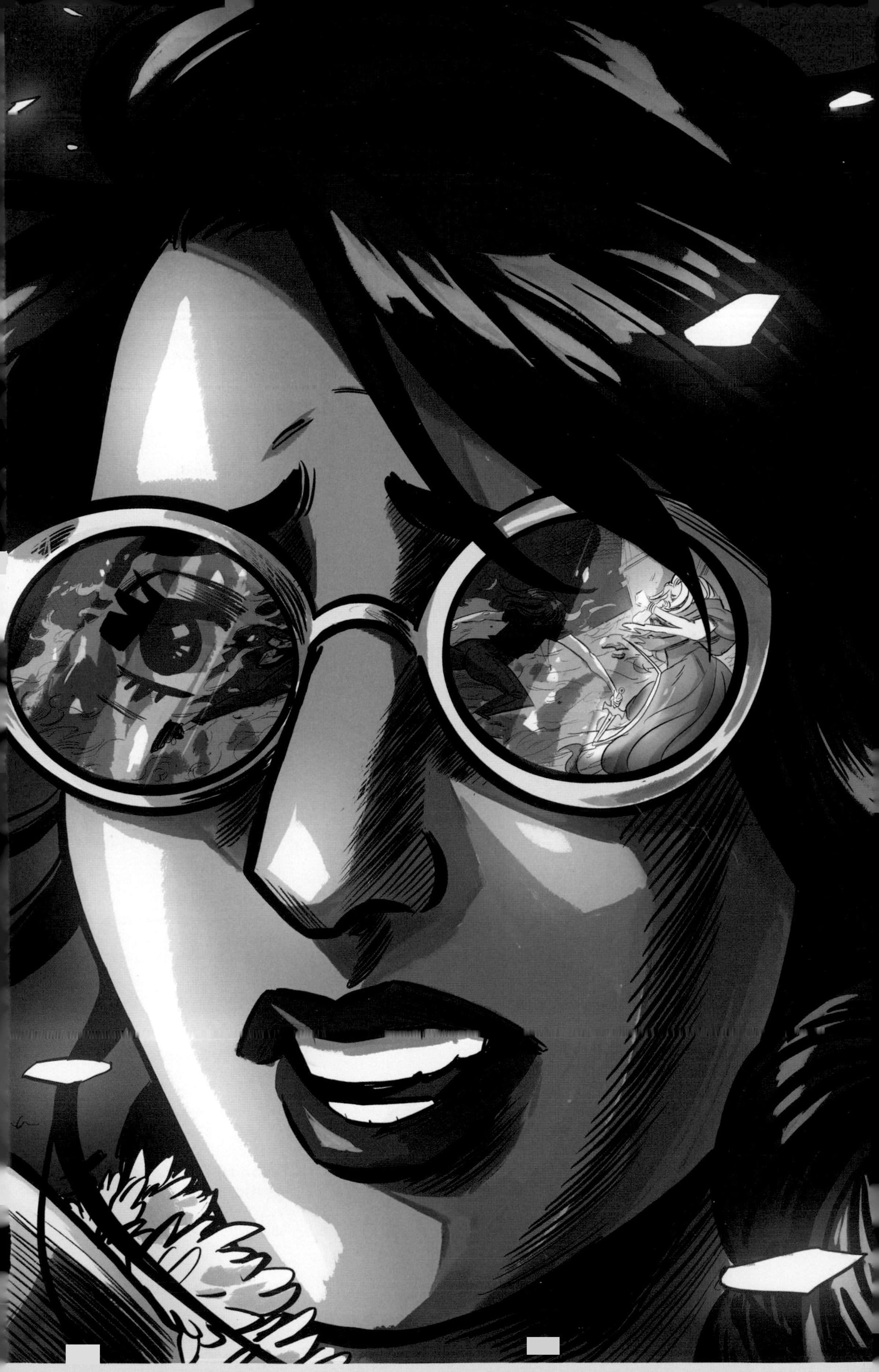

Issue Twelve Variant Cover by **Sina Grace** with Colors by **Cathy Le**

DISCOVER
ALL THE HITS

STEVENSON • ELLIS • WATTERS • ALLEN
LUMBERJANES
BEWARE THE KITTEN HOLY
NEW YORK TIMES BESTSELLING SERIES

Allison + Treiman + Cogar
GIANT DAYS
VOLUME ONE

From a writer of Disney's Moana
RIBON • FISH • PEER
SLAM!
VOLUME ONE

Hope Larson • Brittney Williams • Sarah Stern
GOLDIE VANCE
"Scoot over Nancy Drew..." —Los Angeles Times
Volume One

JAMES TYNION IV • RIAN SYGH • WALTER BAIAMONTE
THE BACKSTAGERS

TYSON HESSE'S
DIESEL
IGNITION

BOOM! BOX™

AVAILABLE AT YOUR LOCAL COMICS SHOP AND BOOKSTORE

To find a comics shop in your area, visit www.comicshoplocator.com

WWW.**BOOM-STUDIOS**.COM

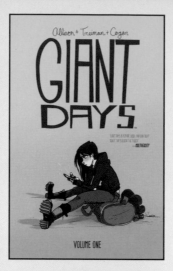

Lumberjanes
Noelle Stevenson, Shannon Watters, Grace Ellis, Brooklyn Allen, and Others
Volume 1: Beware the Kitten Holy
ISBN: 978-1-60886-687-8 | $14.99 US
Volume 2: Friendship to the Max
ISBN: 978-1-60886-737-0 | $14.99 US
Volume 3: A Terrible Plan
ISBN: 978-1-60886-803-2 | $14.99 US
Volume 4: Out of Time
ISBN: 978-1-60886-860-5 | $14.99 US
Volume 5: Band Together
ISBN: 978-1-60886-919-0 | $14.99 US

Giant Days
John Allison, Lissa Treiman, Max Sarin
Volume 1
ISBN: 978-1-60886-789-9 | $9.99 US
Volume 2
ISBN: 978-1-60886-804-9 | $14.99 US
Volume 3
ISBN: 978-1-60886-851-3 | $14.99 US

Jonesy
Sam Humphries, Caitlin Rose Boyle
Volume 1
ISBN: 978-1-60886-883-4 | $9.99 US
Volume 2
ISBN: 978-1-60886-999-2 | $14.99 US

Slam!
Pamela Ribon, Veronica Fish, Brittany Peer
Volume 1
ISBN: 978-1-68415-004-5 | $14.99 US

Goldie Vance
Hope Larson, Brittney Williams
Volume 1
ISBN: 978-1-60886-898-8 | $9.99 US
Volume 2
ISBN: 978-1-60886-974-9 | $14.99 US

The Backstagers
James Tynion IV, Rian Sygh
Volume 1
ISBN: 978-1-60886-993-0 | $14.99 US

Tyson Hesse's Diesel: Ignition
Tyson Hesse
ISBN: 978-1-60886-907-7 | $14.99 US

Coady & The Creepies
Liz Prince, Amanda Kirk, Hannah Fisher
ISBN: 978-1-68415-029-8 | $14.99 US